Juneau Black

Summers End

Juneau Black is the pen name of authors Jocelyn Cole and Sharon Nagel. They share a love of excellent bookshops, fine cheeses, and a good murder (in fictional form only). Though they are two separate people, if you ask either one a question about her childhood, you are likely to get the same answer. This is a little unnerving for any number of reasons.

ALSO BY JUNEAU BLACK

THE SHADY HOLLOW MYSTERY SERIES
Shady Hollow
Cold Clay
Mirror Lake
Twilight Falls

SHADY HOLLOW HOLIDAY SHORT STORIES
Evergreen Chase (eBook only)
Phantom Pond (eBook only)

Summers End

Summers End

A SHADY HOLLOW MYSTERY

Juneau Black

VINTAGE BOOKS

A Division of Penguin Random House LLC

New York

A VINTAGE BOOKS ORIGINAL 2024

Library of Congress Cataloging-in-Publication Data
Names: Black, Juneau, author.
Title: Summers end : a Shady Hollow mystery / Juneau Black.
Description: First edition. | New York : Vintage Books, 2024. |
Series: The Shady Hollow mystery series.
Identifiers: LCCN 2023048928 (print) | LCCN 2023048929 (ebook)
Subjects: GSAFD: Cozy mysteries. | Animal fiction. | Novels.
Classification: LCC PS3602.L293 S86 2024 (print) | LCC PS3602.L293 (ebook) |
DDC 813/.6—dc23
LC record available at https://lccn.loc.gov/2023048928
LC ebook record available at https://lccn.loc.gov/2023048929

Vintage Books Trade Paperback ISBN: 978-0-593-47053-4
eBook ISBN: 978-0-593-47054-1

Book design by Christopher M. Zucker

vintagebooks.com

Printed in the United States of America
10   9   8   7   6   5   4   3   2

For Helen

Author's Note

You have picked up this book out of a sense of curiosity, or perhaps even a sense of wonder. What is this world of Shady Hollow? A place in the deep woods, surrounded by mountains and shot through with rivers, with little towns throughout where you may find foxes and bears, mice and birds, squirrels and deer all living together in a civilized manner . . . except for the murders, of course.

How does this world work? How does a moose run a coffee shop, how does a raven run a bookstore? How do a sparrow and a snake pass each other on the street with good cheer? How does an elk fit into a chair in a rabbit's home so they can play a friendly game of cards?

Our only advice is to let such mundane matters go. From the moment you open these pages, you are invited to step away from your world and into a new one.

So welcome, dear reader, to Shady Hollow.

Cast of Characters

Vera Vixen: *A foxy reporter who chases down stories—and criminals—in pursuit of truth. She also chases down coffee and treats, in pursuit of deliciousness. She finds both at Summers End.*

Lenore Lee: *Vera's good friend, a raven who leaves her beloved bookshop for the chance to see Summers End and winds up confronting more of her past than she expected.*

Athena Standish: *Thena shadows Vera to learn the ropes of journalism. But this clever vole is also very interested in murder.*

Gerry Rosewood: *The proprietor of the lodge nearest the historic site of Summers End, this squirrel has seen pretty much everyone and everything over the years.*

Cora Rosewood: *Gerry's partner in business and life, Cora cooks up meals for all the guests, and possibly cooks up some other mischief as well.*

Chief Lawrence C. Buckthorn: *This deer keeps the peace in the sleepy town of Summerhill, but is he up to the task of solving a murder?*

Deputy Titus Poole: *A bad-tempered wolverine who seems to hold a special malevolence for certain nosy reporters. Does he have a secret to hide?*

Emmeline Greenleaf: *A white rabbit who runs the Bronze Feather, an antiques shop that offers rare goods other stores just can't match.*

Roxanna Cobb: *As the owner of a shop offering divinations and fortune-telling, this pika sometimes clashes with the more skeptical professors. Did one argument go too far?*

Lefty: *A masked raccoon who's got his paws in a number of petty schemes and is willing to share what he knows . . . for a price.*

THE ACADEMICS

Ridley Durham: *A bighorn sheep in charge of the Summers End archaeological dig. The ram views it as his personal domain, and he rules with an iron hoof.*

Augustus van Hoote: *Not just an expert in ancient languages, he's also a cousin to Shady Hollow's own Professor Heidegger, and perhaps has an even bigger ego.*

Isaiah Ford: *A bearded dragon with a penchant for antiquities and little patience for fools.*

Ligeia Lee: *A professor who uses qualitative methods to fight with her colleagues, and her wickedly sharp wit to fight with her sister, Lenore.*

Keats Loring: *A peacock who wields poetry like a weapon. For someone with so many accolades, why does his work seem so slight?*

Adelaide Chesley: *A porcupine and an archaeoastronomer who's so busy watching the stars, she never watches her back. With all those spines, maybe she doesn't need to.*

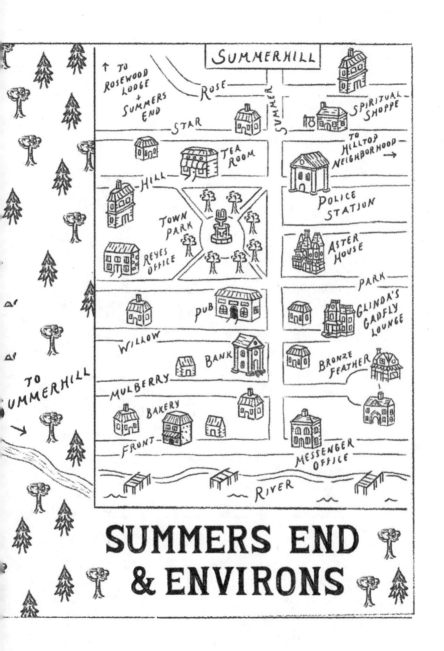

SUMMERHILL

↑ TO ROSEWOOD LODGE + SUMMERS END

ROSE

SUMMER

STAR

SPIRITUAL SHOPPE

TO HILLTOP NEIGHBORHOOD →

TEA ROOM

HILL

POLICE STATION

TOWN PARK

REYES OFFICE

ASTER HOUSE

PARK

PUB

GLINDA'S GADFLY LOUNGE

WILLOW

BANK

BRONZE FEATHER

TO SUMMERHILL →

MULBERRY

BAKERY

MESSENGER OFFICE

FRONT

RIVER

SUMMERS END & ENVIRONS

Summers End

Chapter 1

A fine summer day is a gift. And not just any gift, but the sort of gift that is given for no reason, for no special occasion, not out of any sense of obligation. It is a gift that surprises and delights the recipient. That stunning blue sky? Better than jewels. The warm breeze rustling the leaves and pushing the grasses into waves? A marvel. The golden disk of the sun moving along its track like a queen progressing through court? A treasure to be cherished, for there will be days ahead that will not be so warm nor so gentle.

Vera Vixen was not typically in such a poetic frame of mind, but as she sat in her living room, rocking in the chair near the (unlit) fireplace with her front door open wide, she wanted to appreciate both the glory of summer and the fact that she was in complete solitude, a state she couldn't expect to achieve again for quite a while.

For the fox had done something that many others would never dream of doing, a thing not for the faint of heart or weak of spirit.

She'd agreed to chaperone a school group.

Specifically, she'd agreed to join the upper class of Shady Hollow High School on their annual field trip, a weeklong excursion, held just before the fall term started. This year, the students were going to Summers End, a famous prehistoric monument near a town two days' journey upriver. Vera had recently read about it but had yet to see it for herself. Her best friend, Lenore, the proprietor of the town's bookstore, Nevermore Books, had waxed euphoric when the site was chosen for the school's trip, and she persuaded Vera to join her among the chaperones.

"Are you sure?" Vera had asked, rather surprised that the raven would want to hover over a crowd of raucous, restless young creatures.

"It'll be fun. There are several chaperones in addition to the teachers, so it's not like we're roped to the little beasts all the time. And Summers End is absolutely incredible. You have to see it to truly experience the power of it."

"Are you just saying that because it's essentially a big grave?" Vera was simplifying the situation, but it was true that Summers End was a burial site, and Lenore was quite interested in all things macabre.

"It's so much more than that!" her friend protested. "And this trip is special, because we'll be able to be at the site on the *actual day* of Summers End! The one morning of the year that the whole monument was designed around. Lots of folk will never get a chance to see the sunrise there. These students don't know how lucky they are!"

So Vera signed up along with Lenore. While initially skeptical, she was looking forward to it now.

After getting up from her chair, Vera walked to the door and pulled a straw hat with a wide brim off its hook. She set it on her head, then grabbed her trusty bag and headed outside. She didn't lock the door, of course. Shady Hollow was not the sort of community where folks locked their doors.

She strolled through the streets on her way to the offices of the Shady Hollow *Herald*, where she worked as a reporter. Vera wanted to make sure everything was squared away before she left on the trip. A week was an almost unimaginably long time for a reporter to be gone from her beat!

Practically the moment she walked in, a black-and-white head popped out of the editor's office. "Vixen! Get up here!"

She rolled her eyes but did as directed. BW Stone ran the paper with an eye on the bottom line, and he rarely overlooked the potential for a good story. When Vera stepped into his smoke-filled office, she waved a paw in front of her snout and said, "Morning, boss. Want to talk about the Summers End story?"

The skunk gave her a level look. "I'm still not sure that there's any story to be had, Vixen. It's all well and good for you to gallivant off for a week, but what if a big story breaks here? And meanwhile you're poking around old rocks and tunnels from centuries ago. Talk about old news!"

"Don't worry, BW," she told him. "If a story breaks—which it won't—you've got other great reporters to cover it. Why, Barry Greenfield can write a feature news story in his sleep."

"Hmpf." (This is what BW said when he knew a thing was true.)

Vera went on. "Besides, I bet a lot of folks will enjoy an article on Summers End. I'm going to talk to the scholars working on the site and the townsfolk nearby to get some good info. Plus, remember that I'll have a university student shadowing me for the whole trip. That's important, too . . . mentoring the next generation and all that."

BW puffed on his cigar, then said, "I suppose. The feel-good stories do all right. But what I wouldn't give for some tragic accident or horrible crime."

"Boss!"

"For the *headlines*, Vixen. I'm not a monster. Remember, more papers selling means more work for reporters. I'm just looking out for everyone, aren't I?" he said, sounding wounded and sorely put-upon.

"We don't need tragedies, BW. We need curiosity," Vera told him. "A story about . . . I don't know, a boating contest . . . can be just as gripping as a murder. It's all in the way it's written."

He harrumphed again. "Spoken like a true reporter. But let me tell you, Vixen, that sales go up when bad things go down. Like clockwork!"

"Well, don't look to me for any dirt on bad things. All the bodies I'll be reporting on have been dead for at least a millennium. I doubt I can reveal anything new about *them*."

"Just come back with a great article, Vixen. And your little shadow, too. If I publish their first byline in the *Herald*, at least the family will buy some extra copies."

She left BW sitting morosely in his cloud of smoke and went to her own desk. It was easy enough to tidy the few papers left there. She covered her typewriter with a cloth to keep the dust off.

"Whole week, Vera?" a voice said near her. "Careful, you might never want to come back to work."

She turned to see an older gray rabbit standing next to her desk in a worn waistcoat with a stack of papers in his paws. "Fat chance, Barry. Besides, this isn't a vacation. I'm chaperoning the students and I'll be writing a story on Summers End."

"I went there once, when I was young," Barry said, his normally sardonic tone softening for a moment. "I don't remember all the details, but I remember waking up before dawn to go and see the sun rise. It was all gray and misty—bad luck, huh?—but I stuck around after all my siblings left to go back to the lodge. The sun broke through for about three minutes, just long enough to hit the stones around the hill so that the mist was striped in sun and shadow, and the hill rose up like it was an island in the sea. I'll never forget that."

Vera noted that the plain-spoken reporter got awfully flowery when it came to the famous site. It must really be something. Aloud, she said, "Were you there on the day of Summers End, when the sun shone into the monument itself?"

"Unfortunately, we were a couple weeks too early for that. Anyway, as a leveret I'd have been too scared to go into a burial mound with bones everywhere. There's a host of spooky stories about the place, you know. Ancient spirits of those sacrificed on the altar! Filmy ghosts floating through the mists to haunt the tourists!"

"Did you feel haunted?" Vera teased.

"Not a bit," Barry retorted. Then he hesitated. "But I did feel . . ." He shook himself, his ears flopping. "Eh, never mind. It's the sort of place you've got to see for yourself. Have fun, Vera. See you next week!"

She bade goodbye to Barry and left the newspaper office, turning toward the bookstore.

Nevermore Books stood at one end of Walnut Street, a tall, narrow building that had once been a grain silo but now stored something much more enticing: books. Vera walked in, finding the place silent.

"Lenore?" she called. "You here?"

A cloud of black wings fluttered down from an upper floor, using the open space in the middle for a clear flight. Lenore landed with nary a bump. "Hey there, all ready for the trip?"

"I'm packed," Vera said. "But I wanted to know if there was anything else I should get before we board the ferry upriver. It's going to be hard to think once we're surrounded by students!"

"Have you got a book for the journey?" Lenore asked shrewdly. "That's all you really need."

"I've got my notebook, the history of Summers End you sold me earlier this year, and that collection of short stories that won all the awards."

"Then you're set. I'll meet you at the ferry dock at eight sharp tomorrow. With luck, we won't lose too many young ones overboard before we get there."

Lenore's humor tended toward the dark and dry.

Vera laughed. "See you tomorrow. We're going to have a great time."

"Yup. Ancient tomb, rowdy students . . . what could go wrong?"

Chapter 2

The next morning came very quickly. Vera was ready for the trip, but she had to get to the dock to get her assignment and find out which students she was chaperoning. With the exception of the regular Shady Hollow High School teachers, who were actually responsible for the educational part of the trip, most of the adults volunteering were members of the community who were not familiar with the students. Once they arrived at Summers End, there would also be professors from the local university around, although they would be there to lecture, not to look after the students.

The trip was carefully planned so that they would have plenty of time to make the journey to the town of Summerhill, near the monument. Then, on the sixth of the month, they'd see the sun's light shine through the site's specifically laid out boulders into a long tunnel, where the sun would briefly illuminate a special stone. That moment marked the end of summer. Old traditions set that day as being exactly between the summer solstice and the autumn equinox, signaling the shift from the long, lazy days of high summer to the part of the season when crops ripened in earnest and folks had to begin thinking of the harvest.

Vera sighed with relief as she boarded the ferry with time to spare. There was a festive air on the boat as the students chattered with each other excitedly, and the chaperones gathered to get their assignments. The fox was pleased to see that Arabella Boatwright, the librarian from Mirror Lake, was in charge of the field trip's chaperones. She was organized and had an air of authority that should work to keep the younger participants in line. Vera recognized only a few of the students. There was always a Chitters or two, from her friend Howard's enormous family, as well as several of Ms. Boatwright's nieces and nephews. Most of the others were strangers to her, although she had seen them around Shady Hollow at various events with their parents.

There were several other chaperones gathering around the librarian, who held an official-looking clipboard. Vera stood in line to receive her assignment. As she waited, she noticed Calliope Standish, the vole who served as director of the local theater group, the Shady Hollow Players. Just then, Calliope spotted her and waved excitedly.

Vera realized that another creature standing next to Callie was watching her—also a vole. Vera walked over to them both.

"Hi, Callie," she said. "Who's this?"

"Hello, Miss Vixen!" the younger vole said. "I'm Athena

Standish, Calliope's niece. It's such a privilege to be mentored by you. I'm a big fan of your work."

"Oh, it's so nice to meet you at last, Athena," Vera said. "Let's sit and talk more about the mentorship once the ferry gets under-way. First, I've got to get my assignment from Ms. Boatwright."

Athena nodded and said she'd be with her aunt until then. Vera was pleased that the vole seemed so enthusiastic. Journal-ism favored those who weren't afraid to step up and ask ques-tions. While some might call this fine attribute "pushiness," Vera preferred to think of it as "spunk."

It didn't take long to receive her list of names from Arabella, who also whispered some advice to the novice chaperones. "Doesn't hurt to be a little scary at the beginning. You can be nice later. But you want everyone to know who's in charge!"

Vera was in charge of four students: Joshua Chitters (mouse), Vick Sumner (stoat), Georgette Ashbridge (partridge), and CJ Mapleton (chipmunk). The students all responded quickly when she called their names, gathering in front of Vera.

"Hello, there," she began. "My name's Vera Vixen, and you can call me either Vera or Ms. Vixen."

"We know who you are, Ms. Vixen!" Chitters piped up.

"And now I know who you are," she responded, with mock severity. "So I expect that you will follow all the rules set by the grown-ups, and that if I ask you to do something, you'll do it quickly and without argument. We're going to a very important and special site, with lots of historical significance. You'll have to be respectful, even if you're excited to be there. I trust you *are* all excited?"

"Oh, yes!" Georgette said. "Summers End is unique and we're really lucky to get to be there for the special sunrise. Our teacher said we'll pick names the night before. One student will get to go into the monument tunnel first to be there when the sun hits the calendar stone, and I want to be the winner!"

"Well, maybe you will be," Vera said. Clearly, the partridge was ready for the field trip.

"I've heard there's just piles and piles of bones," Vick said, his eyes gleaming.

"They aren't in piles," Joshua Chitters corrected. "They've been placed in ossuaries throughout the site, whether on the ground or in niches on the walls. Each species is kept separately."

"Wow, I can see that you all have done the reading on the site," said Vera. "And you're correct. The bones are kept in ossuaries."

"Still a lot of bones," Vick said. "Maybe I'll grab one as a souvenir."

"No!" Georgette shrieked. "You'll get a curse on you if you do that!"

"More importantly," Vera added, "it's against the law to take *any*thing from the site. Not a bone, not a pebble, not a leaf. And I'll have you and your things searched if I get even a hint that someone's taken something. Got it?" She spoke to everyone but kept her gaze on Vick. This one would need watching. She was glad Arabella had given her the hint about being stern!

"Just joking," Vick muttered.

"How reassuring to hear. Now why don't you all get settled for the trip upriver. It's a long one, so make yourselves comfy. And don't get in trouble!"

The students wandered off, so Vera looked around for Calliope and Athena.

"Nice to see you again, Callie," Vera said to the older vole.

"No plays to direct now?" The most recent one had been *Ah, Wilderness!* performed this past spring.

"The Players always take a break in summer," Callie explained. "We'll get started on rehearsals for *The Lion in Winter* shortly after I get back from this trip. I do love chaperoning! It keeps me young to see all the students, and with Thena along as your shadow, it will be an even better time."

"I've always known that I want to be a journalist," Athena said eagerly. "A real journalist who breaks big stories, like you do, Ms. Vixen."

"Call me Vera," the fox told her kindly.

"And everyone calls me Thena," said the vole.

"If I remember your application correctly, you write for the college paper."

Thena nodded. "Yup. Not that it's very hard-hitting news. But you have to start somewhere."

"That's true," Vera agreed. "My first jobs weren't glamorous, either. But I learned a lot, and I hope you'll learn something this week, too."

"Oh, I know I will!"

Just then, Vera saw Vick throwing something into the water off the side of the ferry. She sighed. "Excuse me, won't you?" she said to the others before hurrying off. It was going to be a busy week indeed.

On the afternoon of the next day, the boat docked near Summerhill, the town nearest the monument. The chaperones all led their charges down the gangplank and onto the path into town.

"Come on, everyone!" Arabella called. "Follow me to our lodgings, and then you'll have some free time before dinner."

The long procession of students and adults made their way to the heart of Summerhill. It was a quaint place, with a high street of shops and restaurants to serve the many tourists who visited. Because this was a school outing, the whole group had rooms at an inn called Rosewood Lodge. It was situated a short distance from the town itself, on the end of its own street called Rose Lane. Rosewood Lodge looked rather like an overgrown cabin crossed with a ski chalet. The building was two stories, made of whitewashed boards with an overhanging roof to keep out rain and snow. Baskets of pink geraniums hung from big iron hooks next to every door, while ivy climbed up the pillars and crept across the walls. The doors to all the rooms on the ground floor opened directly to the outside, and the upper rooms to a long common outdoor walkway that also served as a sort of shared balcony.

"Nightmare," Lenore muttered, as she strolled next to Vera.

"What is?"

"The layout! With outside doors, we'll have students sneaking out of their rooms the moment we turn our backs. There's no way to corral them."

Vera chuckled. "Well, then we just have to wear them out during the day so they're too tired to even think of sneaking out at night."

"You don't spend much time around young folks, do you?" Lenore cawed loudly to get her charges to follow her to their assigned rooms, and Vera did the same with her little group.

Both Vera and her group had rooms on the ground floor, which would help. Further, it turned out that Vera would be sharing her room with Calliope and Athena, so there would be extra eyes on all the restless youth. Good!

Lenore's group was on the upper floor, and soon the whole place was crawling with excited students dashing in and out of their friends' rooms, trying to decide which ones were the best (despite them all being virtually identical). Vera liked Rosewood Lodge. It was no-frills but homey, and everything was kept scrupulously clean by the Rosewoods, a squirrel couple who looked over the crowd with unfazed expressions.

"Come on," Vera said to her mentee. "Let's interview the caretakers and see if there's anything interesting to learn."

They walked over to one of the squirrels (his wife had dashed off to help with some luggage). He introduced himself as Gerald Rosewood. "Gerry will do," he added.

"Worked here long?" Vera asked.

"Practically my whole life," he said. "My grandparents started the place, and now my wife and I live over at the caretaker's cottage there." He pointed to an adorable house off to the side, sheltered by huge trees and surrounded by a cottage garden full of roses. "Not exactly an ivory tower, but I'll take it!"

"Is it always this full of students?" Thena asked, pulling out her own notebook and pencil.

"Off and on. Busy week now because of the Summers End Day happening tomorrow. The younger student groups thin out as school begins in the fall and the weather gets worse. But we've always got a few college students and off-season tourists. Some researchers, too, though the regular professors who work here during dig season like to stay at the fancier place on Summer Street." He looked away as he said the last bit.

"Which one is that?" asked Vera.

"Called Aster House. Big tall place with lots of gables and whatnot. Can't miss it. They do have a very nice dining room," he added, with professional courtesy, "if you want more elevated fare than we make here."

"I'm sure what you serve is great," Vera said. "Our organizer mentioned that everyone likes the food. And students are rather harsh critics."

"Simple but filling," Gerry said proudly. "My wife is the chef."

"Looking forward to it." Vera turned to Thena. "Since my charges officially have a few hours of leisure, want to explore the town with me? I always think it's important to get the lay of the land before writing an article."

Thena beamed. "I'd love to!"

So fox and vole walked from the lodging house back onto the main thoroughfare.

Summer Street ran perpendicular to the river, with the docks on the east end, just visible from their vantage point. All along the way, buildings nestled next to each other. Most were shops or businesses of some sort, with a few private homes sprinkled in between, though it appeared most residents lived on the numerous side streets, which were tree lined and comfortably shaded with sunny spots that could support a cottage garden or a plot for vegetables to grow.

There was a general store, a pharmacy, a small bank . . . typical businesses. But Summerhill supported a higher than usual number of shops and restaurants as well, thanks to all the visitors who came to see the monument. Vera and Lenore passed a bustling pub, a tearoom, a bakery, and a candy shop. Among all these were shops that sold gifts and souvenirs: postcards, drawings, and pottery with depictions of Summers End, books about the site, and seemingly endless items emblazoned with the name Summers End or a picture of the monument. Vera spotted a tea tray with a painted scene of the monument at dawn, and Thena tried on a hat embroidered with the words *Summers End Is Endless Fun.*

"Ooh, that's an interesting-looking shop," Thena said, pointing to a storefront that was just off the main street and set back a bit from the sidewalk.

Interesting *is one word for it,* Vera thought. The clapboard face was painted purple, spangled with yellow stars. A round wooden sign painted to look like the full moon had been attached to the fence, and read:

ROXANNA'S SPIRITUAL SHOPPE

"Got an extra *p* and *e* at the end," Vera said dryly. "Must be special."

"There's an occult shop near the university," Thena replied. "I get all my teas there. Wonder if this one has any."

Before the pair could even cross the street and venture in, they saw a small group of figures leave the boutique bearing shopping bags and laughing. A pika wearing a black hat (complete with the distinctive cone shape and wide brim) followed them out and waved cheerily, calling, "Good luck, and thank you for coming!"

A porcupine was walking along the sidewalk as the group moved away, and she made a face at the proprietor of the shop. "The hat's a bit much, don't you think, Ms. Cobb? It's bad enough you charge folks for nonsense, but to do it in costume? Hmpf!"

The pika stamped her back paw on the stoop and glared back at the porcupine. "If you're so certain, *Professor*, why not come in and see what the stars have in store for you?"

"Ha! As if I'd waste the money, you charlatan! There's only one expert on stars in this town, and it's sure not you!"

"Too bad you're not an expert on manners!" With that retort, the pika whirled around and retreated into the shop in a decidedly dramatic way. Meanwhile, the porcupine continued on, huffing loudly. She went straight toward Vera and Thena, who actually had to hop backward to avoid getting brushed with her spines.

"Excuse me," the porcupine muttered, not sounding like she meant it.

Vera decided that the owner of the *shoppe* might have a point about the porcupine's expertise in manners. "Come on, Thena. Let's keep exploring."

Thankfully, their path took them in the opposite direction of the cranky creature. In general the mood of the town was friendly and welcoming, and the summer sun beamed down, broken up only by a few fluffy clouds. They bought some nut brittle from a vendor working from a small, wheeled cart under a massive oak, and walked on, nibbling the sweet and salty treat.

"Oh, look! That must be Aster House," Thena said, pointing to an impressive multistoried, white-painted structure stacked with gables and chimneys and crusted over with decorative details under the eaves. It was set back slightly from the street, allowing a small garden to flourish between the sidewalk and the wide porch. The front doors were open, and they could hear the sounds of creatures talking inside. With the wistfulness of a student on a budget, Thena added, "It's the fanciest place to stay in town. I wonder what the rooms are like."

Just then, an owl strode out of the doorway, exclaiming angrily and gesturing with his wings. "Total idiocy!" he squawked. "If I have to listen to one more word from that pathetic excuse for a scholar . . . ! *Research*, she calls it. I've seen better research in my compost pile. Mining old ditties and badly metered poems is not research, it's fraud!"

He was voicing these complaints to his companion, whom Vera had first overlooked because he was as low to the ground as one could get. Then he cleared the porch and elevated his upper body, and Vera saw that he was a lizard.

"Goodness, van Hoote! What's the fuss? It's not as if you've never heard Professor Lee's theories before." The lizard, who Vera was almost certain was a bearded dragon, seemed amused by his companion's pique.

The owl was still complaining: "Her so-called theories demean the whole field of archaeology. Perhaps all of academia! She ought to be thrown out, and yet here she is, basking in getting tenure."

"A worthy achievement to bask in," the lizard replied (and lizards know all about basking).

The two approached the sidewalk as they were speaking, and soon Vera and Thena would have been forced to step aside to let them through. But then the owl recovered his manners and offered a courtly bow. "Do excuse our somewhat hasty progress, ladies. I didn't intend to be rude and knock you down!"

"We're both quite nimble," Vera said with a smile. "I take it that you are professors here to study Summers End?"

"Yes, we're among the few," the owl confirmed. "You'll meet the others soon if you wander the streets long enough. Earlier, I was just talking to Professor Chesley. She's an archaeo-astronomer studying the layout of the site and its relation to the stars."

"Um, would she happen to be a porcupine?" Vera asked.

"Indeed she is!" the owl said, looking surprised.

"I think we did meet her," Thena said. "Well, sort of. She almost stepped on me."

The lizard gave a snort. "She does tend to only look up." By his wry tone, it seemed that he guessed it was not inattention that caused the near accident, but he wasn't going to call out a fellow professor when she wasn't there to defend herself.

"And what do you study?" Vera asked them both.

The owl proclaimed, "Professor Augustus van Hoote, at your service. Ancient languages are my specialty. And my colleague here is Professor Isaiah Ford, archaeologist nonpareil!"

"Pleased to make your acquaintance," the lizard said, with his head making a bobbing motion that approximated a bow. "Are you with this week's school group?"

"Yes, up from Shady Hollow," Vera told them.

"Ah!" van Hoote said, fluttering his wings. "Do you know Ambrosius Heidegger?"

"Oh, yes indeed," Vera said. "He's helped me in my own work on several occasions."

"Wonderful! He's my cousin, in fact, as well as a colleague. What is your work? Are you a scholar?"

"Miss Vixen is a journalist," Athena interjected eagerly. "A very good one. And I'm shadowing her this week as part of my student internship!"

"Then we shall see you both at the site, I'm sure," Ford replied. "A significant date to be here. The sunrise should be most illuminating."

"In every sense of the word!" van Hoote chimed in with a chuckle. "I hope to make a great advance in my own studies when I see the sun hit the calendar stone at the back of the chamber."

"You wouldn't advance in your studies if the sun hit you full in the face," a new voice interjected.

Without anyone noticing, another creature had joined the group. A raven with glossy feathers and a furious expression, who must have just come out of the inn.

Van Hoote whirled to meet the challenge. "Oh, shut your beak, Lee. Prancing around with your make-believe sources and shoddy scholarship . . ."

"It's called qualitative research and it's real enough for the committee—"

"Committee-schmitty!" van Hoote interrupted with a snort. "Publicity-chasing hacks, the lot of them."

"You didn't say that when they granted *you* tenure," the raven pointed out.

"A different time, my dear."

"Very different," she agreed, with a sly grin. "So long ago that it's amazing that anyone still remembers. Soon you won't be teaching ancient languages, you'll be part of the curriculum!"

"Why you—" The owl lunged toward the raven, but the lizard slid his bulk between them, faster than Vera would have thought him capable of moving.

"Now, now," he said. "This is no way to behave in public. What will the good folk visiting Summerhill think of us?"

The raven broke away first, tossing her head and preening a few feathers in a show of disdain. "I'm just stating facts."

"Facts! As if!" van Hoote grumbled but seemed to give up the fight.

The raven turned to Vera and Thena with a now-polite smile. "Goodness, what a scene to wander into. I trust our spirited little discussion hasn't given you the wrong idea about academia."

"You certainly all seem passionate," Thena murmured. "What do you study, Professor?"

The raven was just about to reply when Vera heard a familiar voice beside her.

"Oh no!" Lenore said in dismay. "Don't tell me *you're* here!"

The other raven looked just as disgusted. "Of course *I'm* here. It's my job. What's your excuse, Lenore?"

"Wait!" Vera said. "You two know each other?"

"All too well," Lenore practically spat out. "This is none other than big-time fancy university professor Ligeia Lee . . . my sister."

Chapter 3

A short while later, Vera and Thena were seated in a cozy corner of a local pub, watching Lenore across the table. The raven was still annoyed at the unexpected encounter with her sister. And since Vera hadn't even known Lenore *had* a sister, she was naturally interested in her best friend's plight. Thena was simply watching, wide-eyed.

"There's a reason I opened my shop in Shady Hollow," Lenore was explaining over an untouched glass of fizzy elder-flower soda. "It was a town where no one in my family lived, so it was a place I could get away from all their criticism."

"How could they be critical of you owning a successful bookstore?"

"Because it doesn't take several advanced degrees to do so. In my family, the question wasn't 'Are you going to go to college?' It was 'What have you chosen for your second and third PhD?' I was asked this as a hatchling, mind you."

"Yikes," Thena said. "My parents were excited when I chose to go to college, but they wouldn't have cared either way."

"Rejoice in your family," Lenore said in a flat tone. "I had a different experience. And my choices were not exactly greeted with enthusiasm among my parents or my siblings."

"How many do you have?" Thena asked. "Er, siblings, not choices."

"More than anyone deserves. But Ligeia is the closest to me in age."

"Let me guess," Vera said. "She followed the chosen path."

"Waltzed down it strewing flowers in her wake. Ligeia is a professor at the university and has published several books, none of which I'll stock at my store."

"Isn't that a bit petty?" Vera asked gently.

"No, it's just business. You know how much her press charges for a book? You'd be able to dine out for a week on the cover price. Ah, academia!"

"I have to say," Thena noted, "we've only been here half a day, and nearly all the professors we've encountered do seem . . . argumentative."

"I think it's part of the job description," Vera said.

"What's Ligeia's area of expertise?" Thena asked. "She's here at Summers End, so I assume it's related to archaeology."

Lenore said, "She studies the funeral practices and afterlife beliefs of prehistoric woodland culture, which includes the time period when Summers End was built. Ligeia gets really excited about little things, like when a grave includes two bone sewing needles instead of one. My stars! Whatever could it *mean*?"

"That it's nice to have a spare if you misplace one?" Vera guessed.

Lenore cackled in amusement. "And *that's* why you're a reporter and not a professor. A professor can spend twenty years vigorously interrogating the potential reasons for having a certain number of needles and then viciously attacking anyone who doesn't agree with them."

"Attacking?" Thena squeaked.

"In print. Professors aren't the most physical of folk, so combat is conducted within the confines of academic journals."

"Safer for everyone," Vera noted. "So you don't speak to your family much?" (Earlier, about ten seconds after Lenore arrived, Ligeia had huffed that she had somewhere important to be before flying off, leaving Lenore standing on the sidewalk.)

"Not if I can help it. They cluck with disappointment over my wasted potential, and I can barely keep from banging my head against a wall to get some relief from all their yammering. No, Ligeia can have all the fun of academic pursuits. I don't care at all!"

Vera didn't say anything, but she could tell that there was real hurt under Lenore's breezy dismissal. The two sisters must have been close in the nest. For all that Lenore put on a show of not needing anything from her family, no one liked being cut off.

At that point, the clock near the door of the pub chimed.

"Oh no!" Thena said. "We're supposed to be back at the lodge for dinner soon!"

"Yeah, let's go." Lenore quaffed her soda and slid out of the booth. "I'll take students over professors any day!"

On their way out of the pub, the group of visitors moved to one side as a large peacock entered. He swept past them as if they weren't there and strutted over to an empty table. Vera stared after the bird, marveling at the rich azure color of the feathers on his head and body. His tail was closed in deference to the close quarters of the pub, but the green and blue feathers were magnificent.

Thena took note of the object of Vera's fascination and said to her in a low voice, "That's Professor Keats Loring. I had him for Introduction to Language Arts when I was a first year. He's a published poet and quite a character. In class, he made it clear that he didn't expect any of us to be good enough to even attempt a solid composition, let alone a poem."

Vera studied the creature while waiting for Lenore to put on her hat. He was dressed in flowing robes, and their severe black only served to highlight his vibrant plumage. What an interesting academic community there was here in Summers End! The town of Shady Hollow was a rather small one, and although it contained many different types of creatures, there was a limit to how many different species lived there. She would make a point of interviewing Professor Loring if she could. When Lenore called her name from the door of the pub, she realized that she had been lost in thought and the rest of her party was ready to go.

After leaving the pub, they all hurried back to the lodge. Lenore flapped her way up to the second story, while Vera and Thena went to their room to get ready for dinner. Vera changed to a warmer wrap (the evenings were occasionally cool in the woodlands, even in summer).

She found her four charges and directed them to the large patio at the back of the lodge, where long wooden tables were arranged, with benches on either side. When the weather was good, meals were served outside due to the number of creatures staying at the inn. Close to the patio was a small building known as the summer kitchen. A squirrel wearing an embroidered apron over her outfit was minding the big stove and oven, and a few creatures were already carrying out platters of food that were sitting ready on the wide countertop window. Her chef's jacket read CORA ROSEWOOD, ROSEWOOD LODGE.

"Why don't you go see if you can help bring food out to the tables," Vera suggested to Vick and CJ, who were already sniffing hungrily at the air.

The two scampered toward the kitchen, while Vera led the others to a table where Lenore and her own charges were already sitting. Thena and Callie joined them, with a few more students trailing along. It didn't take long before all the seats were filled and the tables were covered in dishes.

The hungry young ones eagerly passed baskets of freshly baked rolls around to put on their tin plates, and the chaperones took on the task of serving soup from big stone crocks on each table. The soup tonight looked to be a sort of garden vegetable medley, and it smelled absolutely delicious. The tomatoey broth was rich with basil and other herbs, and chunks of peas, carrots, zucchini, and mushrooms filled each spoonful—it was summer in a bowl.

Vera quickly finished her soup, wiping up the dregs with torn bits of bread. She hadn't realized how famished she'd gotten!

"Main course ready!" the squirrel called from her kitchen.

"I'll get ours!" Vick said, leaping up from his seat. CJ followed an instant later.

The second course was a simple but hearty meal of grilled vegetables on skewers, laid over a warm and spicy purée of summer beans. Vick laid the platter down almost reverentially, while CJ brought over a bowl of smoky-sweet sauce for drizzling over the food.

The students chattered happily as they ate, talking of the coming school year and how they intended to spend their last precious few days of vacation after the trip concluded. The grown-ups talked about Summers End itself, and what about the monument attracted them.

Vera noticed the same porcupine that she'd seen earlier now standing with a few students at the edge of the patio. She was pointing to some star in the sky, and Vera guessed this must indeed be the astronomer van Hoote had mentioned. She recalled that a different instructor was scheduled to be available each evening to answer any questions the students might have. Tonight must be Professor Chesley's turn. The porcupine didn't look particularly comfortable with younger students, to judge by how prominent her needles were.

Then Vera refocused on the conversation at her own table.

"After all," Lenore was saying, "it's got to be compelling to make us put up with this crowd of miscreants!" She glared at her charges, who just giggled.

"Whatever, Ms. Lee!" a sparrow chirped.

Just then, someone tapped a glass, drawing the room's attention to a spot at one end of the patio. Some folks had to twist in their seats to see what was happening.

Arabella stood up on a bench and called for silence.

"Everyone, I'd like to introduce you to a very important figure here at Summers End. Professor Ridley Durham is the leader of all the research being done on the site, and he's worked hard to allow student groups like ours to visit, so many different folks can learn about this significant place. Please welcome Professor Durham!"

Everyone applauded politely as Durham stood up and turned

toward the crowd. He was a stocky bighorn sheep, with impressively curled horns on either side of his head. His eyes blazed with intelligence, though he wore a friendly smile.

"Welcome, indeed!" he said, and it sounded like a chuckle. "I am so, so delighted that you could join us here at Summers End. As your organizer mentioned, I am the head of research here, and it is such a privilege to work on this unique site. I'm sure you know the basics, because you *love* studying up during a school break, don't you?"

The students all laughed, and Durham grinned wider.

"He sure knows how to win over the audience," Lenore muttered to Vera.

Durham went on. "Summers End is possibly the most important prehistoric monument in the woodlands, a place of great significance for the very founding of civilization in this area of the world. It takes cooperation to build such a structure. Bears provided strength to lift and set stones. Elk and moose helped haul heavy materials from the river and the surrounding land to the site. Smaller creatures aided in marking out and digging the main tunnel and all the other parts of the monument. And of course, birds flew above to judge distances and make sure everything was being built according to plan. It was a group effort."

"But it wouldn't have happened if it weren't for the bears!" a voice shouted from the crowd—very likely the burly young bear Arabella was chaperoning.

Durham chuckled again, but said, "It's true that bears helped a lot, just as *all* creatures did. And it's true that one of the chambers in the underground part of the monument contains only bear bones. Why should that be? It's one of the many aspects of Summers End that we're still studying. And who knows? Maybe someday one of you will be working here as a researcher or professor. Maybe one of *you* will make a great discovery about Summers End!"

"Oh, wow," Georgette breathed, enraptured by the speech. "That's what I want to do!"

Lenore leaned over to Vera, whispering, "Ligeia said the same thing when she was young. Hasn't turned out quite that way, and according to what I hear, he's the reason."

"You mean Durham?" Vera whispered back, looking at the jovial ram.

"Yup. That's what the gossip is."

"How do you know the gossip about academics when you avoid academia?"

Lenore gave her a wink. "You think it's easy to escape family news? Believe me, ravens have their ways of getting the word out. Haven't you heard the old joke? *How is a raven like a writing desk?*"

"Um, how?" asked Vera.

"Mmmm, come to think of it, the joke is probably only funny to ravens. Never mind."

Meanwhile, the ram was telling the story of Summers End, one that Vera already knew from her reading. He was saying, "Summers End is not just a burial mound. In fact, the graves and ossuaries throughout the site are only of secondary importance to its real purpose. Who can tell me what that is?"

Paws and wings shot upward as students vied for attention. "Yes, you," Durham said to a chipmunk.

"It's a calendar!" the chipmunk said excitedly. "The sun shines directly into the chamber on only two days, the beginning of summer and the end of it."

"Exactly!"

"But why isn't the place called Autumn's Start?" another student queried (without bothering to raise a paw).

Durham gave the student the tiniest look of censure for butting in. "A fair point. Partly it's convention. Folks have called this place Summers End for so long that we have to assume that's the name it always had. And the last day of summer is key because that was the signal to everyone living around here so long ago that it was time to begin preparing for those cold fall and winter nights ahead. The days are still long and warm, but the weather can fool you. However, the sun and stars are reliable. The prehistoric civilization we call early woodland culture wanted to be sure they knew when fall was on its way, so they could manage the harvest and be ready for the future. They built the monument and the mound—which is technically called a barrow—above it as a big alarm clock, powered by the sun itself. And today we come to study their very clever work, because it teaches us about our own history. Which I think is one of the most noble pursuits there is . . . though I might be biased!" He gave a laugh.

Professor Durham then wound down his talk, taking more questions from the students. He seemed quite at home up there and answered every query with aplomb and good cheer. Could such a creature really have upset Ligeia Lee's career? Vera would have to look into it.

Georgette was frantically waving her wing to get noticed by the ram. He finally looked over and pointed toward her. "Yes, you. The pretty little partridge there. You look like you've got something on your mind."

"Thank you, Professor, yes! I was wondering when you will make the selection for the student who gets to go into the monument first on the morning of Summers End."

"Ah, excellent question! As a matter of fact, I think we should get started on that right this moment. My graduate assistant has the wooden box that we use for lotteries here. Myron, bring it on up!"

A rat with sleek dark fur bounded up to where Durham was standing. "Got it, sir. And paper and pencils!"

Durham nodded as he took the box from the rat. He announced, "If any of you are interested in putting your name in, please do so on a piece of paper. Only once, please! We are fair-minded and want everyone to get an equal chance. The winner will be selected tomorrow morning just before we all go into the monument. So it will be a fun surprise!"

Many of the students immediately lined up to put their names in the box, Georgette and Joshua among them. As Vera watched the procession of eager students, she noticed Professor Ford speaking to Professor Chesley. They both looked rather put out, but Vera was too far away to hear a single word of their exchange. Was it just more academic chatter, or something else? One thing was for sure: Summers End had just as much mystery in its present as it did in its past.

Chapter 4

After dinner, Vera made a point to check on her charges before she settled in for the night. Georgette and CJ were sharing a room right next to Vera's, and Vick Sumner and Joshua Chitters were roommates a couple of doors down in the other direction. Vera checked in with all of them, gave them firm warnings about sneaking out, and assumed that once they were in their rooms that they would stay there. (Some readers may notice that while the fox was an excellent reporter, she had little experience with teenagers.)

Vera changed into her favorite striped pajamas and brushed her teeth. She was already exhausted, and this was only the first day. She could hear deep even breathing coming from both Thena and Callie. She planned to mull over the interesting information she had learned that day: that Lenore had a sister and was estranged from most of her family, and how all these academics dealt with one another. Despite her best efforts, though, Vera nodded off almost immediately.

Sometime later, in the deepest part of the night, she was awakened by a door slamming and some high-pitched giggling. Someone was out of bed! Groggily, she pushed her paws into her slippers and grabbed her robe.

"Not on my watch," Vera mumbled as she made her way into the hallway. Several students were gathered on the patio behind the lodging house. Vera marched over to the group (only Vick was technically under her charge) and instructed them in no uncertain terms to get back to their rooms. There was some shuffling and some grumbling, but they did as they were told. Vera sighed in relief. Where had that bossy tone come from? It was like she was channeling her mother.

Vera realized that she had been standing in one spot without moving for several minutes. She shook herself out of her reverie and looked around to make sure that all the miscreant students had returned to their beds.

As the fox turned to go back to her room, she spotted a shadowy figure near the caretaker's cottage. Did no creature sleep around here? At first she assumed it was one of the Rosewoods, but the way the creature moved seemed rather furtive. Common sense told her to ignore the figure and go back to bed, but Vera was not wired that way. The curiosity that made her a good reporter would not allow her to leave without investigating the scene.

As she neared the caretaker's cottage, the figure that had attracted Vera's attention had withdrawn to some part of the woods where she couldn't see them anymore. Vera was annoyed that she had not gotten a closer look. She couldn't even identify the intruder's species. Some detective she was! She had assumed that it was another student sneaking out for whatever reason. But what if it was a creature with a more nefarious purpose?

Vera turned back to the lodge, then spotted yet *another* creature who was not in their room. This time, however, the fox had no trouble recognizing the raven who was just touching down in front of where she was headed.

"Lenore," she hissed, doing her best not to wake anyone else. "What are you doing? Do you have any idea what time it is?" Again, faint memories of her own mother saying much the same thing came to Vera.

The raven looked startled, but then she spotted Vera huddled behind the lodge in her pajamas and slippers.

"I was checking on my students, who were trying to sneak out," Lenore said. "But then I saw something weird. A figure running along the path toward the monument."

"You too?" Vera responded. "This place is crawling with mysterious shadows, but I don't think we'll have much luck chasing them now. Maybe we can look for pawprints in the morning. Let's go back to bed."

They were just about to turn around when Vera saw something else move. "Wait!"

The pair held their breath, watching the figure coming from the lodge toward them.

"That can't be the same creature we were following," Lenore said after a moment.

"No . . . it's Professor Chesley." Vera had just picked out the silhouette of the porcupine hurrying their way. She was carrying an awkwardly large case with her. It bumped against her frame with every other step.

"Professor, where are you off to?" Vera asked, stepping out onto the middle of the path.

The porcupine stopped, but she didn't seem overly startled by their unexpected presence.

"Oh, you're chaperones, aren't you? I saw you at dinner." She didn't mention the near run-in on the sidewalk earlier, so Vera assumed she'd forgotten it happened.

"Vera Vixen, Lenore Lee," Vera said quickly.

"Ah. Ligeia's sister" was all Chesley said. "I'm headed to the site, of course."

"So late at night?"

"I'm an astronomer," she reminded them. "Naturally I work when it's dark. I'm going to set up my telescope on top of the hill, as I always do on clear nights. I should have excellent stargazing."

"That's a big case," Lenore noted. "Do you need help getting it there?"

"Goodness, no," Professor Chesley said, putting a protective paw on top of the case. "I'm used to it. Besides, I don't like anyone other than me touching the case or the device. It's very expensive to replace."

"I'm surprised you don't keep it closer to the site," Vera said. "Don't you have facilities there?"

The porcupine harrumphed. "Yes, but the safest place for it is with me! Now, if you don't mind, I need to get going so I'm ready in time. I'm studying the summer constellations and they've already started to rise in the east. Good night!"

They bade the professor good luck but remained standing there for a moment after she'd left.

"She's not exactly friendly, is she?" Lenore asked. "Even when she's talking about her work, you get the sense that she'd rather be anywhere else."

Vera nodded. "Still, there's nothing suspicious about an archaeoastronomer working at night."

"Then why does it *feel* suspicious?" Lenore asked.

"Because we're already on the hunt for misbehaving students. But they don't seem to be out and about anymore. So I think we can safely go back to bed!"

Happily, there were no more outbreaks of giggling, mischief, or shenanigans for the rest of the night. Vera awoke very early, since the chaperones had to rouse the students and get everyone to the site in time for sunrise. Callie stirred the moment that Vera got out of bed, while Athena rolled over and blinked several times before she also got up.

"We've got just under an hour to herd all the students up and walk the path to Summers End," Callie said, looking at the small clock in the room. "Should be enough time."

Vera stepped outside, noting with relief that the sky was mostly clear. There were some ragged clouds, but a helpful wind was pushing them away at a rapid pace, and there would be no impediment to a clear sunrise.

The chaperones walked up and down the outside of the lodge, knocking loudly on doors, calling for the students to get up. Some came eagerly, some very slowly, but finally everyone gathered on the patio, standing around, munching on hearty muffins that had been baked by their hosts. The adults had been provided coffee or tea in ceramic mugs with cork lids so they could be taken along. Vera was immensely grateful for the innovation. Her mug was a lovely sky blue with stars painted on it.

"Everyone here?" Arabella called out, glancing at the paling sky. "I sure hope so because we're walking over now! Vera, take your group first, please, and Lenore, can you take yours last and keep watch behind you in case any stragglers are trying to catch up? Okay, let's move!"

Vera led her group through the woods, along the broad path that led the way to the monument. Georgette was practically beside herself with excitement, and kept fluttering up the path a ways until Vera called her back to the group.

"Not that there's any danger here," Vera noted one time, "but I really don't want to lose any of you."

Finally, the whole group reached the site. The woods thinned abruptly as they approached, and the quickly brightening sky made it easy to see the landscape, which shortly before had been all charcoal and shadow.

Vera got her first look at Summers End.

First and most noticeable were the dozens of standing stones forming a ring around the edge of the site. Some were so big and heavy that no one was quite sure how they'd been moved and put into place. Just beyond this impressive circle was a slightly wider ring that tourists didn't really notice because the stones comprising it were much smaller: round white rocks placed every few feet or so. They marked the border between the site and the surrounding woodland, but otherwise didn't seem to have a purpose.

Then Vera turned her attention to the center of the site. It was dominated by an artificial hill known as a barrow. It was flat topped and oblong to accommodate the burial chambers beneath the surrounding earth, and most importantly the long tunnel that served as the pathway for the sunlight on this special day. This mound was also called Summerhill, and there was something very mystical about it . . . or maybe that was just because the late summer mists were currently swirling around its base, obscuring the lowest portions. It made the hill seem more like an island rising above a calm sea.

But then a breeze sprang up and pushed the mist away bit by bit, until the whole hill was revealed. At the base, on one end, was a doorway cut into the hill itself, framed with three huge stones on the top and sides. In front of the doorway, a few paces away, was a long, low stone, only about a foot or so high. Vera remembered that it was called the altar stone.

Flanking the altar stone on each side were the two massive vertical stones. These served to block the sunlight on the "wrong" days, so that on this particular day the sun could shine all the way into the doorway and straight down the long tunnel to hit the so-called calendar stone at the end, verifying the end of the summer season.

It was all quite elaborate for a prehistoric culture, Vera thought. It was hard not to be impressed. She readied her camera, which she'd brought along for the trip. She'd taken pictures along the way, but she was hoping to get several of the inside of the monument if the light and shadow allowed.

Standing nearby the tall stones was Professor Lee, looking rather vexed. Beside her, Professor Ford was looking around the site, his tail curled up in protestation against the cool mist.

"You're here!" he said to the group. "And just in time. Wonderful. Is Durham with your party?"

"Professor Durham?" Vera asked, puzzled. "No. I thought

that the plan was to meet all the scholars here at the site. I haven't seen him this morning. Anyone else?" She looked around at the other chaperones but got only shaken heads.

Arabella frowned. "That's odd. He told me specifically that he'd be here waiting well before sunrise."

"Well, I've been here for nearly an hour," Professor Lee said tartly. "And it's been a long, lonely wait, until Isaiah here joined me about twenty minutes ago. Plus, I was worried those clouds wouldn't disperse. Thankfully they did, but we could have just as well had rain."

"Good morning, all!"

The group turned as one, but the cheerful greeting came not from a bighorn sheep but a peacock. Professor Loring had a notebook at the ready, apparently hoping that the sunrise would spark some poetic inspiration.

"Morning, Keats," Ford rasped after a moment. "You didn't happen to see Durham on the way, did you?"

"Not at all," the peacock replied. "I'd have assumed he'd be here long before."

"It's not like Durham to be late," the lizard said, flicking his tongue nervously. "This is his favorite day of the whole year."

"Well, we can't wait around for him," van Hoote said, flapping down to join the group. "The sun certainly won't wait. About ten minutes is all we have."

"Let's pick the winner of our lottery," Arabella said, holding up the wooden box from last night. "And then the first group can line up to accompany the researchers inside the barrow. Now listen, everyone. This is a very important and sacred site. There are creatures buried here, so show respect! No touching, no talking, no messing around. It's a great privilege to come here. Don't make me send you home to Shady Hollow with a note to tell your parents that you desecrated the most important site in the woodlands! Looking at you, Sumner!"

"What?" Vick spread his paws wide, looking innocent.

"Ms. Boatwright, pick the name!" a sparrow urged.

"Oh, right." Arabella opened the box lid and put a paw in, deliberately tipping her head up and looking anywhere but the box. She pulled out one folded piece of paper.

"Callie, can you read the name, please?"

The vole took the paper, unfolded it, and proclaimed in a pleased tone, "Georgette Ashbridge!"

"*Yes!*" Georgette nearly swooned with joy. "Yes, yes, yes!"

"Okay," Vera said, before the little creature fainted. "Let's assemble so we get to our places in time."

Ligeia Lee stepped up to the tunnel. "It's a long way, and the ceiling is low. We will not use lanterns this time because we need to have the *only* light be from the sun. Larger creatures will have to hunch down or crawl at points. If you've got claustrophobia, you may wish to stay outside. I'll go first, then Ford, van Hoote, then the students, led by Ms. Ashbridge, and chaperones. Let's move safely but briskly to be at the stone before the sun hits."

CJ and Joshua both raised their paws. "Er, we're going to stay out here," the mouse said.

"Yeah, where it's less haunted," CJ added.

Arabella snorted but volunteered to remain outside with any students wary of going in. Loring also said he'd stay in the sun, muttering something about watching the delicate golden light strike the altar stone.

Everyone instinctively crouched down as they entered the tunnel. Vera was hit with a clammy coldness and got a sharp reminder in her gut that this was a mass grave. She took a deep breath to clear her head and started moving on all fours into the gloom.

Vera inched forward as the creature in front of her did, pausing to take pictures whenever she had a moment, or when something looked interesting. She only hoped that the pictures would come out. It was quite disconcerting to be with so many others in almost complete darkness. Time was of the essence, since they all wanted to be in place to see the sun hit the calendar stone.

The fox looked up as she heard an imperious voice (perhaps van Hoote?) say to someone up ahead, "Excuse me, please. Can you move out of the way? You're blocking everyone's view!"

At that moment a beam of sunlight shot through the tunnel and illuminated the burial chamber.

"Everyone to the sides of the tunnel!" another professor's voice called. "Allow the sun a clear path."

There were involuntary cries of awe as the sunbeam hit the calendar stone, the brightness illuminating the ancient circular carvings, creating a thin line that corresponded exactly to two grooves in the stone—the confirmation that this was the moment for which the whole monument was designed.

How amazing, Vera thought, snapping a few more pictures, *that prehistoric creatures could be so precise.* It really made one wonder if there was such a difference between so-called modern life and life long ago.

Then suddenly, the murmurs of awe turned to horrified gasps as the chamber grew bright enough to see the thing that had made some of the observers grumble. The thing that had been obscuring a full view of the historic event.

That thing was a dead body.

Chapter 5

There was a great deal of shrieking and jostling from the students as they panicked at the sight and tried to get out of the tunnel that they had just come into. Meanwhile, Vera remained in place, snapping picture after picture almost without thinking. Her reporter's eye was taking in the details of the scene in front of her. What a shocking and gruesome start to the field trip that all of them had been so excited about.

"Thena," she whispered to the wide-eyed vole standing next to her. "Take note of everything you see and hear. It could be vital."

The large supine figure of a bighorn sheep lay directly in front of the calendar stone. The body was surrounded by burned-out candle stubs, strangely carved rocks, and small bone figures of various creatures lying in a circle. It looked like some sort of ancient grisly ritual had been conducted in the darkness of night. A ritual with a grim ending, for the ram was lying in a dark pool of his own blood.

"Professor Ridley Durham has given his last lecture," Lenore muttered in Vera's ear, after she'd checked for a pulse and found none.

The remaining watchers were silent for a long moment. None of the professors seemed to know what to do, so the fox took charge.

"We can't do anything now for Professor Durham," Vera said. "But to help the police, we need to block off access to the crime scene, get all the students back to the lodge, and then contact local law enforcement. No one touch anything. Just turn around and leave as quickly as you can."

The professors, chaperones, and Athena lined up to exit the burial chamber. They obeyed Vera much like her younger students had. Van Hoote, Ligeia Lee, and Dr. Ford all went single file back through the tunnel without saying a word. As she followed the rest of the group, Vera turned back to take another look at the silent form of the ram, now bathed in the golden light of the rising sun. All the exuberant life had been drained from him. And those mysterious objects surrounding the body! Who could have done such a thing?

She took a few more pictures, moving around the scene to catch every possible angle. There was a chill in this chamber that had nothing to do with temperature. Vera shivered a little and then hurried to return to the daylit world.

When the group was once more standing outside the barrow, the professors seemed to recover a little. In contrast, the students were shaken and nervous, several of them asking if this was a trick, or part of some game. Georgette, the partridge who had won the lottery, had been afforded an unexpectedly close view of the corpse, and was now rocking slowly on her little feet as she whispered something to herself.

Professor Loring, Arabella, and the students who hadn't gone inside were demanding to know what had upset everyone, and this resulted in a new round of pandemonium.

"Durham dead!" Loring shrieked. "What an ignoble end! And yet . . . striking!"

The chaperones all did their best to calm the students, while Arabella counted them off to make sure no one had run off into the woods, or worse, remained stuck in the tunnel of the barrow.

Ford was pacing back and forth as he fretted. "This is horrible!"

"I'm sure it was a great shock," Vera said in a soothing tone. "He was a friend as well as a colleague to you."

"No, no! We've missed the sunrise! Now everyone will have to wait months to measure and observe in the tomb. Durham would have been incensed to know his death interrupted our research!"

His attitude struck Vera as a decidedly weird one, but then again, perhaps he didn't know how to react in the moment.

A subdued van Hoote volunteered to fly to the Summerhill Police Station to report the crime, and Ligeia and Lenore, not really speaking to each other but working together, made sure the entrance to the tunnel was blocked off with a barrier made of planks that had been hauled over from a nearby shed.

Then the chaperones, with the exception of Vera and Lenore,

gathered all the students to walk back to the lodge. Georgette was still beside herself, while the rest of the youngsters looked around the trees nervously, as if they were expecting something to jump out of the forest as they passed.

Vera, as the designated expert on crime scenes, stayed behind with Lenore and the professors to make sure no other creature entered the burial chamber until the law arrived.

"Hey, where's Professor Chesley?" Lenore asked, looking around. "Shouldn't she be here, too?"

"She must have slept in," Ford said. "Though I'm surprised she'd miss the sunrise this morning. It's an important astronomical event!"

"I hope nothing bad happened to her," Vera said, recalling that the porcupine had been stargazing the previous evening, on top of the very same hill Durham's body had been found inside. "We should verify that she's all right. Does she have a room at Aster House, too?"

Ford confirmed it and said that he'd check on his colleague as soon as he returned to town, adding, "But we must wait for the chief now."

The creatures lingered around the now-blocked doorway. Ligeia in particular looked distant and almost perplexed, casting looks toward the entrance of the tunnel as if she wanted to go back in.

"Did you see something strange in there?" Vera asked the raven.

"You mean besides the very contemporary body amid all the old bones?" Ligeia snapped back.

"Well, we all saw that. Did you notice anything else?"

"I don't want to talk about it," Ligeia said, looking away almost angrily.

Ford moved over to the pair. He fixed Ligeia with his gaze. "You were the first to arrive."

"So?" Ligeia asked. Vera noticed her feathers ruffling. She was getting defensive.

"Did you see anything when you got here?"

"Like a deranged murderer running away from the site? If I had I would have *said*, Ford! Honestly." She turned away and strutted a few steps, making it clear that she had nothing more to say on the matter.

Still, it was an important consideration. Ligeia *had* already told them that she arrived first to the scene, which would have meant she was waiting alone in the darkness before dawn.

"Professor Lee," Vera asked, keeping her tone polite so as to not annoy her. "Can you tell me if you noticed any light from the tunnel while you were waiting outside? There were all those candles around the body. I wonder if they were still burning when you arrived."

"No! As I said, if I had noticed anything out of the ordinary, I would have mentioned it. And I certainly would have noticed light from the tunnel! Those candles must have burned out hours ago . . . if they were even lit."

"What makes you say that?" Vera asked, curious. Why wouldn't the candles have been lit?

"Nothing," Ligeia said, her manner tense. "I'd rather not speculate."

"About what? The body?"

"The whole mess."

Just then, they all heard a new sound, the rhythmic beat of approaching hooves. Vera turned to the path leading to Rosewood Lodge and beyond that, the town.

A figure was coming quickly through the trees, and Vera

soon saw what she'd already guessed. The local law enforcement officer was a deer. Specifically, an enormous buck with a
rack of sharp antlers towering over an admittedly noble form.

When he reached the small group, he slowed to a walk.
Van Hoote soared above and landed silently nearby.

"I hear we have a problem," the deer said. He looked around
at the various professors and then to Vera, Lenore, and Thena.
"You three I haven't met."

"Lenore Lee is Ligeia's sister. I'm Vera Vixen, and this is
Athena Standish," Vera explained. "We're with the school group
here this week, but we are also journalists." Next to her, Thena
straightened up with pride to be included in this professional
designation.

"Reporters?" the officer asked with a frown. "I don't want
this to become some opportunity for gawkers."

"No, sir," Vera agreed quickly. "I simply meant that we're
good at recording details, and that may be helpful at some
point."

"Hmm." He gave her a long, considering look. "I'm Chief
Lawrence Buckthorn. Both the town of Summerhill and this
site are in my jurisdiction, and I'll insist that everything happens
according to my rules, and under my authority. Is that clear?"

"Absolutely," Vera said, silently adding *so long as the freedom of
the press is respected!*

Thena was already nodding, clearly impressed by the massive
buck.

"All right," Buckthorn said in a different tone. "Van Hoote
mentioned a body was found. Where?"

"Inside the monument," Ford said. "The victim was Ridley
Durham."

"Professor Durham?" the chief repeated, in a startled tone. "I saw him only yesterday!"

"We all saw him last night when he spoke to the students during dinner at the lodge," Vera said. "He was supposed to meet us here earlier this morning for the sunrise, but evidently he'd got here well before, because his body is all the way inside."

Buckthorn looked troubled. "Well, let's go see it. Move that board, please. And can someone light a lantern so we can see when we're inside?"

The board was easily moved, but no light was forthcoming.

"All our candles are missing!" van Hoote reported, after checking a small supply hut near the site. He carried a glass lantern, but there was nothing inside it.

Vera produced a candle and a pack of matches that she had in her bag. (As an amateur detective, she liked to be prepared for things.) Buckthorn nodded approvingly, took the candle from the fox, placed it in the lantern, and led the way back into the monument to view the crime scene. As she reentered the tomb, Vera noted almost in passing that the brightness of the sunlight had already changed to a softer, more diffuse glow most visible near the entrance.

The going was slow as the larger animals had to crouch down to make their way through the tunnel. Vera happened to catch sight of what looked like a blood trail in one of the side corridors that opened off the main tunnel. Not wanting to disrupt the chief's examination, she said nothing at the moment but made a mental note to point it out later. Perhaps someone else had been injured, maybe even the killer.

Chief Buckthorn reached the body first and cautioned everyone else to stay back for a moment. He walked around it, holding the lantern high, taking note of the ritualistic objects placed carefully around the corpse.

"I've seen some odd things in my career, but this is one of the strangest," he said at last. "Looks like some kind of ceremony. Are these little things—the rocks and the bone figures—are they familiar to anyone?"

"The bone figurines look like ones we've dug up all over the site," van Hoote said. "We find them in the course of our excavations from time to time and move them to storage for later research. But they shouldn't be *here*."

"If it's a ritual," Ford added, "it's not one I've ever read about. Ligeia?"

Vera looked around at the professors and realized that both van Hoote and Ford had turned their attention to Ligeia. Of course! Ligeia was a researcher of the death practices of ancient woodland culture.

But at the moment, she was completely unforthcoming, staring angrily at the scene before them all. Vera noted the pool of blood, almost black in the poor light, and how it was centered around Durham's head like a halo. *Not a very large pool of blood,* she said to herself, filing the fact away for later.

"Professor Lee?" the officer inquired. "I know that this place has historical significance, but it's up to you faculty at the college to tell me what it all means. I can't begin to guess at what all these figures and bones might indicate."

"They indicate nothing!" Ligeia said coldly. "Absolutely nothing!"

She then stalked down the tunnel and back to the bright, warm world.

Chapter 6

The rest of the group remained still.

"She must be very upset," Ford said after an awkward moment of silence.

"I'm afraid that she really is best placed to tell us what this . . . arrangement might mean," van Hoote added. He swept one wing toward the grim scene. "I confess that I can't make heads or tails of it. Have you ever read about such a ritual, Ford?"

"Never," the lizard admitted. "It's singular."

"All right, then," Buckthorn said. "Why don't you all go back out, and I'll conduct my questioning in a more comfortable venue. I'll have some questions for you, too, Miss Vixen. You seem like a sharp-eyed creature."

Most of the professors were anxious to get away from the body, with its staring eyes and uncanny stillness. They proceeded down the tunnel once more, and Vera paused when she passed the same side chamber where she'd seen the blood. She almost pointed it out to Buckthorn, but she held her tongue, remembering past events when the local law had not always been pleased with her assistance.

In fact, Vera was feeling a little queasy. She really wished that Orville were here, instead of this imposing deer. What was it about her that attracted murder? She had been anticipating a fun field trip with the students, not this horrific crime. It really made a creature think about how short life could be. Professor Durham had been charming and confident just last night, and now he was cold and silent.

Emerging from the dark tunnel, Vera blinked at the strong light of the late summer morning. The air was already warm, and the puffy clouds overhead belied the sinister reality of murder.

"I suppose," Thena said slowly, "that it couldn't have been an accident. That he couldn't have just slipped and hit his head . . ."

Vera shook her head. She knew exactly how the vole felt, and she was familiar with the urge to deny terrible things. "It would feel better to believe that," she said gently. "But no one simply falls down in a circle of candles and artifacts. And I can't imagine that Durham's head wound was either self-inflicted or the result of a random mishap. He was struck from behind and hit on the one spot where he was vulnerable and couldn't see an attack coming."

"But, Vera, the . . . the things all around him! It's like some awful nightmare!"

True, the presence of the ancient carved stones and bone figures in the shapes of creatures was eerie. Why had someone placed them there, and how did they get them?

She looked over at Ligeia, standing sulkily by a tree, waiting for Buckthorn to question her. It would be a while. He'd first called van Hoote, who seemed as willing to chat as his cousin Heidegger.

Vera told Thena, "Wait here. I'm going to do a bit of constructive eavesdropping." She then drifted closer to the creatures talking, hoping she could hear a bit of the conversation.

Buckthorn was going through fairly standard questions with the owl, asking him to reiterate when he arrived on the scene, who was present already, and if van Hoote had noticed anything unusual about the site.

"Just that Durham wasn't waiting right outside. He lived for this day every year! Er, I mean, he did live . . . until this year."

"Okay, what about how things looked inside? Except for the body, was anything out of place?"

"As I told you, those objects surrounding him had no business being there! The killer must have brought them into the monument, though I've got no possible notion of what they intended by it. It looks like something out of a bad play. Cults and séances and who knows what! Don't approve, not at all!" Van Hoote actually stomped his clawed foot on the ground to register this—it made Vera wonder if any student at the university ever passed his classes.

Buckthorn thanked van Hoote for his cooperation, then asked Isaiah Ford to join him. The questions were much the same, though Ford had more to say about the bone figurines.

"They shouldn't be there at all! Not just in the tunnel, but on the site at all. Not loose like that."

"Is it possible that one of you excavated them and had stored them somewhere short-term until you could bring them back to the university at the end of the dig season? I know you all pack up in a few weeks to get back for the semester." The officer sounded quite knowledgeable about the academic schedule.

"So many, though?" Ford said, shaking his head. "We share our finds, even though we work in different fields. Any items found should be properly labeled and stored. No reputable researcher would keep such a discovery a secret."

"Maybe there was a misunderstanding somewhere," Buckthorn guessed. "I do hope the answer comes to light during the investigation. But I'll need to keep all these figurines as evidence until we know more."

Buckthorn seemed to disregard the poet Loring as a useful witness, to the peacock's obvious relief. He then motioned to Ligeia Lee. "Ma'am, I'm most anxious to hear from you. Please join me for a little chat. According to the others, you were first at the site today."

Vera saw that everyone was listening in now—the facade of a private conversation was just that, a facade.

"I told you that," Ligeia noted sourly. "What else must I regurgitate? That Durham and I fought from time to time? True! That he was an insufferable boor? Also true! Did I kill him? No!"

"No one's suggested that," Buckthorn said, although his tone implied that maybe someone should. "Now, your specialty is what?"

"Death and funeral practices of prehistoric cultures," she said.

"Grand. Then maybe you can tell me if Durham's death seems to, er, follow any pattern? Or resemble something you've seen before? After all, Summers End is a mass grave, right?"

Ligeia frowned. "That's an oversimplification. There are bones buried throughout the site, yes. And we know that certain honored creatures were taken inside the monument for a final rest in ossuaries. But it's not merely a grave, as such. It's a calendar, and a sacred place. The ancients would be appalled by the idea that someone was murdered in there!"

"So the candles that burned out, and the stones, and the figurines . . . they were just there by happenstance?"

"How should I know what the killer intended? All I can say is that *I've* never read a credible report of such a thing. It's a gruesome joke, that's what it is."

"You think his death is a joke?" Buckthorn asked softly.

Buckthorn didn't directly accuse Ligeia of anything, and that was somehow even more of a condemnation.

She sneered. "I think this is all a joke. Including your so-called questions."

He shook his head. "I do hope that you will be of more help to my investigation later, Miss Lee."

"Professor Lee," she corrected in an icy tone. "I hold a doctorate."

"Of course. Wouldn't want to forget that." He made a note in his book, though Vera doubted it had anything to do with Ligeia's title. "A small matter that we'll have to cover is that one of your colleagues, Professor van Hoote, mentioned that you had a spat with Durham in the pub last night. Is that correct?"

Ligeia stepped back, growing wary at last. "I told you; I had a spat with him every day. That's just how it was between us. I didn't kill him!"

Buckthorn cast a look toward Vera and Thena, but then glanced at the sky. "I'm afraid that you'll have to come with me for some further questioning . . . Professor."

"Hold on!" Vera said, moving forward. "You can't be making an arrest already!"

"No one's under arrest. Yet," he added. "But what I've got here is a dead body, a scene that looks like a funeral rite, and the professor of funeral rites, who just happens to constantly be fighting with the victim. And has no alibi to speak of."

"This seems rather hasty," Ford objected, though he didn't move or offer an argument against the police officer's decision.

"I suppose we must trust the officers of the law to know what's best," said van Hoote, looking like he didn't altogether believe his own statement. "And I'm quite sure that the facts will show that Ligeia is completely innocent."

Vera wasn't at all sure of that. Whether during her time in the city or in the woodlands, she'd seen far too many creatures take the easy path. Police officers, lawyers, and judges . . . It didn't matter where they sat on the path of justice, they often skipped important steps in order to make their own work a little easier. It wasn't necessarily corruption. For instance, Vera guessed that this Chief Buckthorn was just going for the fastest and most obvious option: blame someone who didn't like the victim. But it was *far* too early to come to any conclusions!

"Chief," Vera said, trying for a calm tone, "surely you intend to conduct a full investigation. Aside from getting statements from all the workers on the Summers End site, not just Professor Lee, what other steps are you planning?" She'd pulled out her notebook and held her pencil to the page, just as if this were an ordinary interview.

The deer seemed to respond to that unspoken cue (elected officials often did). He said, "I'll see that everything is examined and done according to protocol. My deputy will be here shortly to secure the site. I let him know what had happened when I left with van Hoote. And we'll get the town doctor out to examine and move the body."

"Is your town doctor trained in autopsies for criminal cases?" Thena asked, her own pencil poised. (*Excellent question!* Vera thought.)

"Er, I'll have to ask," Buckthorn faltered. "Murders are very rare around here. I'll check with Dr. Reyes when I get back to town."

"Perhaps Ford and van Hoote can help by replacing the wooden barrier in front of the tunnel doorway, to keep the scene safe until you can arrange for the body to be moved," Vera said.

"I was just about to order that," the deer replied. He glanced at the two professors, who nodded quickly and moved to carry out the instruction.

Buckthorn went on. "I've got to send word to a few folks about what's happened here. I must go back to the station with Miss—er, Professor Lee. I'll have more questions for you as well, if you can come when it's convenient. It's the green building on Hill Street."

"We'll be there," Vera said.

Then he left, bringing Ligeia along with him. Though she hadn't been physically restrained, it was clear that she was not just going for a casual stroll. The onlookers all watched her go, with the suppressed excitement of those who know they just witnessed a juicy tidbit of gossip.

Vera noticed Lenore staring after the pair, with an expression of rage that she'd rarely seen on the raven before.

"How *dare* he! He'll regret this," Lenore cawed softly. In the still summer air, it sounded like a portent.

Just then, a wolverine in a stiffly starched uniform emerged from the woods and hurried up to the group.

"That's Deputy Titus Poole," van Hoote whispered to Vera. "He's . . . well, you'll see."

To say that Poole did not take kindly to the presence of journalists was an understatement. "Reporters, eh?" the deputy snarled at Vera and Thena when van Hoote explained who they were. "More like gossipmongers! If I catch either of you snooping around anywhere you don't belong, I'll haul you off to the jail myself."

"What's off-limits?" Thena squeaked out. (Vera herself preferred not to ask such questions, because then one could claim ignorance.)

"The murder scene, the whole grounds of Summers End, the town, and the forest between."

"But that's everywhere!" Thena protested.

"Exactly! Stay at the lodge with your school group until your boat comes to take you back. I don't need meddlers poking around during the investigation. And don't go bothering folks with your questions. Like vultures, you are!"

Thena looked puzzled. "I don't think vultures are particularly drawn to journalism, are they?"

"He means—" Vera began to explain.

"Never mind!" Poole growled. "Just get out of here! Now! I don't want to see your faces again, understand?"

"We couldn't fail to catch your meaning," Vera said hastily. She ushered Thena away and gave Lenore a quick look to tell her to come along as well.

As the trio moved through the woods, Thena was still considering Poole's comment. "Why vultures?"

"He's just being rude. Very rude," Vera said. "It's alleged that back . . . way back . . . vultures were . . . um, carrion feeders."

Thena's jaw dropped. "Ewwwww!" she exclaimed. Then she gasped. "So he was saying that reporters . . ."

"It's best not to think about it," Lenore told her. "What we do know is that Poole is *not* our friend."

"That's clear enough," Vera agreed. "At least Buckthorn seems a bit more reasonable."

Thena turned toward Vera with an anxious expression. "What do we do now? I've never written a story on a crime before!"

"The story is the least of our worries." Vera snapped her notebook closed. "You, Lenore, and I . . . we have to make a plan."

"A plan for what?" asked Thena.

Lenore finished, with unexpected heat: "A plan to make sure that my sister isn't jailed and put on trial for murder!"

Chapter 7

A few hours later, Vera, Thena, and Lenore sat in the afternoon warmth at a table in the town park. Partly out of habit, Vera had stopped at a little bakery for supplies. They now had a basket of scones on the table between them, but no one was eating.

The good news was that Ligeia was with them. Although Buckthorn had questioned her closely and written down every word she said, he had not taken the step of formally arresting her. Yet.

"He told me I better not leave town," she reported. "And I told *him* that I have no intention of leaving until we close up for winter! After all, we've got work to do on-site and in our laboratory, regardless of what happened to Durham."

"Good for you," Vera said. "I'm glad you made it clear you weren't intimidated."

"Well, he then tried to hint that I was callous for talking about work after a murder, and I just reminded him that ravens had never been known as sentimentalists."

But then Lenore shook her head and said, "Anyway, what can we do to get this cop to *not* decide that Ligeia is the first and only suspect?" Lenore pecked at her blackberry scone, but then pushed it away.

Ligeia sounded both angry and fretful. "He's going to charge me with the murder, I just know it!"

Lenore frowned at her sister. "Could he? Did you do it?"

"How can you even ask that?" Ligeia seemed insulted by the very notion. "We're family!"

"What's that got to do with anything? Besides, our family isn't exactly the warm and friendly type. So. *Did* you kill him?"

"No! Not that I haven't dreamed about it from time to time. The real surprise is that he lived this long. I wasn't the only one to fight with him, anyway. Everyone hated his guts."

"Why?"

"Because he bossed us all around. Deciding who did what, and who got credit for finds. I can't tell you how many times some poor student dug up an artifact, only for him to snatch it away for cataloging. And it was always his name on the record, or at best 'Durham and assistant.' It's difficult to make a name for yourself when someone else keeps putting their name there instead!"

Vera didn't mention how bitter Ligeia sounded. But it was worth asking the other scholars about the matter. Maybe they'd have something to say about Durham's practices when it came to who worked where at Summers End . . . and who benefited or lost due to Durham's controlling nature.

"Listen, Vera," Lenore said then. "I know that Ligeia and I might not be all cuddly together, but she's my sister, and I can't just sit back while the law stumbles around and pushes her into a jail cell. Can you put your investigative skills to work to clear her name? We *need* to find the real killer!"

Vera nodded firmly. "I'm going to get to the bottom of this whole story. I want to write about it for the *Herald*, but I'm sure that the evidence will prove Ligeia had nothing to do with it."

"Speaking of evidence," Thena said, gesturing to Vera's camera, "did you get a lot of pictures? We can look at them to see what Buckthorn and Poole might miss. But I don't know if there's any way to develop the film here in Summerhill."

"There's a room in the lodge you can use," Ligeia said. "In prior years, when professors stayed there all summer, the university had the place set up with all the facilities we would need for a dig, and we've taken plenty of pictures of artifacts and structures and graves and whatnot."

"Good," said Vera. "I think those pictures will be vital, since I doubt we'll be allowed back into the monument again."

Lenore cawed with ironic glee. "You think? The prime suspect, her sister, and two despised reporters? I'm surprised Poole hasn't thrown us all in jail already."

"Let's not give him an excuse," Vera said, remembering how the wolverine had glared at her. "Everyone be careful about what you say and who you talk to."

Vera followed Ligeia to Rosewood Lodge, where the professor retrieved a key to the darkroom from Cora. "Lock yourself in," the raven advised. "Mostly because at least one of those students will barge in and ruin the exposure process. We used to have a sign that said 'Keep Out,' but that's like saying 'Come On In—Free Snacks' to a student."

"You could put up a sign that says 'Supererogatory Study Hall.'"

Ligeia laughed. "That would mean the students would have to know any vocabulary words at all. Well, if I'm not in prison next semester, I'll suggest it. Good luck. I think we'll learn a lot from those pictures . . . assuming they turn out and it's not all just sheets of black film."

Vera shook her head at the similarity between Ligeia's and Lenore's outlooks. Neither raven was an optimist. The sisters were more alike than they pretended.

She went into the darkroom and dutifully locked the door. Back in Shady Hollow, the *Herald* had staff to do the processing, but Vera had learned to develop film when she first started out as a reporter. She still preferred to process her own photographs. Sometimes the subject matter was sensitive (like crime scenes), and she wanted to be the first creature to see the evidence. The process of developing film required darkness and not being disturbed. In other words, it was an excellent time for Vera to sit quietly and ponder all that had happened since she woke up before dawn. It had been a day of unexpected twists and turns, to say the least. While she waited for the rather stinky solution to work on her precious film, Vera recounted her first impressions of the crime scene in her head.

The various professors and researchers who worked at the Summers End site were the most likely suspects, in terms of opportunity and motive. From working in a newsroom, Vera understood all about professional rivalries. They could quickly get out of control, and some creatures would do anything to get ahead at the expense of their colleagues. Was that what had happened here? Clearly Ligeia had plenty of reasons to dislike Ridley Durham, but just because she had had an argument with him the day before the murder didn't mean she was the only one with a motive. It was quite possible that van Hoote or Ford or another researcher hated Durham even more. Maybe they were just a little quieter about it than Ligeia was.

Isaiah Ford in particular proved difficult for Vera to assess. He was circumspect in attitude. While van Hoote used every opportunity to spout off about anything and everything, Ford seemed content to observe, not allowing others to know what he was thinking. And then there was Chesley, who was very aloof—not to mention conspicuously absent during the all-important sunrise. To say nothing of Loring, who seemed to hover on the edge of the academic circle here—ostensibly one of their number, and yet clearly not truly part of the group.

She'd have to figure out how to get some background information on all the professors. Unfortunately, the university was too far away to travel to at the moment, though she could send a request to someone there to help out. Actually, it would be a perfect project for Athena, since she was a student at the university and could ask questions without arousing any suspicions. She could simply say she was looking up professors' backgrounds for a journalism assignment. Which was technically true!

While Vera was musing, she worked patiently with the film, dipping the pictures into the various vats and timing the steps by the clock on the wall. She knew better than to look at the pictures until they were done—everything would be hazy and confusing until the end.

She jotted a few notes down to remind her to tell Thena to ask some useful questions, then continued to think about the crime scene and everyone's reactions. Van Hoote had been quite shocked, to judge by his behavior. But that could have been some fine acting. She could tell that van Hoote held an inflated opinion of himself. If Ridley Durham had withheld funding or credit from the owl, he might have felt that the head of the department had to be removed.

There were a few others who worked on the site, assistants and students getting their field credits. Vera wanted to get all their names and question them, because if Durham had mistreated his colleagues, she could only imagine how he treated those he saw as underlings.

But most of all, Vera would have to return to Summers End to really understand the layout of the place and how creatures might come and go. Clearly, those few hours at the end of the night had been crucial. She hoped someone had seen something useful that could point to the correct suspect. She resolved to ask van Hoote to show her around the site as soon as possible. It would be a good way to subtly question him while getting the lay of the land.

A short while later, Vera pulled the now dry pictures off the line, eager to get back outside and examine them in the light. When she got to the door, she opened it just a crack, peeking to see who might be out and about (she was aware that she'd been neglecting her chaperone duties all day). Luckily, it was calm. The students must all be in their rooms or herded out to the patio in the back. It would be dinnertime soon enough, and Vera did still have certain responsibilities.

The fox hurried to the room she was sharing with Callie and Thena. Both of them were out, so she took the opportunity to spread the newly developed photos out on her bed. The images were black-and-white but surprisingly crisp considering the challenging light Vera had to deal with underground.

She ordered the photos so that they more or less matched her progress down the tunnel, from the doorway with its giant

flanking stones all the way to the flat calendar stone against the
far back wall of the tunnel. Vera paused at one image, which
showed the sun's rays hitting the stone just in the middle of a
series of concentric rings etched onto its surface. She squinted
at several small spots, wondering if they were also part of the
design . . . until she realized with a start that they were blood
drops.

"Ugh," she said, replacing the photo on the bed. She moved
to another, this one of Ridley Durham's supine body. The bighorn sheep had fallen onto his back, his sightless eyes staring
up at the ceiling. Placed in a semicircle around the head, several inches away from it, was the collection of carved stones
and little bone figurines. The pattern was simple: stone, figure,
stone, figure. There were a dozen in total, perhaps to signify the
number of months in a year? Vera grabbed her notebook and
scrawled down her guess. She would bring it up later when she
consulted with Lenore and Thena. She then got her magnifying
glass out of her luggage and held it over the photo, hoping to
see the objects in more detail. If a creature chose these particular things to mark Ridley Durham's death, perhaps the objects
themselves could reveal who did it!

But even after several minutes of intense scrutiny, Vera
couldn't tell much. She was pretty sure one of the stones had a
carving of wine or mead on it, but the other stones were either
tilted away from her lens or the shadows were too deep for her
to make out the images etched on them. The figurines were a
bit easier. There was one sheep (though a lowland sheep, not a
bighorn), placed near the top of the semicircle. She could also
identify a mouse, a raccoon, an egret, and an owl. The species
didn't suggest anything to Vera, but maybe Ligeia, as the expert
in funeral customs, could explain it.

Vera rifled through the rest of the photos, hoping to glean something from the murder scene itself. She saw that Ridley's body was exactly in front of the calendar stone, and remembered the moment just before the sunrise, when the occupants of the tunnel jostled around, each thinking that the body was simply an inconsiderate creature who was blocking their way. But poor Professor Durham couldn't have moved if he'd wanted to.

Then Vera paused over one image, taken while she stood near Durham's head, looking back along the tunnel. His curling horns took up the lower foreground of the image, but that wasn't what Vera noticed. Instead, she seized her magnifying glass and studied the empty stone passageway beyond Durham's hooves.

The stone floor had a strange shadow all along it, going back to the entrance. But nothing could have cast that shadow. Then she sucked in a breath.

That wasn't a shadow. It was a stain. The blurry darkness was a long trail of smeared blood going from the very entrance of the tunnel to where the body lay.

Ridley Durham hadn't been killed inside Summers End.

He'd been killed elsewhere and moved.

Chapter 8

Vera's find made her heart race. Ridley Durham was not a small creature. If the killer moved his body, then it meant they had to be strong enough to drag a full-grown bighorn all the way down the tunnel, and possibly much farther than that. Or that they'd used some other method to move the body.

She wanted to talk to Lenore about the discovery, but she knew that her friend was staying close to her sister. Vera couldn't interrupt that.

But just then, the door opened and Thena and Callie walked in. The older vole said, "Ah, there you are, Vera. I was beginning to get a little worried."

"I was just looking at the photos I developed," Vera explained.

"Ooh, anything interesting?" Thena asked, already moving toward the pictures.

"Absolutely," Vera assured her, pleased at Thena's investigative instincts. "I've got a lot of questions about Durham's death."

"Is that wise?" Callie asked. "It sounds dangerous to flush out a murderer, and anyway, isn't that a job for the Summerhill police?"

"Chief Buckthorn is on the case," Vera acknowledged. "I'm just . . . helping."

"Did he ask for help?" Callie inquired, more skeptically.

"An officer of the law is always happy to receive assistance from a citizen," Vera said, with a wink.

"Oh, goodness." Callie shook her tiny head. "I'm going to speak to Arabella about what we should do tonight. The students will surely feel uneasy when it gets dark. I'll leave you two to chat. And Vera . . . remember that Thena is to be mentored. And good mentors don't put their mentees in harm's way."

"Wouldn't dream of it!" Vera said, crossing her heart with a paw.

Callie hesitated and then spoke quickly, as if she had been thinking about something. "Vera, I know that investigating this murder is important work, so you should talk to Arabella about your chaperone duties. Maybe we can shuffle around the responsibilities, so the students are being watched adequately. Parents are counting on us to keep their young ones safe. And I'm counting on you to keep Thena safe!"

When Callie left the room, Thena said, "Don't listen to her! She's acting like I'm still a helpless newborn. I'll do whatever it takes to get this story."

"Hold on," Vera said. "She's right; you need to be careful.

But you should still look through these photos and we should discuss your reactions. And I've got some tasks for you. Don't worry, they're proper journalist tasks: research and talking to sources."

"You mean on everyone's backgrounds and motives? I'm already on it!" Thena pulled out a little notebook and opened it, showing a chart with all the names of potential suspects.

"Great," Vera said. "We need to start as soon as possible, because I think that Chief Buckthorn is going to move fast as well."

"You mean he'll blame Ligeia for it, no matter what he finds."

Vera nodded.

The vole said, "I'll reach out to some folks at the university and ask about the professors. I know someone in the Archaeology Department, and there's an assistant in administration that I spoke to about an article I wrote for the college paper."

"Excellent," Vera said. "As a journalist, you can never have too many sources. You never know when one will prove useful."

Thena grimaced. "I'll have to send all my questions via wing-mail to get answers in time. This could get expensive!"

"The _Herald_ will pay for it," Vera assured her. "I've got some money you can use for the messages. Just save all the receipts—that's another journalism tip."

Thena chuckled. "This internship is going to be more educational than I ever expected."

Once Thena left, Vera tidied up the crime scene photos and prepared to head down to the dining room for some tea to fuel her next step, which would be to find out where Ridley Durham was actually killed. But before she reached the patio, she spotted what looked like a bundle of feathers off to the side of the walkway. Sobs came from the bundle. The fox realized with a pang of guilt that she was looking at Georgette, one of her charges. Callie had been right to remind her earlier. She had been so caught up in the investigation, she had forgotten that she was at Summers End to chaperone. She was responsible for the well-being of four young creatures.

Vera got down on the floor and lightly touched the partridge with her paw. The sobbing grew louder. She decided to go with the brisk approach.

"Georgette," she said in a firm tone. "What's going on? Why are you making all this noise? Aren't you supposed to be working on your field report about Summers End?" (All the students were supposed to write an essay while they were on the trip.)

The small bird sniffed and looked up at her chaperone. "But, Miss Vixen," she wailed, "how can I focus? It's just so awful! Professor Durham is dead! Someone bashed in his head! What if I'm next?"

"Now, now." Vera fished in her pocket for a pawkerchief. "There's no need to worry. The police are investigating the murder. You and the other students are perfectly safe."

Georgette took the proffered piece of fabric and wiped her eyes while Vera sat down next to her. The bird said, "Please, Miss Vixen, you've got to figure out who the murderer is. I'm scared, and I don't think that the police know what they're doing." She sniffed again, and added in a heartbreaking voice, "And I *really* want to go home!"

Vera comforted the partridge while patting her on the head. It was in fact a grand idea to send all the students home. Not only would it be safer for them, but then Vera would be able to devote all her time to investigating the crime, without the guilt that came from neglecting her other duties. She wasn't cut out for this chaperoning business. Once Durham had been discovered, she had forgotten all about the young creatures that she was responsible for. Not just Georgette, but Joshua Chitters, Vick Sumner, and CJ Mapleton. It was a good thing Arabella was in charge of the trip, and not her. But Vera did make a note to talk with Arabella as soon as she saw her and argue for sending the students home early. Even a few days could make a difference.

Vera reached out to Georgette and helped her up off the floor.

"Why don't you come with me," the fox said kindly, "and we'll get you a snack. Something to take your mind off all this. I'll speak to Ms. Boatwright about when you and the rest of the students can go home."

The little partridge gathered her things and followed Vera. They went to the dining area, and Vera ordered some lemonade and molasses cookies for them both. There was really no ill that could not be cured by molasses cookies.

While they were eating, another student came up to them, and said, "Georgette, we need a fourth for our card game. Want to join?"

The partridge nodded and went off with her friend. Secure in the knowledge that she'd be with others, Vera felt like she could leave the inn again.

In a meditative frame of mind, Vera walked back to Summers End, hoping to examine the area before the sun set. As she approached, she saw Poole, the cranky deputy. Unfortunately, he also saw her.

"Hey, what are you doing here? The chief gave orders that everyone has to stay away!"

"And that was very smart," Vera said. "It's important to keep the area pristine so that evidence isn't lost. But I think I discovered something important, and it would be wonderful if you could help to confirm it." She was not above buttering up, if it got her closer to the scene of the crime.

The wolverine did not look even slightly buttered up. "You need to leave the site, or I'll arrest you for trespassing."

"But you're passing up a prime chance to uncover vital evidence! Look here," Vera said, pulling out the photograph depicting the trail of blood. "Do you see this dark streak? I believe it's blood, which means that Durham wasn't killed inside the barrow. He was killed somewhere else, and the murderer dragged him inside. If we can locate where he was actually killed, there could be clues pointing to the murderer's identity! You've been patrolling all day, haven't you? Have you seen any spots here on the grounds that looked suspicious?"

Poole shook his head abruptly. "The only suspicious thing I see is a nosy reporter trying to do the job of a cop. Now get!"

"But, Deputy Poole, don't you want to solve this crime?" She took a gamble, appealing to both his sense of justice and his desire for promotion. Hopefully at least one of those things would resonate with the wolverine.

He snorted. "So what if I do find some clue, and it points right to your raven pal?"

"Then the law has to take its course. Please, there's a little bit of daylight left. Help me look for the place where Durham was killed. It can't be far, and it might even be right here at the site."

"I don't know. I've got orders, and the chief doesn't like it when folks ignore what he says."

Just then, Professor Ford, accompanied by one of the graduate students, the rat named Myron, emerged from a low building not far from the site and walked toward them. "What's going on?" he asked.

Vera explained that they were looking for some hint of where

Durham might have been struck, before being taken inside the barrow. Ford instantly volunteered to help, and the younger rat did as well. Poole still looked highly skeptical of the whole thing, but Vera pointed out that they only had about half an hour of sunlight left, so it was unlikely that they'd find anything. "Then you can enjoy telling me how much I've wasted your time," she said.

The deputy did seem slightly cheered by the prospect of chastising a reporter, and he allowed the search. Vera suggested the three of them start at the entrance of the barrow. "We'll each take a different direction, heading toward the outer ring. If anyone sees anything out of place or suspicious, give a holler."

"I've been patrolling all day," Poole said, frowning. "You saying I missed something obvious?"

"Not at all," Vera replied. "You've been here with the goal of keeping random folks from accidentally messing something up. But now you've got new information, so the situation has changed. I think that we should all look for any dark spots that might be blood. Or flattened grass, or fresh tracks. And most of all, anything that looks like it could have been used to hit Durham on the back of the head."

The quartet worked their way slowly out from the barrow entrance, moving more or less along the cardinal directions. Vera's path took her north, and she zigzagged in an effort to cover more ground. Every few minutes, she glanced up at the lowering sun, all too aware that night was coming.

"Wait a second!" Ford called out from his quadrant. "Come on over! There's something wrong here. See that hole in the ground? There's a stone missing. It's one of the border stones! I know it was here yesterday; I pass by here every day!" The professor looked incredibly upset.

The other three abandoned their own searches and hurried toward Ford.

Vera looked from the small hole in the ground to the nearest intact border stone, which was half buried in the earth, its white top rising about six inches above the surface. She remembered reading that the stones served to divide the sacred space from the surrounding ordinary world. According to the book she'd read about the site, there were over a hundred of these stones that made up the outermost circle. And if her hunch was right, one of them had been dug up and put into use as a murder weapon.

Vera told the others to start examining the ground nearby. "Okay, same plan as before, but more focused. Let's all work our way out from this hole. I bet the stone isn't far away. Even though it wasn't big, it must still be rather heavy."

The group spun outward, each of them focused on the ground. Twilight was approaching rapidly, the sky turning to liquid amethyst as the sun's last rays vanished. The surrounding woodland loomed near, and the deep shadows under the trees made everything within hidden and unknowable.

"We'll have to come back at dawn," Vera muttered to herself, "and hope that the murderer doesn't use the darkness to cover up evidence they couldn't get to today."

She was about to give up when she came to a clump of ferns growing under the spreading limbs of a huge elm tree. She pushed aside the long arching fronds, and amid the gloom, a rounded white shape was revealed.

Vera gave a yelp of excitement, bringing Poole, Ford, and Myron quickly to her side.

"That's definitely a border stone!" Ford said. "See how the lower half of it is dark?"

Myron said, "That's the half that was buried. It was in the ground for centuries before last night!"

"Okay, all of you, step aside," Poole ordered. He whipped out a big square of clean cloth and carefully wrapped it around the stone, then lifted it up.

He grunted slightly. "Wouldn't want to carry this too far."

"It's about ten yards from the hole it was taken from," Ford said, measuring by sight.

Poole carried the stone several feet back toward the clearing, then set it down on the grass where they could all see it in more detail. In the last remaining light, one big splotch on the side of the stone commanded attention.

Poole poked a paw at the edge of it and then bent forward and sniffed.

"Yep, that's blood. We found the murder weapon."

Chapter 9

The next morning, Vera ate her breakfast in haste, though it was something of an injustice to Cora's excellent blueberry muffins and the lodge's strong coffee.

After the discovery of the rock that had been used to kill Durham, Deputy Poole had shooed them all away, with orders not to tell anyone about what they'd found. He'd rewrapped the stone and carried it back to the spot under the ferns, presumably to show Buckthorn where it had been located.

Although Poole had doubtless made a report to Chief Buckthorn, Vera intended to go visit the police station herself. She wanted to show him her photos and discuss whether the discovery of the weapon changed the case. It might narrow down

the list of suspects quite a bit—or at least make him realize that
Ligeia wasn't the only creature he should be looking at. Yes, the
raven could have wielded the rock. But was it a natural choice
for a weapon? Vera thought that most winged creatures would
opt for something both lighter and easier to use.

She put on a hat, since the sun would still be hot even this late
in summer and gathered her things in a straw bag. The moment
she stepped outside, Arabella hailed her.

"Vera, I wanted to speak to you."

The fox was pretty sure Arabella was going to take her to task
for neglecting her chaperoning duties, so she said, "I know I've
been running around working on this story about the murder—"

"I'd expect nothing less," said Arabella, to Vera's surprise.
"You may have signed up to watch over some students, but your
skills will be put to better use as an investigator."

"You're not upset?" Vera asked.

"No reason to be," Arabella replied. (Rats are very logical
creatures.) "It's obvious that a horrible crime was committed,
and folks deserve to know the truth of what happened. You'll
be able to do that when you write about it for the paper."

"But my four students . . ."

"Oh, I've already made adjustments to the roster so that
you and Lenore won't be full chaperones. She's much too worried about her sister to focus anyway," Arabella said.

"Wow, you're sure?"

"It's all sorted."

After thanking the rat for her understanding, Vera dashed
away down the path to town. The gravel track was wide and
well traveled, though at the moment she was the only creature on it. She reached Summerhill and walked a few blocks
before she found the police station, which was exactly where

Buckthorn had said it would be. Hill Street intersected Summer Street, and in front of a green-painted two-story building a white sign read:

SUMMERHILL POLICE

SAFETY IN ALL SEASONS

Vera opened the gate and went up the wide path, which was paved with big, flat stones with sparkly flecks of mica in them. In the morning sun, the building's paint was shiny and pristine, as if someone washed it down each week. The windows even had flower boxes, now full of blooming lavender and trailing ivy. It looked more like a bed and breakfast than a police station. She idly wondered if Orville would agree to window boxes back in Shady Hollow, then immediately discarded the notion based on the expression she imagined Orville wearing the moment she brought it up. ("And who's going to water them? My imaginary deputy?" he'd probably say.)

The front door had been propped open with a large brick, so Vera continued inside, where she saw Chief Buckthorn sitting at a big desk in the middle of the main room. Behind him there were three doors in the back wall, with small windows cut into the top of each and cheerful signs nailed on them: CELL ONE, CELL TWO, and CELL THREE. The signs were decorated with different flowers, and Vera had to squint to notice that the word *cell* had been painted over the word *spa* on each. She was starting to get very curious about who was sprucing up the local constabulary's space.

"Chief, I'm sorry to interrupt you, but I've got important information about Durham's death."

The deer looked up at her. "Is it the name of the killer?

Because that would be helpful." He pushed aside the papers he'd been working on. "Miss Vixen, I was hoping I'd run into you today. Have a seat and tell me what's on your mind."

Vera appreciated that he was willing to listen, so she smiled as she made herself comfortable in the visitor's chair, which sported a cushion embroidered with ivy leaves. "Er, I have to say that this is the most *decorated* police station I've ever been in."

Buckthorn gave her a wry grin. "We inherited the building. It used to be a salon. But it turned out the salon owner hadn't paid taxes in forty years and had no plans to start. They skipped their hearing, absconded downriver in a boat, and we took the property in lieu of payment. But the town council felt that purchasing new furniture or supplies would not be a worthy use of funds. So. Here we are." He held up a mug that said *Keep Calm and Call Your Stylist* and took a sip of coffee. "Can I offer you something to drink?"

"Not at the moment, thanks," Vera replied, being well acquainted with the quality of coffee in a typical police station. "I had coffee at the lodge with my breakfast."

"Oh, sure. Cora makes good coffee." Buckthorn regarded his own mug a little sadly.

She said, "I expect Poole told you about finding the stone used to kill Durham?"

"Yes, last night when I relieved him of his patrol duty. Showed me the spot where it had been found and where it had been dug up from the circle. I sent a note to the doctor—he'll do his best to match the blood, though I don't think there's much doubt it's the weapon. But what's got me curious is how you knew to look for it."

Vera pulled out the photo she wanted to show him. "When we went into the monument, I had my camera with me. I'm a reporter and I wanted to chronicle both our school's trip and the sunrise. So I took a bunch of pictures, and I developed them yesterday afternoon."

Buckthorn frowned. "I wish you hadn't taken pictures, Miss Vixen, particularly without asking permission. It is a crime scene." Then he sighed. "But of course you didn't know that when you started, and your reporter training must have kicked in immediately. May I gently request, though, that, in the future, you refrain from doing similar things until we discuss it first?"

Vera nodded. Buckthorn's approach was certainly different than Orville's had been. The first time Vera told him she had pictures of a crime scene, he'd practically chased her out the door! "I do respect that you've got a job to do, Chief. And I hope you respect that I do as well. I may work at the Shady Hollow *Herald*, but news can happen anywhere." She offered the photo to him.

He took it and scanned it carefully. "Durham's body," he noted, with regret in his tone. "A loss to this community, Miss Vixen, I can tell you that. But what's in this image that we didn't see at the site?"

"You may have seen it, Chief, but I didn't notice till I looked at the photo. The dark streak down the tunnel floor . . . it's blood. Durham's blood."

Buckthorn's eyes widened and he held the photo up, examining it even closer. "I do believe you're correct, Miss Vixen." He flung the photo down on the desk. "Who would do such a thing?"

"And why use a border stone as a weapon?" Vera added. "Why did the killer not use a knife, or something *designed* to be a weapon? Even the nightsticks you and Poole carry would be better than a half-buried rock. It makes me think that maybe the killer didn't plan the murder. It was a spur-of-the-moment decision, and the rock was the closest item they could reach."

"Possibly," Buckthorn mused. "But dragging the body inside surely indicated that the killer wanted to hide what they'd done."

"Not exactly, Chief. Remember, it was the night before the biggest event of the year for the site. The killer had to have known that the body would be discovered first thing the next morning."

"Then is that why they made that nasty tableau surrounding the body?" the deer asked. "I don't like it, not at all."

"No one likes a murder, Chief. But I think this evidence should cast a lot of doubt on your assumption that Ligeia Lee is the culprit. She couldn't haul Durham's body very far! Plus, now you'll need to look at where Durham was killed. It was on the far side of the clearing, the opposite side to the path everyone uses to get to Rosewood Lodge and back to town. You'll need to talk to witnesses who were in that area and collect alibis from those in the vicinity."

"I know how to do my job, Miss Vixen," Buckthorn said coolly.

Belatedly, Vera realized that she'd grown used to talking with Orville about police work, and that she'd overstepped with the deer.

"Sorry," she said. "I'm sure you do. I just feel strongly that particularly when a crime like this has occurred it's important to be careful, so that justice can be served."

"I happen to hold the same view," he noted, still a bit frosty. "You might have noticed, for example, that I did *not* arrest Professor Lee. Because I am being careful."

"Right." Vera nodded. "Er, I'll just go then, shall I?"

"That might be best. Please stick to your profession, Miss Vixen, and let me pursue mine."

"You got it." She was about to excuse herself when she saw something else on his desk—a single glossy black feather.

"What's that?" she asked, pointing to it.

He quickly pulled a sheet of paper over the item, but Vera wasn't going to give up meekly.

"That's a raven feather, isn't it?" she continued her questioning. "Why's it on your desk? Where'd you find it?"

"That's none of your business, Miss Vixen."

"I'm a member of the press, and I'm writing a story on a crime, and you're an officer of the law investigating that crime. So it's exactly my business!"

The deer narrowed his eyes, and tilted his head in a way that suddenly made Vera aware of just how sharp the tips of those antlers were. But then he sighed. "I'll tell you, but you'd best keep it quiet till I make a formal announcement."

"Announcement for what?"

He disregarded that particular question. Instead, he removed the sheet of paper that briefly covered the item. He said, "When Dr. Reyes, Deputy Poole, and I moved the body from the tunnel yesterday, this feather was found . . . underneath it."

Too stunned to talk after that, Vera hightailed it out of the police station and moved quickly down the street, eager to get away from the annoyed chief and the shocking bit of evidence on his desk.

How did Ligeia's feather end up under Durham's body? Was the raven lying? Was she the killer after all?

No, Vera told herself. Lenore wouldn't have rushed to defend her estranged sister if she had any doubts about Ligeia's innocence. And Vera did believe Ligeia when she said she didn't do it. But the feather was real, and its presence had to be explained somehow.

Buckthorn had told her to stick to her specialty. But what Buckthorn didn't know was that Vera's specialty was sticking her nose in other folks' business. Orville told her so all the time!

So Vera headed toward Aster House, the inn where all the professors seemed to have rooms. She was hoping to find van Hoote, and wondered if the owl had already gone to bed (if he held to typical nocturnal hours).

Before she saw him, though, she encountered the stargazing porcupine.

"Professor Chesley, I'm glad I've found you!" Vera said. "We were worried when you weren't at the site for the sunrise event yesterday. We thought you might have been in some danger."

The porcupine looked surprised at the very notion. "Danger? Why should that be?"

"Because you were watching the sky through your telescope the night before, possibly right when Durham was killed. Or possibly just before, depending on what the doctor concludes about the time of death."

"How distasteful to contemplate," Chesley said, frowning at Vera.

"Well, what concerns me is whether you might have seen or heard anything that night that could help us identify the murderer."

"Isn't that a matter for the police?"

Vera shrugged, saying, "Of course, I'll share what I learn, but isn't it better to have more help rather than less? We all want the killer caught."

"Do we?" Professor Chesley gave her an odd, penetrating

look. "I could name several creatures who'd probably give the killer a heartfelt thanks. Durham wasn't universally loved."

"So I've heard. Do you want to tell me who specifically had issues with Durham?"

"Some might put Ligeia Lee on the top of that list. But I don't gossip about colleagues."

Vera tried another angle. "Did you see anything on the ground while you were stargazing? You'd have had a perfect sightline if anyone came near the hill."

"That's true. But the fact is I didn't see anyone. You know, I told Chief Buckthorn all of this yesterday when he came here to get my statement. Not that I had much to say. I wasn't anywhere near the site when the murder occurred. I was asleep in my room! So I don't know why it matters what I might think. Honestly, just leave me out of the whole mess."

"Just so I can eliminate you from my list of witnesses, how late *did* you stay?"

Professor Chesley made a *hmmm*ing sound and looked to the side. "Probably about three thirty or so? The sky gets light in the east well before sunrise, and you'd be surprised how few stars are visible."

"Oh, I assumed you would usually stay till dawn."

"Well, yes, *usually*," Chesley said, her expression growing miffed. "But there was a bit of a rain squall that came through. Clouded everything up and there was no point in staying. I don't care for getting wet."

"Okay, that could be helpful in determining the time of death. Thank you, Professor." Vera paused, then asked, "If you don't mind me saying, it's a *little* strange that you weren't at the site yesterday morning. I mean, the most important day of the year!"

The porcupine sighed, perhaps annoyed that she had to explain her work to a nonexpert. "The sun's path is well known, and not particularly relevant to my own research, which focuses on whether ancient civilization understood precession and, if so, how."

"What's that?"

"The polestar isn't always directly above the pole—the whole globe on which we live sort of wobbles a bit, after many thousands of years. The effect is called precession. It can affect how we see stars in the sky, depending on where you're standing and what time of year it is and how extreme the precession is. So I have to take very precise measurements here at the site to find out if some of those stones in the outer ring were placed because of where a particular star rose or set during the night."

"So you don't care about the day of Summers End at all?"

Chesley shook her head. "For my work, all that matters is that I know the date. The stars' paths and their relation to the ring of standing stones on the site are far more intriguing to me." She gave a slight, unexpected laugh. "You know, it's a common failing of academics, and indeed all creatures, that the brightest object gets all the attention, leaving so much else ignored. Good day, Miss Vixen."

With that pronouncement, the professor walked away, leaving Vera to stare at her spiny, uncommunicative back.

Chapter 10

After speaking with Chesley, Vera resumed her search for van Hoote. She got lucky and found him lounging on the big back porch, pensively rocking back and forth on one of the swings designed for avian guests.

He lifted a wing in greeting when she called out a hello.

"I trust you're recovering from the shock," he said, his tone serious. "I've scarcely been able to put two thoughts together since poor Ridley was found."

"You two were close?"

"Worked together for many years! Naturally we got to know each other. Can't imagine who would dare do him in!"

Interesting choice of words, Vera thought. *Not who would want to do him in. But* who would *dare*. Aloud, she said, "You don't think it was Ligeia?" She was still very disturbed by Buckthorn's revelation about the black feather being found under the body.

Van Hoote gave a derisive snort. "Goodness, she's all show and no snap. Ligeia would want him to stay alive so she could keep arguing with him. Even supposing she did want him dead . . . why wait till now? She's been here the past three dig seasons. She's had plenty of other opportunities to do away with him in a less obvious manner. And trust me, those two never got along."

"It was rather dramatic, wasn't it?" Vera asked. "Do you find any of the other professors or workers on the site to have a flair for drama? Loring, perhaps?"

The owl frowned, considering the idea. "Hmmm. Not sure about that. He's mostly concerned with his own poetry, and he had nothing to do with the dig, so why would he have a grudge against Ridley?"

"He's not part of the dig?" Vera asked in surprise. "But he's a professor at the university, just like the rest of you . . ."

"He's with the university, but he's got no connection whatsoever to the Archaeology Department," van Hoote pointed out. "The peacock showed up in Summerhill about a week after we all did, and said he was here to *absorb the landscape into his soul* or some such. He spends all his time wandering the town and the woods and jotting things down in his notebook. Got some grant to write a collection of poems based on Summers End. But I think he's just using that as an excuse for a vacation."

"That's interesting," Vera said, jotting it down in her own notebook. "I assume he's staying here at Aster House with all the other professors?"

"No, actually. He rented a room with someone in town.

Guess his grant wasn't *that* big," van Hoote added, with professional smugness.

But that gave Vera an idea. "Ridley Durham did have a room here, though, correct?"

"Oh, yes, 401, the suite on the top floor." A look of annoyance flashed across his face. "Which honestly, they should reserve the top floor for birds, don't you think? *Much* more suitable."

"He must pay extra. Or have paid, rather."

"Perhaps. Maybe he got funding to cover it. I only know that the suite is quite expensive."

"Funny that you all don't stay at Rosewood Lodge," Vera said. "It's so much closer to the site."

"We all *used* to," van Hoote said, with a flap of his wings.

"Oh, right. Ligeia did mention that," Vera recalled. "Why the change?"

"Rosewood Lodge was more convenient, that's true. But Ridley got into a huge fight with the Rosewoods a few years ago, and Gerry wouldn't allow him to stay at the lodge any longer. So Ridley retaliated by moving *all* the professors' rooms over here to Aster House, just to keep the Rosewoods from getting any money from the university. He couldn't stop the student groups from using the lodge, though. It's the only place big enough for them, and Aster House is much too fancy for students anyway."

"Wow, it must have been quite the row. What was it about?"

"Couldn't say. Ridley could be awfully hardheaded sometimes. I guess those horns made him think he could fight anyone and win."

Maybe that's why someone hit him from behind, Vera thought. She also filed away the fact that Ridley Durham's room was on the top floor of the inn. Possibly the room held clues about who had motive to kill him. Vera wished Orville were here. If he were in charge of the investigation, he'd search the rooms right away, and he'd probably allow Vera to help, or at least share his findings. She very much doubted that Chief Buckthorn would extend the same courtesy. However, Vera was also used to edging around pesky regulations when justice demanded it.

She said to van Hoote, "You know, I actually came here to find you. I was just thinking that I've had no opportunity to really see Summers End properly yet, and now it's very important to do so, in order to understand how the murder could have occurred. Do you have a little time to show me around?" She was not above a little flattery and deployed it now. "Professor Heidegger always spoke so highly of your gift for explaining difficult concepts to nonexperts." (In reality, he'd done no such thing.)

Van Hoote did everything he could to avoid puffing up his chest, which still inflated slightly at the praise. "Well! I do have the afternoon free, as you may observe from my leisure here. I'd originally been scheduled to discuss the latest findings from our observations of the sunrise with Ridley . . . but obviously that's no longer going to happen."

"It's too bad the murder disrupted your research."

"Indeed! Ridley would have been furious. He hated losing an opportunity for scholarship. But we'll adapt. Luckily, the sun will rise on Summers End next year, too!" Van Hoote hopped down from the swing and gestured with one wing for Vera to proceed back down the walk. "No time like the present! Let us go while the sun shines, and you will gain a wealth of knowledge under my tutelage!"

He and Vera walked on, and she had to admit that she did

gain a wealth of knowledge, for van Hoote talked constantly. At first, he shared tidbits about the town of Summerhill itself. He mentioned where the best neighborhood was ("All the oldest families live in Hilltop, mostly so everyone can see their houses perched up there!"), where the finest drinks could be had ("Glinda's Gadfly Lounge. You have to go down the side alley and knock on the door and then say, 'I've flown pretty far for a drink,' and they'll let you in."), and where to find muffins and donuts fresh baked at dawn ("The Front Street Bakery is smaller than the one on Summer, but they're ready with divine donuts just when I like to head off to bed. Perfect snack!").

"You sound like a local," Vera observed.

"Of course. I know the town well, you see, having summered here—so to speak—for the last six years. Tremendous advances in my field, thanks to my work here at the site."

"And your field is ancient languages, yes?"

"Yes. I study the ebb and flow of language to better understand how the woodland culture came to be. The goal is to determine how we moved from being separate species with our own calls and cries, to a civilized society where we all can communicate."

"And Summers End will teach you that?"

"It's a major turning point in our history," he said. "No single species could have built it, so by definition, all sorts of different creatures had to be able to communicate with each other to get the work done. That means such language capabilities existed *before* the site was built, whether written or spoken. I'm looking for clues as to what the language they used actually looked like by studying the items left behind and the monument itself."

"Is there writing at Summers End?" she asked. "Where?"

"Oh, I'll show you. It's exciting to view."

"Was Professor Durham interested in your work as well?" Vera asked.

"He was very supportive. Advances in any of our fields helped the whole project."

"But then why did he bicker with some of the others?"

"Well, we all get passionate. And if you're referring to Ligeia, I must admit that not everyone found her research to be as . . . central to our mission."

"Wait. Isn't Summers End a burial site as well as a celestial clock? Ligeia studies burial customs!"

"Oh, yes, and there's nothing wrong with that. But Durham thought she was a bit too . . . open-minded when it came to assessing facts. She's liable to accept folklore and nursery tales as sources and value them just as highly as she would an artifact dug out of the ground."

"But aren't stories and songs and rhymes important, too? That's how creatures pass on knowledge from generation to generation. I bet the Summers End builders would have approved."

Van Hoote gave a little snort. "Ask Ligeia who *she* thinks built Summers End! Then you'll see."

Before Vera could pursue that comment, they reached the site. The wolverine on guard duty rushed up to meet them, but he wasn't exactly a welcoming party.

"Oh, no, not again! No one is allowed on-site unless they're on official business!" he barked. "That fox has to leave!"

Van Hoote brushed aside Deputy Poole with an airy wave of his wing. "Not allowed? Don't be absurd. I'm on official business, and Miss Vixen is my official guest!"

"Nope, nope, nope." Poole looked so fierce about it that Vera wondered if he had gotten into trouble for allowing her and

Ford to look around the previous evening, despite their search uncovering an important clue. He went on. "Chief Buckthorn made it extra clear this morning that no one is to be let loose on the site."

The owl hooted in offense. "Let loose? Do you see any looseness? You do not, and that is because all the youngsters have been sensibly contained at the lodge. I am conducting a *tour*, dear sir. If you wish to complain about my conduct, you may certainly scurry off to your superior."

Vera was pretty sure that the suggestion that Titus Poole *scurried* anywhere would cause the wolverine to have a fit. But he contained his rage and glared at her. "Very well, but no sneaking around and poking into things. I'll be watching your every move, reporter."

"How terribly reassuring," she muttered.

"*Manners*, sir." Van Hoote gave the wolverine a golden-eyed glare that had some effect, for the deputy finally stepped back. "Ah, good. Come along, Miss Vixen. Prepare to be dazzled."

Chapter 11

Van Hoote led her inside, out of the noonday sun. The humid warmth was quickly replaced by cool air that was just this side of damp. Unlike her first experience, which was crowded and then panicked, this time Vera could sense a kind of calm in the atmosphere. Van Hoote held the lantern high, and there was no sound other than their soft shuffling along the stone floor.

"It's so much quieter than I expected," she murmured. "Even with the stone all around. Stone usually creates echoes."

"It's the packed earth surrounding us," the owl explained. "And this stone absorbs some sound, as well as moisture and smell. The ancient woodlanders chose their materials well. These stones have remained here for thousands of years, with nary a crack to show for it. They have been set with care, so that heat or frost, wet or dry, they'll stay in place. Ah, here we are."

He paused at the center of the tunnel. On either side of him, an open doorway led to a side chamber.

"I read about these," Vera said. "They're the smaller burial chambers."

"Yes. Each contains the graves of creatures from multiple species, as well as a host of objects buried with them. The most common are the so-called symbol stones, each carved with the image of something the dead would like to have in the afterlife. We believe that not only did this practice mean the living cared about their dead, but that creating symbolic versions rather than using the goods themselves was also a deliberate choice."

"So rather than bury a loved one with a fancy necklace they cherished, you'd carve a picture of a fancy necklace and place it with the body."

"Exactly. It cut down on grave robberies, because there was nothing in here that a living creature would want. Extremely clever and practical, yes? We're fortunate that we've all got such wise ancestors!"

Coming from an owl, this was a strong statement indeed. Vera said, "May I peek inside? I didn't get the chance to see any of these side chambers before."

"Certainly!" He held the lantern up and indicated the left chamber.

Vera walked into it and was startled to see the walls bright with colors. "It's been painted!" she exclaimed.

"By many different artists, over centuries. We think the earliest images date from not long after the site was built, but it's clear that subsequent generations added their own art. Some of it depicts legends and fables, others seem to commemorate battles or significant events. See here." He indicated a spot where an artist had drawn a mountain range with a white arc above it. "We suspect this image is a comet. Such an event would have been seen in the night sky for weeks and there would have been all sorts of superstitious ideas about what it might foretell."

"That's amazing," said Vera. "I had no idea the site was so complex, with so many different features."

"A scholar could spend a lifetime here and barely scratch the surface," van Hoote said with a solemn nod.

"But only if Durham let them," Vera added. "Right?"

"He was certainly the authority here. Not sure what will happen now."

"Do you think his death makes things easier or harder? I heard that he was excellent at getting funding."

"Oh, that's true enough. And he was a good ambassador, very skilled at selling the idea of Summers End. But you're right. Don't let all the jolly smiles fool you," van Hoote said. "He runs—er, ran—this site like it was his own personal kingdom, and he parceled out grant money and awards to his favorites while leaving others out in the cold."

"Could he do that?"

"His name carries a lot of weight," van Hoote explained. "He can—well, he could—get another scholar thrown off a dig here. Or he'd decide who got to put their name on a paper to be published. And publishing more papers means you're more likely to get tenure. Might not seem important, but for us . . . it's a matter of life and death."

"In this case, death."

Van Hoote coughed uncomfortably. "Well, I didn't mean it like *that*."

They came out into the sun again, and van Hoote gestured to the hill above them. "Looks different now, doesn't it? When you know all that lies beneath it, the hill isn't so simple."

"Definitely not," Vera agreed.

"Come along, please. There's one more part of Summers End I want to show you."

Vera followed him away from the hill and toward the edge of the forest beyond. Summers End was a large site, so it took a few minutes of steady travel to reach their destination: a long, low building that Vera hadn't even noticed before, despite having looked around the area carefully.

"What's this place?" she asked.

"Our workroom. I don't always end tours here, but I think you'll appreciate it," van Hoote said, ushering her into the low building tucked into the trees at the edge of the Summers End clearing. The inside was utilitarian, designed for work and not for show. Several long wooden tables filled much of the space, with various tools nearby: brushes of all sizes, tweezers, scalpels, and more. Not to mention the stacks of notebooks and binders and many boxes, all waiting to be used.

Van Hoote said, "Any artifacts that are uncovered at the site are brought here to be cleaned, identified, and cataloged. At the end of each dig season, we bring all the boxes of artifacts on the boat to come back to the university with us for further study."

"Where do you keep them till then?" Vera asked as she looked around.

"That closet," he said, pointing to a set of double doors at the end of the room. "On the day we found Professor Durham, I came here and discovered that the doors were unlocked, and a few boxes were missing. All those stones and figurines around the body . . . they were taken from our storage facility. I suspect the killer took Durham's key and opened the doors, since they didn't appear forced."

"Did you tell Buckthorn that?"

"Yes. He put it into a report."

Continuing to examine the researchers' laboratory, Vera moved to the next table and picked up a small pitcher with a rounded bottom and a narrow neck. There were elongated triangles pressed into the clay, creating a rather striking pattern.

"What's this?" she asked. "Was it found here at Summers End?"

"Ah, that!" Van Hoote looked quite pleased. "Very fine example of its type, and in one piece as well! We diggers don't often get that lucky. Yes, this little pot was uncovered here at the site. If I recall, it was in a side chamber inside the hill, hence why it was found intact. Most pottery got discarded or buried, and so usually we find only shards, which we have to reassemble painstakingly."

"How does a pot help you study languages?"

"The makers sometimes put a mark on the bottom or added a word or two to the design. This one doesn't have it, but there are examples of creators carving words into the clay, such as a charm like *May this pot never break* or sometimes a bit of wisdom like *Water is life*. I use those to map the changes in language over time."

"I understand. It's a very pretty pitcher."

"It is. You see that distinctive pattern? The triangles? We have ascertained that they were made by birds' beaks clamping down on the soft clay before it was glazed and fired. The result is the distinctive, and dare I say *elegant*, pattern you see there. We call it

Beakware, and it's absolutely the best indicator that a site dates to a particular period. A century earlier, the pottery was done in quite a different style, with more emphasis on color rather than texture. And a century later, the pottery itself is different, since the makers had learned to add small amounts of fine sand into the mix, which strengthened the pot during the firing process. Yes, Beakware and Summers End are closely linked!"

"It sounds special. How much would such an object cost? Not that I'm implying it's for sale!"

"Certainly not!" van Hoote agreed with a squawk of concern. "Such items are far too valuable to scholarship to consider selling. Though there are always collectors eager to add a trophy or two to their hoard," he added, ruffling his feathers in distaste at the very concept.

"Would this be of interest to a collector? It's not a rare or valuable material . . . Just clay."

"Not just clay, madam! It is history solidified! There are those who pay for the thrill of touching the past. Just think, it may well be that one of the makers of Summers End held that very object in their paws during a sacred ceremony. Does that not stir something in you?"

Vera did feel awed at the possibility, the faint hint that by holding the small clay pitcher she could feel time fold in upon itself, collapsing the past into the present. "It's an honor to view it," she said at last.

"Exactly!" van Hoote said with a nod. "Which is why we must not allow these . . . *shoppers* . . . to treat these marvelous objects as mere trinkets. In the city, there are unscrupulous types who'd sell this little item for hundreds, perhaps even thousands. But that doesn't begin to match its worth as an artifact, as a key to knowledge. That's why we ensure the site is protected at all times. Durham was adamant that all protocols be followed to the letter, and he insisted that we work with local law enforcement. If we can find the killer, we'll also find the thief. At least that's what I hope."

Vera asked, her interest piqued, "Hold on! Are you saying there have been *thefts*?"

Van Hoote shifted from one clawed foot to the other, clearly uncomfortable about what he had just revealed. "Er, yes, unfortunately. A few items disappearing from time to time. For a while, we thought it was a matter of the recordkeeping being in error. Or perhaps an absent-minded colleague was putting something in the wrong drawer. But we went through the whole workroom a few times this season, and several artifacts weren't anywhere to be found. That's when we realized someone had got in and stolen them."

"That's awful. What does Chief Buckthorn have to say about it?"

"He takes it seriously, but he's not able to do much in terms of investigating because we're not sure *when* the objects went missing. But he told us he spoke to all the boat captains in the area to ensure they don't accept unauthorized shipments from the Summerhill docks. And he's told us that there's no hint of strangers from the city visiting and showing an unusual interest in artifacts."

Vera nodded, but privately she thought that it was a thorny path for the local law. Boats were only one way to get folks and goods in and out of the town of Summerhill. And no one could guard the whole forest if a creature chose to travel over land or air! Plus, some of the artifacts from the site were as small as they were valuable. A creature could easily tuck a symbol stone away in a piece of luggage or wrap up a little figurine and slide it into a purse. No officer of the law could search everyone and everything traveling through the town.

If the thief was smart, they'd have left town already.

Unless they *couldn't*, because a sudden disappearance would be suspicious, especially if the thefts could be linked to the murder in some way! And who had more cause to protect their reputation than a university professor?

Chapter 12

Vera left van Hoote in the workroom and walked away from the site in a thoughtful mood. She noticed Deputy Poole glaring at her while he patrolled, but she ignored the wolverine. Some battles were better left unfought.

At the lodge, she was delighted to learn that there were sandwiches left over from lunch. Though some of the young creatures joked and chatted at the tables outside, the overall mood was still subdued.

Cora offered her a tray that held a cheese and vegetable sandwich on toasted sourdough, along with a little cup of soup. Vera gratefully accepted it and made her way to a table. Before she even sat down, Vick and CJ joined her.

"Miss Vixen, are we going to get sent home? They're saying it's too dangerous to stay in Summerhill!" Vick informed her.

Vera was about to reply that *of course* it was no more dangerous than two days ago when they'd arrived. Whoever killed Durham was not likely to also target a visiting student from a random village. But then an idea glimmered in her brain—an idea worthy of a chaperone.

She put on a sober expression and said, "We can't afford to ignore the possibility, Mr. Sumner. This is an unprecedented situation, and who knows what's in the killer's mind?"

"We got reassigned to a different chaperone," Vick said, looking rather put out. "I bet it's because you're going to solve the murder."

"Well, I'm going to investigate and write some articles," she said. "But whatever Ms. Boatwright decides to do, while you're here I'll be counting on you both to help keep the other students in line. After all, some of them are rather immature. But I expect you'll keep your heads and stop anyone from doing anything silly."

Vick and CJ looked flattered, and CJ said, "Yes, Miss Vixen! We'll keep an eye out for you!"

"Thanks, that makes me feel better. Now you go and relax. I think one of the professors is planning on giving a talk, since we've come all this way, but that's not until later."

The two creatures ran off, allowing Vera to munch her sandwich in peace. Shortly after she finished, Arabella came up to her and said, "You've probably heard, but I'm working on bringing the students home early. It's a matter of a few days, honestly, but parents have already sent wingmails because they heard about what happened, and they're worried."

"The students are worried, too," Vera said. "Even though I don't think there's much danger for them. Durham was killed for a specific reason."

"Well, it seems that an early exit will be best for everyone. I've got to find out if there's an earlier downstream ferry with enough space for us all. It's always something, isn't it?" The rat bustled off, no doubt hacking away at all the tasks the changed itinerary meant for the group. Vera admired her efficiency.

Having eaten, Vera returned her tray to Cora and decided to find Lenore. She had a lot of clues to ponder, and at the moment, it seemed that they didn't fall into any particular pattern. She was pretty sure Lenore would be with her sister, so she headed back to Aster House. Lenore was indeed with Ligeia, in her room, the curtains all drawn closed.

"I'm about to take a nap," Ligeia explained. "I was tossing and turning all night and this bright sunlight isn't really my thing anyway. Excuse me. I'll probably feel better in an hour or so."

Vera and Lenore withdrew and went downstairs.

"She's very upset, even though she's pretending she doesn't care," Lenore whispered. "This is exactly what she used to do when we were younger! Can't stand to have anyone see her looking out of sorts."

"Sounds like someone else I know," Vera teased. But she also saw how upset Lenore was about the possibility that her sister could be accused of a crime she didn't commit. To distract her friend, she proposed a walk through town, so they could get away from all the drama. Outside, however, it was surprisingly busy, with a stream of creatures flooding the main street.

"Oh," Lenore said at last. "I get it. A passenger ferry must have just docked. These folks are day-trippers here for shopping and dining."

"And the history," Vera added. "Though they'll be surprised to learn that Summers End is off-limits today."

"I bet most of them won't even bother to go to the site. They'll pick up a postcard and think it's just as good." Lenore sniffed. "After all, they're here to go *antiquing*. You know the type: the kind who will run you over to get to the rusty farm tool on the wall behind you because it's *just darling* and would look so good on the porch." The raven ruffled her feathers.

Vera chuckled. "Come on. I'm sure it's not as bad as all that."

"You are blissfully ignorant, Vera! You don't have folks coming into your bookstore asking to purchase lots of books by their *spine color*. Not a care for what's inside, all that matters is that it's blue!"

By this time, they had reached a street called Mulberry Court. It was a cul-de-sac with several buildings on it, most of them at least partially commercial, though it appeared that the upper stories of many were private residences. Perhaps the owners lived above their shops. Each small front yard featured the sort of antiques that were impervious to weather, and one store displayed fabrics draped all over the porch railings and fence, making the whole structure look like a house-sized quilt.

A shop with the sign that announced it as the Bronze Feather, however, was more sedate in appearance, with no hint as to what was sold inside. Vera climbed the steps to the porch. The front door had glass set in the top half, but it was etched, so Vera couldn't make out the interior. But there was a sign that read OPEN, so Vera turned the knob and walked in.

She looked around in awe. The whole front room was lined with glass cases, and those cases were filled with all manner of jewelry and trinkets and other glittery things. And more importantly, many of those things were quite old. Vera glanced at

Lenore, who gave her a meaningful wink. She was wondering the same thing as Vera: Were all these real?

"Good afternoon, ladies," a thin yet cultured voice called.

Vera turned to see a slender white rabbit standing behind one case, dressed in an exquisite pale green silk dress with pin-tucking all up and down the front panel. She also wore a heavy silver chain with a short silver magnifying glass attached to it—what was known as a jeweler's loupe.

"Hello, there," Vera said, smiling in her most friendly way. "Are you the owner of this wonderful collection?"

The rabbit nodded proudly. "Yes, I'm Emmeline Greenleaf. Are you with the others from today's ferry?"

Lenore nudged her before Vera could answer. She stepped forward and said, "We've both heard so much about the quality of items in Summerhill. You know, sometimes you go into a shop that claims to have unique finds, and it's all the same old junk. But it looks like you've really chosen your inventory with care."

Vera noticed how Lenore neatly avoided answering the question of where they came from, which was just as well, since Vera didn't want to admit they had been in town for a few days. That might invite questions about the murder, which Lenore certainly wouldn't feel up to discussing.

Lenore had moved to examine the case between her and Ms. Greenleaf and was practically cawing with delight over several shiny little baubles. (The reader will recall that ravens and their ilk have a demonstrated affection for all that glitters.)

Vera browsed the cases while Lenore kept the owner talking about this peridot ring or that engraved pocket watch. Then she stopped in her tracks. One tall case in the corner held what could only be ancient artifacts, including carved stones and little bone figurines in the style Vera had seen inside the monument. No prices were listed.

"Intriguing, are they not?" Emmeline Greenleaf asked, having shaken off Lenore's questions and made her way to Vera's side. "Not as polished as some of our other offerings, but with an innate charm of their own."

"How old are these?" Vera couldn't help but ask. "What I mean by that is, are they replicas?"

Emmeline gave a little shrug. "Naturally I strive to offer only the finest items, and I do have everything appraised. No one can be one hundred percent certain about anything, but every expert I've consulted says they appear to be quite authentic. Summerhill, as you may know, is very lucky to have the site of Summers End, and everything found there is destined for a museum or the university. But private citizens are always finding similar items when they dig up a garden."

"And they just give them to you?" Vera asked, incredulous.

Emmeline chuckled. "Certainly not. They sell them to me for a fair price, after the appraisal. I then clean them up and offer them to other buyers, after a reasonable markup. After all, I pay for the experts to look at them and I have to take the risk of holding them until a buyer comes. But I think it's worth it. After all, each one is a little piece of history, isn't it?"

Vera pointed to a particularly delicate carving. "Dare I ask the price? Say of that snowy owl figurine, the one with the spread wings."

Emmeline told her the price, and Vera did her very best not to faint.

"The mouse on the lower shelf is only half as much," Emmeline said, probably quite familiar with Vera's reaction. "I do try to accommodate a range of buyers."

Lenore's eyes had gone wide at the idea of spending such an amount, and she said to Vera, "We'd better hurry if we want to meet our friends for dinner. We can come back another time."

"Yes," Vera agreed, feeling that a quick exit would be best. "Thanks for showing us your lovely collection, Ms. Greenleaf."

The two left the store and hurried down the short block to get back to Summer Street.

Lenore was still aghast over the prices. "Did you hear how much that bone owl cost?! It's the size of a plum, but I could eat for a year for the same amount!"

"Truly," Vera agreed. "But I was more concerned about the way she fended off questions about the provenance before I could even ask. I didn't get a chance to tell you before, but it turns out that artifacts have been stolen from the dig site."

"Wow, and you think we just saw some of them?"

"Not sure," Vera admitted. "I shouldn't assume the worst, and perhaps there isn't a connection. But do you really think local folks dig stuff like that up when they're planting tomatoes?"

"Even if they did, there are usually laws about treasure troves," Lenore said. "I've read about this. It doesn't matter if you own the land you find an artifact on. You're obliged to at least report it to authorities and then there's a hearing or something similar to decide what happens to the discovery."

Vera frowned, thinking. "So Ms. Greenleaf could be lying."

"Maybe. Or those so-called artifacts were fakes, and the huge price is just a way to gull unwary tourists with too much money. We should look at the other shops in town to see if they've got anything like what the Bronze Feather has. It could be a whole cottage industry in replicas."

The pair strolled through the town, putting Mulberry Court behind them. As they ambled, their conversation shifted from the matter of the artifacts to the murder, and all its possible implications.

"Okay, if we're going to help Ligeia out of this mess, we've got to focus on one part of the investigation at a time," Vera said. "And the logical place to start is with the body."

Chapter 13

In light of the discovery that Durham's body had been moved, Vera knew that she'd have to return to the monument to study the passageway and all the chambers with more attention. Van Hoote's initial tour wasn't going to cut it.

Luckily, she and Lenore didn't have to go far to find themselves another guide. They found Ligeia on the back porch of Aster House, gloomily regarding the lovely backyard with its masses of coneflower, black-eyed Susans, nasturtiums, and pink phlox. From her expression, it seemed the cheerful flowers had personally offended her, but it was more likely that she was worried about getting tossed in jail, where she wouldn't get to see any flowers at all.

"Ligeia, are you up for a couple of questions?" Vera asked gently.

"Why not," the morose raven replied.

"Well, I'm curious about something. On the morning Durham was found, you said you were waiting for forty minutes before Professor Ford arrived and then you both waited another twenty until the main group reached the site."

"Yes, that's correct."

"Why?"

The raven tilted her head, puzzled. "Why what?"

"Why did you arrive an hour earlier than you had to?"

"Er, well, I guess I was excited for the moment."

"I was excited, too," Vera agreed, "but I didn't exactly hop out of bed a moment earlier than I had to. You had a reason to be there early. What was it?"

Ligeia looked away, obviously wishing this conversation wasn't happening. "It's not relevant to the case."

"I think it is. If Professor Chesley left the hill at three thirty, and you arrived an hour before sunrise, which would be shortly after four, that's a very small slice of time that a creature could have moved around the hill or down into the chamber with no witnesses. What you saw, or who you saw, could be vital."

"I saw no one!" Ligeia insisted. She seemed agitated.

"But you expected to," Vera guessed, suddenly picturing the scene. "You arrived early because you had arranged to meet someone there at the site before everyone else got there. Who?"

"You can trust Vera," Lenore told her sister. "She really does care about the truth. And I wouldn't stay friends with her if I didn't trust her myself."

Ligeia considered that for a long moment. Then she sighed.

"You're right. I was waiting for Durham," Ligeia whispered. "But you can't tell anyone that, especially not the police chief. I might as well sign a confession!"

"But if you saw Durham before he got killed, that could help us determine the exact time of death."

"You're missing my point! I didn't see him at all. I'd been after him to tell me about the results of a grant that I'd applied for, that I needed his approval to get, because he's the head researcher here. But he'd been putting me off for weeks. Finally, I got him to agree to talk to me about it, but he said he'd only discuss it that morning, before the sunrise. I bet he thought the timing would keep me away. But I arrived when I said I would. He never did."

Of course not, Vera thought, because the killer had found him first and he'd already been placed in the underground tunnel by the calendar stone.

"One more thing," Vera said. "I spoke to Chief Buckthorn, and he told me that they found something while moving the body."

"Don't suppose we're lucky enough for it to have been a suicide note," Ligeia replied, making Lenore squawk with dark delight.

Ravens! Vera thought. Out loud, she said, "I'm afraid not. It was a black feather. And he seemed to think it belonged to you."

Ligeia gasped. "The cheek of him! If I'd lost a feather anywhere, I'd have known. And if I happened to lose it where I was dragging a body, I'd have picked it up, because I'm not an idiot. But anyway, I wasn't in there!"

"He's a deer," Lenore added. "He doesn't know what it feels like to lose a feather. What type of feather was it? Wing? Tail? Down? Contour?"

Vera shrugged. "Er, wing, I think?"

"Pffft. Probably a turkey vulture's and he can't tell the difference. Anyway, a bird doesn't lose a wing feather without noticing."

"I'll take your word for it," Vera said. "But the fact remains that a black feather was under the body when they picked it up. So maybe the killer intended to frame you from the beginning!"

"Well, that's slightly alarming," Ligeia said, upholding her sister's earlier observation that she liked to appear unruffled. "That means one of my colleagues is willing to go a lot further than I ever thought."

"Vera," Lenore said. "What should we do? We can't count on Buckthorn to do it for us. He'll fall for the killer's tricks."

"You know I'll do everything I can. But right now, I need Ligeia's help." Vera explained to the scholar why she needed to get back into Summers End.

"Oh, sure, I'll show you around," she said. "Let's go right now before somebody tells us we can't, or I get arrested or something."

"I'm game," said Lenore. "But how are we going to get inside? I doubt Deputy Poole is going to allow the prime suspect, her sister, and a nosy reporter to stroll in."

"He patrols the whole site, not just the barrow," Vera said. "I noticed that when van Hoote was showing me around before. We'll wait until he's on the far side."

The trio hurried back to the site. They kept wary eyes on Poole as he stalked his route (once startling Myron, who dropped all the trowels he'd been carrying when Poole swept past him from behind). At one point, the wolverine was blocked from view by a few especially wide standing stones. That's when the ravens flew and Vera dashed to the long barrow's entrance.

"Whooo," Lenore said, after they'd all got inside and replaced the wooden barrier. "Never thought I'd be sneaking into tombs in broad daylight, with the law on my tail!"

"Ah, makes you miss being young!" Ligeia cawed, her mood obviously improving rapidly. "Come on, let's move in deeper so he won't overhear us if he comes by."

Vera lit one of the candles near the entrance (the supply having been replenished for the law to use) and carefully put it in a lantern.

"The side chambers are brimming with archaeological interest," the raven said. "It's a shame that there's so much focus on the central chamber and the calendar stone. Yes, they're important, but you wouldn't believe how folks just skip over the rest."

"It sounds like it would take all night to see everything," Vera said.

"We *can* take all night if we want to. Actually, I like doing my research when all the other know-it-alls aren't hanging around. I often come here at night to work in peace. Van Hoote is the same way, of course, but he's so absorbed in his own research that he rarely bothers me."

"I spoke to Chesley before. She *has* to work at night."

"Yes," Ligeia said. "She's always up on the hill when the sky is clear."

"But you didn't see her when you arrived at the site," Vera guessed, remembering Chesley's insistence that she'd been gone.

"I saw her telescope, but not her. I assumed she was at the other end of the hilltop for some reason."

"No, she said she actually left entirely, because of some rain." Vera frowned, unhappy about some detail in Ligeia's description, though she couldn't decide what. "But even so, that doesn't explain why no one saw her for the rest of the morning, until Ford and van Hoote got back to Aster House. You'd have expected her to show up as usual." What was that porcupine up to?

As they talked, Vera and Lenore moved slowly through the long tunnel behind Ligeia, carefully noting all the things the professor was pointing out.

"So the first part of the passage is marked with carvings on the walls, mostly pictorial, but also some marks we now interpret as words. Very early written language. Van Hoote thinks that most of the words were added later, possibly as long as five centuries after the site was first built. But 'first built' doesn't mean much considering that the creatures living here added to the site and changed things all the time." Ligeia's tone grew in enthusiasm as she spoke, her world-weariness disappearing as she got into her favorite topic.

"The pictures are of all different creatures," Lenore said, swiping one wing gently in front of the images painted on the walls. "Bears and elk, raccoons, squirrels, a moose over here, see? Mice along the bottom, and these bigger ones must be rats. And all sorts of birds, naturally," she said, looking up.

Ligeia nodded. "Yes, these pictures seem to almost be like an artist's signature. We think that it's very strong proof that all these types of animals, and more, were involved in the creation of Summers End. This discovery was probably the key moment for historians in being able to pinpoint where and when our civilization began. It began with cooperation—many different species coming together for a common goal. In this case, the creation of a method to tell time precisely so that the harvests could be started and completed before the cold weather began. This allowed the ancient woodland culture to survive winters *as a group*, and consequently build up their numbers and begin to improve their technology. This culture became a major seat of influence in the area, able to fend off less friendly creatures and to spread knowledge to new groups as they came into contact with them through trade. A lot of the stones we've found here actually come from hundreds of miles away. Not to mention some of the specialized tools found at the site. There's an extremely rare kind of flint that only comes from the river delta down south—but we've found them here, proving that our ancestors put aside differences to engage with total strangers, across language barriers, and probably in spite of a lot of bad feelings from previous fights. Summers End is proof that progress is possible."

"The way you talk about all this, I'm surprised that you're not a sociologist," Vera said.

"I am!" Ligeia said. "Death is one of the most important events in any culture. How folks view death, how they treat the dead, what stories they tell about it. If you want to learn about the living, just ask how they feel about the dead."

"What have you learned from the Summers End dead?"

"A lot! The fact that there are bones inside here, and many burial plots surrounding the hill, shows us that woodland culture cared deeply about their friends and family. It takes work to plan and carry out an elaborate funeral, and to gather a bunch of items expressly for the dead to use in the afterlife."

Ligeia stopped before one of the niches on the left wall. "Take this one, for example. This side of the tunnel is exclusively for small land animals, and the niches are low on the wall, as if to say 'you'll be more comfortable here.' This one is a mouse—obvious from the size of the skull, of course. But see the stones tucked into the niche next to the bones."

Vera and Lenore leaned in. The lantern light revealed several symbol stones. One showed two mice with their tails entwined in a fanciful pattern. The next depicted clothing. Another was a picture of what could only be a wedge of cheese.

"See? These stones were symbols of what the dead would need in the afterlife. Things to wear, little toys, food of course." Then Ligeia pointed to the stone showing the pair of mice, saying, "And the idea that you were not alone. That's very important, and it says a lot about the creatures doing the burying."

Just then, Vera peered again into the niche. She pointed and said, "Wait, you told Buckthorn that you'd never seen a ritual like the murder scene. But this looks similar!"

"Similar, but only on the most superficial level." Ligeia gestured with her wing. "As you can guess, these symbols were all designed for a mouse's funeral. The size of the rocks, the images they depict. And two figurines of mice, one in white quartz and this other in soapstone. In contrast, the stones tossed around Ridley's corpse were totally random! Berries, a scarf, one showing a cat's cradle. The same goes for the bone figurines. Not a bighorn sheep among them. There was one with an eagle on it, and another for a shrew. One showed a raccoon on skis! I can tell you a lot about Ridley Durham, and one thing's for certain, he didn't care for skiing, and he had no special bond with raccoons. I could have picked artifacts out of a sack blindfolded and probably come up with something more suitable."

"How about the candles burned around the corpse?"

"The dead don't need light," Ligeia declared. "That's one thing we *don't* find in burial sites. No real lanterns, no lumps of wax, no flint strikers. Instead, we find images of the sun or fire carved onto stones. Meant to last! Burning real candles was just a way to waste good fuel. Speaking of, the ones the killer used were pilfered from our dig supply. Talk about adding insult to injury! The whole box was empty when van Hoote looked. And I'll tell you this, Durham hated wasting supplies. You don't get grants renewed by telling your funder that you managed your supplies poorly."

"That's interesting. Thanks, Ligeia." Vera pondered the raven's information. It got her thinking about just how much they didn't know about Durham.

She wandered into another side chamber, this one sporting many, many paintings but fewer niches. The far wall didn't have any at all, perhaps because it would have detracted from the life-size rendition of a bear standing on its hind paws.

"Bears clearly had a big influence on Summers End," Ligeia whispered, joining Vera in the little chamber. "This painting here is the biggest single image in the whole barrow, so that suggests it's very important."

"Who is it?" Lenore asked.

"There's no writing or hints to tell us," her sister replied, "though I've got a few theories."

Vera was drawn to the picture, and held her paw up toward the bear's head, not quite touching the surface. She imagined that she could almost feel the creature breathing—it was that skillful of an image. "How amazing," she whispered, her fur standing on end as a chill ran over her. "So long ago, but it could have been painted yesterday!"

Just then, something made a pinging sound. Lenore reached into her satchel and pulled out a watch on a chain. "That's my usual alarm for afternoon tea. Which means it's later than I thought!"

"We've been down here a while, haven't we?" Vera said. "We'd better not press our luck."

"I've got to take care of a few things, and folks will start to wonder where we all are," Ligeia said. "Why don't we meet tomorrow afternoon at the tearoom in town to discuss developments . . . assuming I don't get arrested first."

The trio made their way back to the entrance of the barrow, Vera blowing out the candle in the lantern before it could betray them. Lenore removed the wooden barrier, peeked out for a long moment, then said, "It's clear, if we all go now!"

Ligeia nodded and went first, flying directly up and then winging her way toward town. Vera and Lenore stepped out just at the entrance to the tunnel. "What's on your mind?" Lenore asked when they'd emerged from the darkness. "I know you, and you've got a notion."

Vera nodded. "Let's go to the top of the hill and I'll explain. If Poole sees us, we'll bolt before he can reach us."

Lenore flew up, so she was waiting when Vera climbed the relatively short distance to the top. When the two creatures lay down, they were invisible to anyone looking up from below, thanks to the height of the barrow.

The view was impressive, allowing a creature to turn in a full circle and see the site of Summers End surrounding them. Beyond the clearing, the forest rose up in shades of emerald and dusky green. Farther on, they could glimpse mountain peaks in the distance. One lower range cut through the woods to the south, where Shady Hollow lay. To the north, taller and more jagged mountains rose against the stunning blue of the sky. Those peaks were gray rock now, but within weeks they'd be shrouded in snow, a herald of the winter to come.

For now, all that touched the peaks was sunlight, though the color was already turning to gold as the sun sank in the west. They had only a couple of hours until sunset.

Lenore settled on the soft grasses growing over the top of the mound. "Nice of our ancestors to build this for us. Sure, it's a grave and a calendar. But it's also a picnic spot!"

"Multipurpose," Vera agreed. "Truly a mark of civilization."

The friends laughed, but Lenore grew serious quickly. "Something my sister told you gave you an idea about the murder, didn't it?"

"I think she hit on something without realizing how significant it might be," Vera said. "When she was talking about how wrong everything about the murder scene was—I mean the way this so-called ritual was laid out. It got me thinking that maybe the killer wasn't aware of Summers End's history."

"How could anyone around here not be aware of it?" Lenore asked skeptically.

"The broad strokes, yes. But that display around Durham's body didn't look authentic to Ligeia. Right from the moment she saw it, she knew it was nonsense."

"Yeah, she used that very word."

"So we're looking for a killer who had a rough idea of what to do, by putting the symbol stones and the figurines around the body. But they didn't *really* know, because they didn't use items that would have made sense for Durham in particular."

"What if it was a sort of mockery? After all, they hated Durham enough to kill him. Maybe giving him a skiing raccoon for the rest of eternity was just a final insult?"

"Then what were the candles for? To suggest that Durham was afraid of the dark?" Vera shook her head. "No, I think it's a clue that our killer doesn't know as much as they'd like us to think they do."

"That's interesting. Who knows something, but not everything?" Lenore asked thoughtfully. "All our scholars seem to know a lot about their own fields, and a lot less about their colleagues' specialties. Huh. That eliminates no one."

"That's why I think we need to do some active surveillance of the suspects," said Vera. "If we each follow one of the professors for a day or two, we might learn something important."

"Well, we can talk about it over tea tomorrow."

Lenore left for the lodge to check on her students. Vera decided to walk around the outside of the whole site, hoping to gain a new perspective on the situation. Beyond the great circle of standing stones that ringed the area and the now-incomplete circle of small border stones, the meadow continued for perhaps fifty paces, until the forest abruptly resumed. It was rather like walking into a green wall. There was no zone of shrub or bracken, as often happened in the woodlands, rather an abrupt change from sunny sward to deep shade. While it was surely just a practical choice to prevent the forest from encroaching on the site, the effect was quite dramatic.

Vera found a narrow path that circled the site while remaining under the canopy of the trees. When she heard a voice ahead of her, she slowed. Then she saw Professor Loring standing under a huge oak. The spot was about a quarter way around the circle from where the murder weapon had been found . . . and presumably where the murder took place.

The peacock was speaking as if to an invisible audience, waving one feathered wing out in a grand gesture. Then he hunched over a flat rock and scrawled something in a notebook.

Ah, Vera thought. *He's revising a poem.*

Not wanting to disturb genius at work, she waited from her nearby spot until she sensed some natural break in his concentration. Meanwhile, the bird's recitations floated on the summer breeze to her ears.

> *Upon outstretched wings, frozen as winter*
> *Owl white, ye will rise forever*
> *Owl wise, ye know ten thousand secrets*
> *Break your ancient silence—whisper one to me*

Loring frowned, counted off beats on his feathers, then muttered, "Break your stony silence? Break your sacred silence? Ugh."

Vera almost broke her own silence to agree. This was her first exposure to Loring's work, and thus far she was not impressed.

"Excuse me," she said, when it became clear that the poet had lost the attention of his muse, or indeed *any* muse. "I didn't want to interrupt, Professor, but I was hoping to ask you a few questions for a news article I'm writing."

Loring's head swiveled around, and he quickly shut the notebook. "News article?" he asked, alarmed.

"Yes, I'm Vera Vixen, reporter with the Shady Hollow *Herald*. I'm writing a piece on the murder that happened at Summers End. You're a professor from the university; you must have known Durham."

"I did know him, but just to say hello to. I'm not here to *dig*, you know. I'm here for the setting, to draw inspiration from the landscape for my own poetry."

"Yes, I overheard you writing lines for a stanza of your poem."

He sneered. "To call that a poem is an insult to poetry! It's an abomination!"

Vera was a little taken aback (despite her previous assessment of the stanza's quality). "Don't be so hard on yourself. No one likes their first draft, after all."

Loring chuckled bitterly. "Maybe I'll be able to make it tolerable, but nothing more than that. Now, if you'll excuse me, I have to beat this stanza into submission by my deadline. And I'll excuse you, so that you don't have to endure the ordeal."

Vera accepted her dismissal, but all the way back to the lodge, she thought about the poet. Why did he despise his creations so much? And if he hated what he wrote, why not write something else?

Chapter 14

A soft evening sunset brought the woodlands into shadow, but immediately behind Rosewood Lodge, things were quite lively indeed. Gerry had lit numerous lanterns to surround the patio area, and there was a large fire going in the firepit, as if to ward off any lurking danger, or perhaps the darkness itself.

The students had already gathered, because Professor Ford had offered to give a presentation in the hour before dinner, mostly as a way to keep the students' attention and to give them something other than the murder to think about. Fortunately, the bearded dragon was a highly entertaining speaker, and he'd brought along several interesting items to show the students. An ancient hatchet with an obsidian head was the most impressive, passed from paw to claw with murmurings of surprise at how sharp it still was.

"Unearthed from a site called Red Rock Canyon, where it had been buried by mud when a river changed course and the town was abandoned. And why might a hatchet be a significant find?" Ford asked the group, looking around at everyone.

A bear raised a hesitant paw. "Er, because not everyone had them back then?"

"True! Look at the size of this chunk of obsidian. Quite rare to find one that big. And whoever owned that hatchet could do something most animals couldn't do on their own: chop down trees. This enabled them to push back the woods, creating farm fields and building materials, which you need if you want to raise crops or make a town. Without a hatchet, only beavers had much luck with woodcutting. I'm very grateful that my university allows me to bring it along for teaching opportunities like this one. Take your time looking at it! It just might be the oldest tool you ever get to touch. Even older than your grandparents' kitchen pots, eh?"

A laugh rippled through the crowd, and a few students, encouraged by Ford's casual and unassuming manner, asked more questions. He answered each and every one.

"He's good at teaching," Vera said to Thena, who sat next to her. "I noticed that he said 'my university.' Isn't he affiliated with the same one as everyone else?"

"Nope, he's not actually a faculty member there," Thena said. "I'm checking to see where he is now, but not all the schools are responding quickly to my messages."

"Well, maybe we can just ask him," Vera said. "Since he's here."

Vera stood just as Arabella climbed onto a bench and banged the kitchen gong.

"Students! Please take your places at the tables, so we can serve!" Arabella called out.

There was a scene of controlled chaos as all the young creatures scrambled to find their preferred spots. Vera used the time to approach Professor Ford.

"Nice of you to talk to the students," she said, opening with a compliment.

"They need something to distract them from unpleasant thoughts," he said. "Besides, it's the best part of being a teacher. If you don't share what you learn, what's the point?"

She nodded. "I know you're an archaeologist, but you must have a special interest, right? A focus for your research?"

He gave her an inquiring glance. "Well, since you're curious, Miss Vixen, I'm actually very intrigued by time and how ancient cultures thought about it. Summers End, as well as other sites from this era, usually incorporate timekeeping into their architecture, and I find that especially interesting."

"If that's your focus, why was Durham in charge, and not you?"

Ford gave a chuckle. "Oh, I wouldn't want to be in charge! Far too much paperwork and bureaucracy. I prefer to be in the dirt, where the real work is."

"So you got along with Durham?"

"More or less. He was easy for me to deal with because I don't care about fame. I just want to discover the past."

"Like that hatchet?" She gestured to the object, currently in Vick's paws.

"Exactly. Artifacts such as that are special, and not only to scholars. Just look at how an old chunk of black glass and a wooden stick can excite young minds! I think it's important to foster a love of history in the next generation."

"Your university must be very proud to have you. Which one is it again?"

"Chaparral College, out west. Go, Fightin' Fires!" At Vera's blank look, he sighed. "Not a sports fan? That's okay."

Just then, Arabella hurried up to them, and said, "Professor, please come with me. Since you're our speaker, we've got a place for you at the front table."

The lizard excused himself and followed the rat. Vera turned to find her own table, already filled with dishes and eager diners.

During the meal, Vera leaned over to Lenore. "Once we're sure the students are safe in their rooms for the night, would you be up for a clandestine excursion?"

"Those are my favorite kind," the raven replied, her eyes gleaming in the lantern light. "What's the mission?"

"Earlier today, Professor van Hoote mentioned that Ridley's suite was on the top floor of Aster House. I just thought that there might be some useful information in that room."

"And that the law might not exactly rush to share it with you," Lenore said. "But if there's something that points the blame at anyone besides Ligeia, I want to see it! Okay, I'm in."

"Great. Let's keep it between us for now. I'll find you after the students are tucked in for the night."

Late that night, the lodge grew quiet and even the most restive students gave in to the lure of sleep. Both Callie and Thena were asleep as well, to Vera's relief, since she had no intention of letting the voles in on the plan for breaking and entering. She didn't think it would be good mentorship to get her young intern in trouble with the law.

Vera heard a tapping, as of someone gently rapping, on her chamber door. She quickly got up and opened it to find Lenore waiting there.

"Shhh, I don't want them to wake up," Vera murmured, grabbing her bag and stepping outside. She pulled the door gently shut behind her.

"Sorry, I should have let you come to me," Lenore said, "but I was going stir-crazy. Just thinking about how Ligeia could get the blame for this . . . My mother would fall straight out of the tree, you know."

The two creatures made their way from the lodge to the town, Lenore soaring invisibly through the clear night sky, while Vera used the deep shadow of trees to mask her passage, all the way to Aster House.

The building loomed large, its white-painted walls glowing even in the faint starlight. As Lenore landed next to her, Vera gestured for her friend to follow her lead.

One nice feature of the inn was the proliferation of porches on all sides of the building, not just on the first floor but the upper ones as well. Guests no doubt appreciated the amenity of stepping out from their room to a breezy balcony. Would-be thieves appreciated the ease of access.

Vera moved silently around the side of the inn, careful to watch where she put her paws—a few windows were still alight with the soft glow of a candle or a reading lamp, and she didn't want to attract an audience. She climbed the back stairway to a big screened-in porch filled with comfortably shabby furniture and little tables. She spotted another stairway that went up to the next floor. Here, there was no more screening needed, and pots of ferns hung at regular intervals between the posts. Lenore glided past her on black wings, winking.

Of course the bird would take the easy way! Vera continued her climb, pausing now and then when a floorboard creaked, or she heard a noise come from a guest room. She eventually made it to the top floor, where the stairway terminated at a small balcony that led to a single door. Lenore landed on the railing, then hopped down to Vera's level.

"Is this Durham's room?" the raven asked softly.

"It must be," Vera whispered back. "It's a suite and there's only one room number starting with four."

She leaned over to peer in the window overlooking the balcony, but a lace curtain impeded her view. "Can't see anything," she reported. "Not even if someone's in there."

Lenore simply stepped forward and tapped her beak against the door, once, twice, three times.

"What are you doing?" Vera hissed.

"Knocking. If someone is inside, they'll want to know who's outside on their balcony. And if no one comes . . . the coast is clear."

No one came. Vera gently turned the doorknob. It was locked. But the window had been cracked open for air, and it was easy to slide the sash up and climb inside. She opened the door for her friend, and they looked around the shadowy room.

"Do we dare light a candle?" Lenore asked.

"I think we have to, if we want to search the place." Vera lit one of the small lamps in the room, turning the wick as low as she could. In the soft glow, Durham's summer residence was revealed. One corner held a velvet chair, a stool, and several books stacked up—clearly a reading nook. The alcove on the opposite wall contained a big, messy desk. An open door showed a bedroom beyond, and another door led to quite a large closet (though the sloping ceiling made it impossible to stand up inside). Durham's clothing and personal effects were still there, as if the ram were about to walk back in.

"Nice little nest," Lenore said. "Wonder what it cost for a whole summer."

"Well, if you notice a receipt, tell me. Let's see what we can find."

Vera didn't know if Chief Buckthorn had already searched the place (and if he'd already taken items away as evidence). They'd just have to hope that they'd uncover something useful. Lenore walked to the reading nook, picking up the top book on the reading pile and carefully fanning out the pages. Meanwhile, Vera moved to the desk. Ridley Durham seemed to use this small area as an office, to judge by the carrying case marked with the university's logo and the papers stacked on the cherrywood desk.

Vera started to sort through them. There were half-written grant proposals, notes for academic papers to be written, and several logbooks with terse accounts of the daily dig reports. She read a few at random:

> . . . *continued excavation of northwest quadrant.*
> *Postholes suggest outbuilding. No artifacts . . .*

> . . . *potsherd uncovered with writing. L.L. wants to*
> *crumble a corner for testing. AvH refused. Had to*
> *break up argument . . .*

. . . another figurine dug up (mouse), this time by intern.
Made a huge fuss, of course. Interns always think they're
the first to find anything. Cataloged fig in workroom
closet . . .

Vera sighed. It was all rather banal, and there was enough material to keep her reading for days without knowing if she'd uncover anything. She found the most recent logbook and slid it into her satchel, planning to examine it later.

"Find anything?" Vera asked, picking up a folded paper.

"Nothing useful." Lenore put another book to the side. "Durham never threw anything away, did he? I keep finding torn-up bits of paper used as bookmarks."

Vera unfolded the paper and read the phrase *false owl*. "What?" she murmured, perplexed. "Lenore, does the term 'false owl' mean anything to you?"

"Um, not especially. Unless it means that Durham thought van Hoote was lying about something."

"But why make a note that just says the owl lied?"

"It must link up to something else that Durham was studying. Scholars get weird about their research—it might be a reminder for him but written so that no one else could steal his idea."

"Oh, like a code," Vera said.

She put the cryptic note aside and picked up a letter. She saw the name Ford and started reading. "Lenore!" she said excitedly. "Here's something! Durham was suspicious of Isaiah Ford for some reason. He got a letter from Chaparral College that says Ford is no longer on the faculty there! Which meant he lied to me earlier tonight when I asked him."

Lenore looked very interested. "A professor from nowhere, huh? Then what's he doing here?"

"Exactly!" Vera folded the letter up. "If he's here under false pretenses and Durham found out, that's a prime motive for murder."

"I'll follow him, starting tomorrow," Lenore said. "You can take van Hoote and see if he's the false owl. Oh, no," she said suddenly.

"What?"

"Er, read this." Lenore offered her a letter.

Vera saw the university's letterhead and scanned the typed words: *The board considered your request to deny tenure to Professor Lee. After reviewing the matter, the board concluded that Professor Lee has fulfilled all requirements and only extraordinary events could reverse this decision.* She then read an addendum scrawled in a loopy script: *Be advised Lee knows about this. Someone told her. Watch your back.*

She grimaced. "'Watch your back'? It does sound bad, considering what happened. But it doesn't really mean anything, Lenore."

"Are you joking? It practically predicts that Ligeia was going to whack Durham from behind because he angled to have her denied tenure! For an academic, that's worse than death. Er, you know what I mean."

"I know. But just because this board member used an awkward phrase doesn't mean Ligeia did anything at all, let alone murder. We're going to put this letter back where you found it and not worry about it, okay? Now let's keep looking. We shouldn't stay here much longer just in case someone sees the light and gets curious."

The two friends searched the remaining spots but couldn't find much else that pointed toward any particular suspect. Vera did get a sense that Durham was stretched thin, though. In his correspondence, he constantly referenced needing funds, or expressed concern about getting grants. She'd have to make a note to check on the finances of the dig—money was a powerful motivator, and if someone was upset at Durham's handling of funds, maybe the argument got out of control. But who among the professors would be most likely to know about that?

"Moon's rising," Lenore told her at one point. "We should go soon. It'll be bright as day in less than an hour, and anyone who happens to look will see us."

"Okay. I think we've found all that we can hope to find anyway. Is everything like we found it? I don't want anyone to notice things getting moved around."

"You're saying Buckthorn didn't give you free rein to poke around like Orville does back home?" Lenore asked with a chortle.

Vera shook her head. "He's been pretty tolerant so far, considering I'm a stranger in town. But I don't think it would take much to annoy him."

"Everything looks correct to me," the raven said. "Blow out the lamp and put it back on that side table. I've restacked the books. Come on!"

Lenore went out to the balcony first, and Vera followed. As she pulled the door shut, her eye caught a flash or gleam from somewhere. But when she looked around, she couldn't identify anything among the shadows and the growing moonlight. But she felt that unmistakable shiver that signaled she was being watched. No matter how far society had come, how civilized they all claimed to be, instinct always lay waiting, and instinct told Vera that unfriendly eyes were upon her.

"Lenore, did you see a flash? Or any movement?"

The raven tipped her head this way and that. "Hard to tell," she whispered finally. "But I've got a powerful urge to escape, if that means anything."

"Oh, it does." Vera always trusted her friend's insight.

"Anyway, if we *were* seen, no one's making a big fuss, so let's get while the getting's good."

"Fly," Vera told her. "Then if I get caught leaving, you won't get in trouble, too."

The raven nodded and jumped off the balcony into the air. Vera crept down the stairs and past the doorways of guest rooms, feeling all the while that someone was about to pounce on her and demand to know what she was up to in the dead of night. Her heart in her throat, Vera finally reached the backyard of Aster House, her paws welcoming the dew-laden grass for the way it would muffle her steps.

Suddenly, a light came on in one of the windows nearby.

"What's that?" a voice called. "Who's out there?"

Vera leaped away, toward the shadowed side yard and then to the empty, silent street. She kept glancing over her shoulder as she went, terrified that the proprietor of Aster House would chase after her or cry *Stop, Thief!*

Vera crossed the street in her most casual, I'm-not-up-to-anything-at-this-strange-hour way. The moment she reached the heavy shadow of an oak tree, she exhaled in relief. Now she was fine, far enough away from the inn that she could plausibly say she'd been nowhere near it. After all, it wasn't a crime to walk through town at night, was it?

"What are you doing?"

Vera jumped, but it was only Lenore, swooping in under the lowest branches.

"Lenore, you scared the daylights out of me!"

"Good thing it's night, huh? Come on, let's get back to the lodge before we run into anyone and things get awkward."

The fox nodded, and the two of them fled the town to get back to the friendly embrace of the woods. Behind them, Summerhill was still and quiet . . . but not fully asleep. Some eyes were wide open.

Chapter 15

Vera slept fitfully, her mind full of ideas and her body still jumpy from the breaking and entering stint at Aster House. As soon as it got light, the fox decided to write to Orville. She was interested in his take on everything that had happened. She also wanted to assure him that even though she had become embroiled in yet another murder, she was safe, and doing her best to discover who the culprit might be. The police chief of Shady Hollow worried about her when she was investigating a crime. She often followed her nose into dangerous situations without letting anyone else know what she was getting into. At least now she had Lenore and Thena with her. They couldn't get into too much trouble if there was a group of them. Right?

Vera finished her letter to Orville and walked into town. It was fully light now, but hardly anyone was about. However, the messenger office by the docks was open for business. A box turtle stood behind the counter, nibbling a donut.

"Ooh, where'd you get that?" Vera asked.

The turtle swallowed, then answered. "Front Street Bakery."

"Someone else recommended the place. I'll have to stop by."

"You won't regret it. Now, what can I do for you, friend?"

Vera gave her letter to the clerk and paid for it to be delivered via wingmail. With any luck, she would hear back from her beau soon, perhaps even late today. She had been so overwhelmed by events that she hadn't realized how much she missed being with him. She was used to seeing him almost every day, whether for dinner at the Bamboo Patch or for coffee at Joe's, or just a quick visit to one of their workplaces. Funny how one didn't notice how precious the company of someone could be until it was unavailable.

She also missed his counsel on her cases. He didn't have any more experience with murder than she did, but he had been in law enforcement for many years and knew quite a few things that she didn't.

"Oh!" she said aloud, thinking of something else. *"That's what I've been missing!"*

She requested a fresh sheet of paper from the clerk and quickly penned another letter. There were hints that something illegal was going on at the site, and Vera knew she needed an expert to help her sort through things. So she wrote to Lefty, requesting that the raccoon come to Summerhill as soon as possible. Though an unrepentant petty thief and a perpetual thorn in the side of the law, Lefty possessed knowledge that Vera definitely needed. She made sure that the message included the word *compensation* and told the worker at the desk to send it via wingmail as well.

"You're in luck," the turtle told her. "We've got a packet scheduled for just an hour from now. Your messages will reach Shady Hollow later this morning! Dan is extremely dependable." The turtle pointed to a picture of a golden eagle, with DANFORTH BARTLEBY: EMPLOYEE OF THE YEAR written below it. Vera thanked her and paid the required fee, getting a receipt for Lefty's letter, since she'd have to expense the costs incurred for writing an article. She wasn't entirely sure what she'd need Lefty to look into, but she'd know more by the time the raccoon arrived (*if* he arrived—Lefty was not known for his dependability). But there were enough hints of irregularities in town that there was probably something occurring in the shadows. And if Vera and her friend could illuminate that, they could likely also shine a light on Durham's murder.

Vera took a slight detour back from the messenger office, hoping to see a bit more of the town while everything was so quiet and peaceful. She stopped at a neat cottage with a sign that read DOMINIC REYES, MD. Was this the very doctor Buckthorn had mentioned? The one who was doing the medical examination on Durham's body?

Always ready to seize the moment, she walked up the short path from the street, pushed open the bright blue door, and entered the office. A brown rabbit wearing a tidy uniform looked up from her work and greeted Vera from the reception desk. Her name tag read DONNA.

"Hello, there! We're not officially open for a couple of hours, but do you have an emergency?"

The fox decided to take a chance. "No, I'm not a patient.

However, I was hoping to talk to Dr. Reyes about an important matter if he's available?"

The rabbit nodded and went into the office to speak to the doctor. She came back to her desk almost immediately. "The doc says he has a few minutes, and he can see you in his office. Right through there."

Vera thanked her and made her way down the hall to an open door. She peeked in and saw a muskrat wearing a crisp white lab coat. He stood up when he saw her in the doorway and extended a welcoming paw. His name was embroidered over the coat's pocket in blue script.

"Thank you for seeing me without an appointment, Dr. Reyes." Vera sat down in one of the visitor's chairs opposite the doctor's desk. "I'm Vera Vixen, a reporter from Shady Hollow. I was chaperoning the school group at Summers End. I understand that you conducted the autopsy on Ridley Durham, and I have some questions."

The muskrat's cordial bedside manner vanished. He stood up, his expression indicating that the interview would be short indeed.

"Miss Vixen," he said crisply, "you must know that this is a police matter. I cannot discuss this case with you or anyone else. Buckthorn would be livid if he heard of this!"

"Oh, I've been discussing the case with Chief Buckthorn as well," she assured him. "He mentioned that you intended to run some tests to find out if the blood on the stone I found at the site matched Durham's. Did you get results from that test yet?" She kept her tone easy and confident, hoping to calm the doctor and get him to open up.

However, he just looked worried and shook his head. "I can't divulge anything, Miss Vixen. Whatever I tell Buckthorn, he may decide to share with you, but that's his decision, not mine! He runs this town, you know."

"Of course I understand that you want to follow the law," she said. "But if you do have the answer, it might help us find the killer even sooner. That blood test will let us know that we're on the right track."

"I don't know yet. But Buckthorn told me to report to him, and no one else," Reyes said. "You must understand my position." He tugged at the lapels of his lab coat, looking rather distressed.

"Thank you for talking to me, Dr. Reyes. I'm sorry to have bothered you. I'll see myself out."

The fox trotted quickly down the hall and out the front door. She rushed past Donna, who watched her exit without saying a word. She wasn't sure what she had expected from the doctor, but one thing was clear: he intended to abide by the direct letter of the law. Well, that was fine. Vera could certainly ask Buckthorn for the results of the test later. But what a strange and anxious manner the muskrat had, more like a nervous intern than a full-fledged doctor!

Needing a boost after the unsuccessful interview, she stopped at Front Street Bakery and bought some fresh donuts, still piping hot under the cinnamon-honey glaze. A sleepy-eyed coyote took her money and offered her a punch card. "Every thirteenth bakery item is free," he said. "Baker's dozen, you know."

Considering that she'd already garnered four holes in the card, Vera was confident she'd hit thirteen at least once before she left Summerhill. She returned to the lodge, and offered donuts to Thena and Callie, and soon after to Lenore, who came by the room.

"Hey, Lenore, let's talk for a minute before breakfast," she said, glancing toward the two voles. "I had some thoughts about how to help Ligeia."

Lenore could tell that Vera really wanted to discuss something without the others overhearing, and so readily agreed.

"We'll see you at our table in a bit!" Vera said.

"We'll save some coffee for you," Callie promised.

Vera and Lenore strolled slowly toward Summers End, but only far enough away from the lodge so that their conversation would remain private.

"What's on your mind?" the raven asked.

"Just thinking about our late-night adventure. At the very end, when I felt like someone was watching us, I got so tense and shivery. Prey like, you know."

"I'm familiar with the concept," Lenore said dryly.

"Well, it's just that it got me thinking that maybe nothing's really changed. Sure, we've got towns, and houses, and cafés, and clothing now. We tell ourselves that we've transcended the past. But at the core of it all . . . there's still violence. Still murder. Still lying and mistrust and fear."

Lenore was silent for a moment. Then she said, "Yes, there are still bad things in the world today. But the world is vastly different than it was when animals laid the first stones around Summers End. And the world they lived in was vastly different than the millennia before, when there wasn't any cooperation, or a celestial clock to tell you when to plant or when to harvest. When life just was tooth against claw and everybody eventually lost. Things are better now, even if they're not perfect. We have doctors for when we get sick. We have teachers to pass on knowledge. We have reporters to tell us what we need to know about the things happening around us. We have servers to bring us more coffee when our cups are empty. And when something really bad happens, we have ways of finding justice and restoring order. That's progress. That's hope."

"Funny that you're supposed to be the pessimist," Vera said.

The raven chuckled. "There's a difference between expecting the worst and wanting the worst. Folks call me a pessimist because I'm not surprised when things go badly. But because I've thought about it, it means I've got a plan to fix it."

"You do always seem very prepared, no matter what."

"Well, I wasn't prepared to be defending my sister from a murder charge during my summer vacation, that's for sure." Lenore's air of confidence slipped, and Vera realized anew just how concerned her friend was for her sister.

"We'll find out who really did it," Vera promised. "I mean, after breakfast, of course."

"First things first," Lenore agreed. "That donut took the edge off, but I can't think properly until I've got a full stomach."

After breakfast Vera led her old group of students on a walk through the woods surrounding Summers End (she felt guilty about shifting all the work to others with so little notice). Vick and CJ marched on ahead, excited to be "protecting" the others from danger. Georgette stuck close to Vera but seemed to be in better shape than yesterday. The young partridge recited facts about the site as they went along. Vera kept her eyes out for any poetic peacocks, but she didn't see Loring where he'd been the day before. Perhaps he managed to finish his poem to his liking.

Vera returned her charges to the lodge in time for another talk, this one by van Hoote. Arabella gave her a grateful nod when she saw her. "Thanks, Vera. We'll see you later at dinner."

Vera wondered how to put her free time to the best use.

Before she could decide, she spotted Thena trotting excitedly in her direction.

"Vera! I got something!" she began excitedly.

"Whoa, calm down. Let's sit and talk." Vera indicated a nearby table at one corner of the big patio, which was well away from the others.

Thena dropped into the seat opposite the fox and let out a whoosh of breath. "That Peggy Jeffries is a wealth of information. She just wingmailed me answers to all my questions! There isn't anything that goes on at that college that she doesn't know about."

Vera thought this sounded promising, and she gave the vole her full attention. She also got out her notebook, just in case.

Thena cleared her throat and then launched into her story. "Peggy is the one I was telling you about. She's a hedgehog who's been at the university forever. She's an executive assistant for most of the professors who are connected to Summers End through the Archaeology Department. She didn't seem to be especially fond of Ridley Durham, although she was shocked to hear about his murder."

"So it was news to her?" Vera asked. It was interesting to see how fast information could travel through the woodlands.

"Yes. And she was happy to help me. I asked her if she would mind telling me about the relationships between the various professors, like if there was any bad blood or anything. She said that she wasn't one for gossip, but then she proceeded to tell me all about how Durham would select an attractive female grad student to help him with his research, but then not give her any credit when he submitted a paper."

Vera knew that most college professors usually shared publication credit with a student who had helped them with a project. If such behavior was a regular occurrence, Durham would have become very unpopular indeed. But would a student kill him over the omission of academic credit for a paper? And even if that were the case, the student would have had to be at Summers End to commit the crime.

As Vera listened to Thena excitedly share all that she had learned from the well-informed hedgehog, she took notes as fast as she could. There was no telling what information might lead them in the direction of Durham's killer.

"It's not just Professor Durham who was doing shady things at the college," the vole continued. "Professor van Hoote wasn't always completely aboveboard, either."

"Go on." The fox narrowed her eyes as she listened to her colleague relay details about the owl. Just because he happened to be related to Professor Heidegger didn't mean he was above suspicion. Vera wished that most creatures could be trusted fully, but unfortunately, in her experience, it seemed that many of them had something to hide. That didn't necessarily make the owl a murderer, but it did raise some questions.

The vole paused for a breath and then continued her recitation. "Ms. Jeffries told me that she's usually in charge of organizing all the researchers' visits to Summers End, as well as a lot of trips from area schools, you know, like ours. Professor van Hoote often led these tours, since he knows so much about the monument and ancient woodland culture. The student groups were supposed to submit the fees for these tours directly to Ms. Jeffries at her office. However, on more than one occasion, the money was given to Professor van Hoote here at the site. And sometimes, Ms. Jeffries says, not all the money made it to the university's accounts."

"You mean that he pocketed it?" Vera asked, somewhat shocked in spite of herself.

"That's exactly what I mean," Thena responded. She was quite pleased with the results of her work.

Vera sighed, thinking to herself that, much like earlier investigations, perhaps she had *too* many suspects. She was fairly certain that only one creature was responsible for the death of the bighorn sheep, not a group working together. However, it did appear that there were more than a few nefarious activities going on in Summers End. Good thing she had sent that message to Lefty before breakfast!

She thanked Athena for doing such a great job in contacting Ms. Jeffries and getting her to talk. Privately, Vera thought that perhaps that had not been such a difficult task. The hedgehog seemed quite willing to share what she knew. So much for student and faculty confidentiality!

Thena beamed as her mentor praised her work. "I'm learning so much just from this shadowing work, Vera. I wonder if I should apply for an internship at the Shady Hollow *Herald*."

"Maybe, though I wouldn't want you to have to skip your other classes at the university to do it. But let's focus on the present. Go on to the room and write up some notes related to what Peggy Jeffries shared. It'll help you sort out what's really vital from what's not."

"Will do! Maybe I can start to get a bit of an article out of it," she said.

The reporter was pleased that her mentee was so enthusiastic, and after Thena left, she continued to sit at the table, enjoying the sunshine as she idly watched errant students joining van Hoote's talk at the other end of the patio. Could the owl really be responsible for diverting funds from the tour groups he led? Or was there another explanation?

Vera saw a figure emerge from the woods where the path to Summers End let out. Professor Chesley must have been at the site, for she carried that big, bulky case, though what she was doing with it during the day was anybody's guess. She kept walking, and Vera realized that she intended to walk past Vera's table, so she offered her a friendly nod.

"Are you on the schedule for a student talk after van Hoote's?" Vera asked. "I see you've got your telescope with you."

"I always have it close by," Chesley said. "You never know what you might see through the lens." There was something rather pointed in her tone, though Vera couldn't glean what she was getting at.

"You place a lot of value on observation, don't you? I happened to overhear you in town the other day, when you were, er, discussing things with that pika who was working at Roxanna's."

Chesley actually laughed, a surprisingly warm sound from the usually frosty creature. "That was Roxanna herself, and we weren't *discussing* anything. Her way of looking at the stars is just flat-out wrong! Utter nonsense. It's one thing to make money by entertaining some tourists, but let's not pretend that astrology—or any of the other games she plays—is real. What I do is real!"

"You're very passionate about your work. Have you made a breakthrough of some type? Was the stargazing better last night?"

"You could say that I learned something," Chesley replied cryptically.

"That's great. I only wish my own efforts were going a bit better." Vera was still worried that Buckthorn saw Ligeia as the prime suspect, and she hoped to present some of her findings to him to at least persuade him that there were other possibilities. "I plan to do more work today."

Chesley gave her a skeptical look. "Oh, indeed? Haven't you done enough snooping around?"

"What do you mean?" Vera asked. "I'm a journalist. I'm supposed to ask questions."

"You do more than just ask questions, Miss Vixen. And I for one wonder why. Good day!" The porcupine spun about and bustled off. Vera regarded her spiny back and wondered exactly what Chesley's game was. She clearly knew a lot more than she was telling.

Chapter 16

As they'd agreed to the day before, Vera, Lenore, and Ligeia all gathered at the tearoom.

Vera and Lenore had set off together, and, just outside the building, they encountered Athena, who'd been trailing after van Hoote. Thena could report nothing of interest in the owl's movements.

"He was unlikely to do something incriminating," Vera admitted. "For all his bluster, he doesn't really strike me as a murderer. And as for the thefts, he was the one who first mentioned to me that objects had gone missing. If he was the thief, I doubt he would have drawn attention to the crime."

"Unless he knew that the facts would come out," Thena suggested, "so he wanted to get ahead of it."

Vera smiled at her. "Now, that's reporter thinking, Thena! Always question why someone tells you something. Because sometimes even when they tell you the truth, their reasons might not be exactly pure. Van Hoote did make a pretty strong statement to me about how dastardly these collectors of artifacts were. It could have been a put-on. But somehow I don't think so. His distaste for the practice felt real."

"Then we should look elsewhere until we find another reason to suspect the owl. What about Professor Ford? He could be up to something."

The fox agreed, even though she rather liked the bearded dragon and his unpretentious attitude.

In the tearoom, the efficient yet friendly staff found a table for them that was tucked away in its own alcove, allowing a measure of privacy and quiet. Nearby, the main room was quite full of patrons, and almost every lace-adorned table was occupied. Tiered serving trays offered sandwiches, tarts, and scones, while teapots kept emerging from the kitchen steaming from their spouts. The restaurant was pleasantly noisy with the rattle of silverware and dishes. Although Vera was certain that many of the rabbits, stoats, mice, and myriad other creatures were discussing the shocking crime at Summers End, she elected to ignore that fact. Gossip is inevitable, but almost never enlightening once the main facts are known.

Besides, she wanted to discuss the case with her companions, and for that, she needed a full tummy.

"Afternoon, friends. I'm Mae," their server said with a cheerful smile. Based on the rabbit's resemblance to the portraits in the tearoom's foyer, Vera guessed she was one of the family members who ran the place. "What can I bring out to you?"

"We'll need the full tea," Vera said firmly. "Breakfast was a long time ago, and we've had a busy day. A pot of black and a pot of green will be appreciated, I'm sure. And extra scones."

"With extra clotted cream," Lenore added, sounding worried. (She was worried about her sister's fate. But to an uninitiated creature it sounded as if she was worried about the possibility of a scone bereft of topping.)

"Yes, ma'am," Mae said seriously. "I'll bring more apricot jam as well."

Shortly after that, the group was working hard to fill the void in their stomachs, passing the basket of scones around the table and making sure the little watercress sandwiches were not neglected. There was apricot *and* raspberry jam, as well as the generous portions of clotted cream. As a bulwark against emergencies, a jar of honey was also at the ready.

Vera nibbled at a walnut scone slathered in cream, then took a sip of strong and malty black tea. "Ahh," she said, putting the cup down. "That's better. Now I can think."

"Same," said Ligeia, who'd just slurped down a cup of the delicate green tea. "Most restorative. Now, what do we know about the crime, and what do we still need to find out? Summers End just won't be the same until this is resolved."

"That reminds me," Vera said. "Van Hoote told me to ask you who you think built Summers End. But I got the impression that he thought it was a sort of joke."

Ligeia snorted. "It is to him, because he doesn't like evidence he can't point to on a rock."

"So what was he referring to?"

"There's a very old legend about the founding of Summers End," Ligeia explained. "A sort of fable that takes all the real-life, complex aspects of the creation of the site and makes it into a tidy little story that even distracted students can grasp."

"How does it go?" asked Thena, leaning in.

"Well, long, long ago, in the mists of time, before most animals knew anything other than hunger and struggle, a bear was born. And this was not just any bear, but an important one. Essentially this young bear was a princess, though in those times such titles were not used. This bear was strong, of course. And quick to learn, asking question after question. And very striking in appearance, so that everyone said there was not a more lovely creature on the face of the earth.

"But she was not merely pretty, she was good-hearted, which is more important. She worked to help all the creatures who lived in their part of the world. She studied plants to learn about medicines. She spoke with migrating birds to learn about other parts of the world and get ready for danger. And she noticed always the turning of the Earth and how the seasons followed each other, so that she could help everyone be ready for the inevitable winter.

"Now, as it happened, both the sun and the moon took note of her as well. For as they both traveled through the sky on their usual paths, they looked down and saw Princess Bear (as I shall call her, for we do not know her exact name).

"Both the sun and the moon were astounded by her grace and watched her day by day, night by night. The sun made sure to smile down as warmly as possible and burn away any offending clouds. It turned the world gold for her. Then, at night, the moon turned the world silver in order to please Princess Bear. It pulled the tides to and fro, revealing offerings of rare stones and shells from the sea. The sun would send diamonds sparking over water for her. The moon would get jealous and move in front of the sun, obscuring it in shadow.

"In fact, the sun and the moon were so enamored of the bear

that they quite neglected their duties. The days were whatever length the sun wished, and the months had no rhythm thanks to the moon being so distracted.

"It got so bad that none of the creatures on the Earth knew when to migrate, or gather food, or sleep for the winter. The weather was totally unpredictable, since the sun might evaporate a whole stormfront in order to see Princess Bear beyond it. The tides occurred randomly, swamping whole communities, flooding rivers and plains on a whim. And all because the sun and the moon were being foolish over Princess Bear."

"How long did this go on? Sounds like this bear lived for a hundred years," Lenore commented.

"Shush!" her sister snapped. "It's a fable, it's not meant to be taken literally. The night stars, thankfully, stayed steadfast through all this. Princess Bear had noted carefully how the stars spun in the sky and she realized that she could build a calendar to mark when certain stars rose and set, and this could be used to measure time.

"She told the sun and the moon that she was casting a great spell, and for it to work she needed them both to behave, following the lines marked down by the stones and shining at the proper locations on the proper days. She told them that the greatest gift either could give her was to be reliable. (If it was not clear before, she was *very* clever.)

"The sun and the moon both agreed, not wishing to be outdone by the other. And so Princess Bear built her calendar in a ring of stones that marked the moon's travels and mounded up a hill with a long tunnel inside that the sun could only peek into once a year, shining all the way down to illuminate a special stone."

"I see why van Hoote doesn't care for this version," Vera murmured.

Ligeia gave her a glance to quiet her, then went on. "Now all was going well," she said, "except for the fact that Princess Bear had one more admirer. This creature was a sea mink, and it had decided that Princess Bear was the only suitable choice to be queen of earth and sea."

"I've never heard of a sea mink," Thena said.

"If you let me finish, you'll know why," said Ligeia, waving one wing to silence her listeners.

"The sea mink waited in the darkness of the tunnel at the center of Princess Bear's great invention. When it saw her, it declared its affection, and asked her to join it. Princess Bear refused. It begged and pleaded, pestered and beseeched, all to no effect. Princess Bear had no interest in any suitor, least of all this stranger.

"The sea mink grew so angry at the bear's refusal that it determined if it could not have Princess Bear, no one could. It tricked its supposed beloved and used a moment of distraction to slay Princess Bear. Then it fled."

A few among the audience (which, during the course of Ligeia's retelling, had expanded to the neighboring tables) gasped in horror.

"Not long after, the sun and the moon both appeared in the sky and found the cold, lifeless body of their beloved.

"Enraged by the cruelty of the act, both the sun and the moon agreed to put aside their rivalry to find and punish the miscreant who had slain Princess Bear. While her family and her subjects prepared her body for burial, the sun and moon relentlessly pursued the killer. They used their great eyes to examine each and every creature on Earth, whether animals lived by day or night. All through the mountains, the forests, the plains, and the deserts, the sun and moon traveled. Lighting up rivers and trees, sand and soil, they allowed no object or creature to remain unexamined.

"It seemed that no hints could be found, but at last, the sun and moon arrived on a wide strand by the great ocean, where they saw a sea mink with a trace of Princess Bear's blood on its paws. No amount of scrubbing in the salty water could erase its terrible crime. The sea mink denied its guilt, but the sun and the moon were not to be lied to. The sea mink fled, dashing into dark waters, and swimming into caves. The moon pulled the tides to expose the killer's hiding spot, and the sun shone so brightly that nothing could remain hidden. The sea mink fled again, onto the land where it ran, and ran, and ran, always hiding in shadows until the sun and moon chased the shadows away. Onward and onward, the sea mink traveled, never to rest more than a moment, never to find any shelter from another creature.

"The chase went on, the sun pursuing by day and the moon by night. But at last came a night when the moon's face was dark. The sea mink laughed to itself, for here was its chance, a time when there was no light, and it could escape."

Ligeia looked around at the listeners and paused to take a sip of water before continuing.

"But the darkness holds danger as well, and the sea mink could no longer see any way forward. Or backward. Or at all!

"While running through the murk, it strayed into a mire and got stuck, as if the Earth itself was rendering judgment. When the sun rose the next day, it found the sea mink dead. The moon joined it in the evening, and they knew justice had been served.

They declared that this sea mink would be the last of its kind ever to be born."

"Oh, *that's* why I've never heard of a sea mink," Thena said.

The raven continued, "After witnessing the death of the killer, the sun and moon returned to where Princess Bear died. Her family had laid her out on a bier, and everyone left little gifts in remembrance to her. The sun and moon suggested that she be buried in the place she had crafted with her skill and knowledge. So, deep below the circle of stones they interred her, under the hill she'd made. The sun and the moon left great gifts of gold and silver to honor her, and they swore that they would forever abide by her rules set forth in stone and always follow their paths through the sky with perfect order, never straying and never meddling in earthbound matters again."

Ligeia fell silent, signaling the story was over. The group took a moment to digest what they'd heard.

"That's amazing," Vera said at last. "I can't believe I've never heard it before. Van Hoote seemed to think it was a nonsense story. What do you truly think, Ligeia?"

"I think that stories have power, whether they're true or not," the raven replied. "The legend neatly ties up a lot of aspects of Summers End, and we do know that it's a very old story. A version of it is even depicted on the wall of the south chamber. I don't think we'll ever prove whether there was a so-called princess. It doesn't matter. It tells us what we need to know, which is that folks born a long time ago cared about measuring time and they cared about honoring the great minds of their culture. It explains the extinction of an older species as the world's climate changed over the ages. We know that there have been lots of skeletons of ancient creatures found in bogs or tar pits that look nothing like us. This creature who supposedly designed Summers End . . . that's just an easy way to explain its origins. We know that in reality many, many creatures participated in making it."

"But someone might have had the *idea*," Thena said wistfully. "I mean, a particular creature could have had that spark of genius. I wish we did know if there was a princess or not."

"It would be the discovery of the century," Ligeia agreed. "But as far as I'm concerned, what matters is that the *tale* exists."

"You know," said Vera, "bears figure very prominently in all accounts of Summers End. Maybe . . ."

"Watch out," Lenore warned her. "That way lies speculation and endless blathering over scraps of text and scratches on rocks. Let the academics fight it out. It's what they love."

"You'd have made a good scholar, Lenore," her sister said. "After all, you hate losing an argument."

"Huh, wonder where I learned *that*," Lenore retorted. "Anyway, all this talk of old legends is making me feel like I'm about to be set in stone! Let's get to this food." For in fact, during Ligeia's storytelling, Mae had brought out more trays of little sandwiches and scones and tea cakes. It would be a shame to waste it.

"Good idea," Vera agreed. But even as she got up, her mind was still taken with Ligeia's tale. Fanciful, perhaps. But also intriguing. From her work as a journalist, Vera knew that every story has at least a grain of truth at its core. Once the fable and all the fabulous detail were stripped away, what was the core of this tale?

Chapter 17

After they finished tea, Vera judged the slant of the sun and decided that she ought to check in at the messenger office near the dock, hoping that she would receive some answers to the letters she had sent early that morning. Really, what would the woodlands do without wingmail? It was a testament to how all the creatures could work together to accomplish something. No wonder van Hoote was so interested in the origins of language!

Lenore joined her, and at the office, the same turtle was behind the desk, this time munching on a green-flecked scone.

"Cheddar and chive," she said, once she finished chewing. "Makes the afternoon go faster."

"I'm sure," said Vera. "Any letters for me?"

"I'll check. Yes, there are two for Miss Vera Vixen," the clerk said, and produced them both from a little cubbyhole on the wall behind the desk.

She accepted them from the turtle. On the first, she saw Orville's familiar script on the front. She couldn't wait to get back to her room so that she could read it. "Come on, Lenore. Stop by my room for a moment and we'll see if Orville has any advice."

"More likely it's full of warnings to be careful," Lenore guessed. "How about the other one?"

"That's Lefty's reply. He just says *Be there tomorrow*. Looks like we'll have another reliable assistant to help solve this."

"Lefty? Reliable?" Lenore cawed.

The two of them had barely gotten back out onto the street when Lenore nudged Vera. "Hey, there's Ford! See, he's walking down the other side of the street. I'm going to follow him."

"Good luck," Vera told her friend. "Check back at the lodge when you're done, okay?"

The fox watched Lenore flutter off after the bearded dragon, then headed back to Rosewood Lodge.

Thena was in the room, practically bouncing on the bed she'd been sitting on, papers strewn around her.

"Vera, more news!" the vole announced, her voice quivering with excitement. "Peggy, my contact at the university, did some digging, and she found out something interesting. You know how Loring said he's here because of a grant to write a new collection of poems based on Summers End? There's *no* record of any such grant. Well, after Peggy sent me that message, I got the idea that the grant must be private, so I sent a message to his publisher in the city to ask about the upcoming book.

They replied—and said there are no plans for any new book by Loring!"

"But he's definitely writing poems. I overheard him composing one of them near the site just the other day."

"Then he's doing it on spec. His publisher was clear, and they have no reason to keep a new book a secret."

"Interesting," Vera said softly. "Our peacock is keeping some secrets. Great work, Thena. Really smart to think about contacting the publisher and not just stopping with the university. Okay, let me know anything else you find."

"You got it, boss! Anyone in particular I should start with?"

Vera nodded. "Lenore and I found out something about Ford in our own investigations. We saw a reply to a query Durham made to Chaparral College out west. All the note said is that Professor Ford is no longer an active faculty member, and hasn't been for three years. What do you think that's all about?"

Thena's ears pricked up. "So Durham was suspicious of Ford! He must have thought Ford was lying about something and sent letters to the place Ford claimed to be affiliated with only to find out that he wasn't officially connected to them at all. That fits with my own background research. He definitely used to teach at Chaparral, but he must have left. I'll send another wingmail and ask for the particulars, like if he retired or got sacked or whatever."

"If Ford knew Durham was poking around," Vera mused, "he might have decided to take some steps to silence him . . . permanently. I hope Lenore is being careful. She's following him right now."

"Ooh, then let me follow van Hoote some more!" Thena begged. "Remember, we can't be sure that he's aboveboard, either. I'm good at being unobtrusive, and if he does happen to notice me, I'll make up some questions about archaeology and he won't be able to resist giving me a lecture."

Vera nodded. "That leaves me with Chesley or Loring. I guess I'll go after whichever one crosses my path first."

———————

That evening after dinner, Vera and Lenore met briefly to discuss what they knew. Lenore was excited to report back about following Isaiah Ford. "It was uneventful, mostly. Though I admit that I lost track of him for about an hour. He was wandering around town, and Summer Street was awfully busy since another ferry boat had just docked and a bunch of folks were flooding onto the street. He's so low to the ground that I couldn't see past the crowd. By the time I got through them, he was gone."

"What did you do?" Vera asked.

"Well, I couldn't exactly shout for him, so I flew up and circled a few times, though the tree canopy is so thick this time of year I hardly saw a thing." Lenore huffed in frustration. "So I landed again, and just walked up and down the streets until I saw him. He was going into an antiques shop. Guess which one?"

"The Bronze Feather?" Vera asked.

"The very same. I didn't want to go inside because there's no way to hide in there. So I sort of lurked around the cul-de-sac, pretending to be shopping at the other stores. He came out about a quarter of an hour later."

"Was he carrying anything?"

"Not that I could tell. He looked kind of smug when he left, though. Like he'd gotten the better of Greenleaf in a deal?"

"Maybe." Vera couldn't picture anyone getting the better of Greenleaf. "Where did he go next?"

"All he did was stop at the pub for a drink."

"Do you think he was waiting for someone?"

"I know he wasn't, because finally I got thirsty, too, and walked up there. He saw me then and offered to share his table. And that's how I learned all about his experiences working in the desert canyons of the west, where that one lost civilization I can't remember the name of had their city built into the side of the cliffs. They built a sort of ancient calendar, too, but theirs marked midwinter day. That's why he's at Summers End, actually, looking for any link between the designs. Honestly sounded pretty interesting, and very authentic . . . made me wonder if it's really true that he's no longer teaching. He clearly loves it. But all in all, I'm afraid none of it was helpful to our investigation."

"Hey, you never know," Vera told her friend. "At the very least, you established some link between Isaiah Ford and Greenleaf. Do you want to go back to that store with me? I'm *really* curious about what Ford was doing in there."

Lenore flicked a feather as she said, "If he's one of her 'expert appraisers' he's either unethical or a flat-out crook."

"Let's try to determine that when we chat with Ms. Greenleaf," Vera said. "Maybe if we draw her out, she'll let something slip. If Ford is involved in the thefts from the site, then maybe he's taking the objects to the Bronze Feather so Ms. Greenleaf can sell them."

"And he gets a cut?" Lenore asked. "Or maybe she pays him up front for whatever price he sets."

"Let's not speculate about the details yet," Vera said. "At least, not till after we hear what Greenleaf has to say. Then I'll speak to Buckthorn and find out if he's interested in Greenleaf and her shiny shop. I really hope Lefty gets here soon! If there truly is a black-market operation, he's the only one I can trust to get answers about it."

"Weird when Lefty is our beacon of truth," Lenore said with a raucous laugh.

"Hey, he's an expert in his own field," Vera defended him.

"We should get him business cards."

"Sure, in a case purchased from the Bronze Feather."

———

Considering that Lenore had done her bit by following Ford, and Thena had already promised to follow van Hoote, Vera was anxious to get some sort of information regarding Professors Chesley and Loring. She'd go to Chesley first. Something about the porcupine's story about where she was when Durham was murdered didn't really add up, and her whole attitude was so standoffish that it suggested she wasn't being fully cooperative. The fox wasn't exactly looking forward to speaking with a professor who was both unpleasant and nocturnal. But it seemed that a nighttime stroll to Summers End might be the best way to find her stargazing and allow the fox to ask a few questions. Vera decided that she would set her alarm for two in the morning, giving a warning to Callie and Thena so they wouldn't hurl pillows at her when it happened.

When her alarm went off, Vera silenced it quickly. She dressed in the dark and left the room. Callie and Thena were snoring once again when she made her escape. The fox hoped that her roommates were not too upset with her for waking them.

While Vera trotted to the hill where she had last seen Professor Chesley and her telescope, she composed a mental list of questions she wanted to ask. She didn't want to antagonize the astronomer (at least, not any more than she already had), but the fox knew that Adelaide Chesley was hiding something.

Maybe it had nothing to do with the murder of Ridley Durham, but she had to find out.

"I can't believe that I am climbing this hill when most sensible creatures are asleep in their beds," Vera grumbled to herself. At the moment, she was feeling quite grumpy, and would have no trouble giving the porcupine a run for her money in the disagreeable department.

When she reached the top of the hill, Vera paused to catch her breath. She looked around and realized to her surprise that she was quite alone.

Perhaps she was early? Vera decided to wait a while, thinking that Chesley might have some reason for starting her sessions later. Maybe she even napped for a couple of hours during the first half of the night. At first, Vera didn't mind the wait, walking slowly from one end of the long hilltop to the other and then back again. She had an excellent view of the entire site of Summers End, past the ring of standing stones around the edge, and up to the surrounding forest, which was tinged with silver now, thanks to a thin slice of moon rising in the east. There were no clouds anywhere, so it was a perfect night for astronomy.

And yet, no astronomer appeared.

As the time passed, Vera grew grumpier.

"I got up in the middle of the night, and that creature decided to take a vacation!" Vera distinctly remembered Professor Chesley saying that she went stargazing nearly every night, a comment Ligeia confirmed. However, if she was not out with her telescope, where was she?

Something about the telescope sparked a faint memory in Vera's brain. What was it?

Ugh. It was too late at night for clear thinking. The porcu-

pine's absence made Vera wonder if she in fact did have something to do with the murder of Durham. She was definitely
keeping some secrets, and if she couldn't be trusted to tell the
truth about her usual schedule, why should Vera believe anything else she said?

After an hour went by, the reporter gave up and made her
way down the hill, back toward the lodge and her warm bed. As
she walked, she formulated a new plan to find Professor Chesley. She would go to Aster House tomorrow and wake *her* up
for an interview!

Chapter 18

Early the next morning, Vera and Thena headed to the patio of the lodge for breakfast. Callie hustled them out, saying she'd meet them there. "I prefer a bit of solitude for my morning meditation," she told them. "All the chaos of the past few days has really thrown me off my regimen!"

"Aunt Callie got into meditation as an actor," Thena explained. "She's always after me to try it, but whenever I close my eyes, all I can visualize is unwritten term papers. *Not* restful."

On the way to the patio, Gerry Rosewood flagged them down. "There's a message for you, Miss Vixen," he called, gesturing with a small folded piece of paper.

Vera thanked the squirrel and took the message, planning to

read it over at the table. After her fruitless night, she was sleepy, cranky, and looking forward to a hearty breakfast. With *lots* of coffee.

Lenore had arrived before them and commandeered a table. There were already carafes of coffee and juice on the tables. The fox poured herself a mug of coffee and took a grateful sip.

Before she could read the note, Callie and Thena arrived, taking seats opposite Vera.

"Have you heard?" Callie asked. "Arabella has been going back and forth with some of the ferry services at the docks. She finally got word of a boat with enough room. The students will be heading home later today. With the death of Durham, and the fact that there's an active investigation going on at the site, there's really no benefit to their remaining here."

Thena nodded. "Deputy Poole won't let anyone other than the university employees on the site, and that's only because he hasn't got the authority to stop them. And the professors are far too distracted to devote much attention to teaching our group of students. So home they go!"

"I'm going with the students," Callie said. "They still need chaperones to mind them. But Thena can stay, if you don't mind keeping an eye on her, Vera."

"Of course! I wouldn't let my mentee skip out on her work anyway." Vera smiled at Thena. "A reporter always sticks with the story."

"You got it," Thena said happily, then pointed to the as-yet-unread message Gerry had given her. "What's that note?"

"Oh, right. Let's see." Vera opened it and read aloud:

Please come alone to the Summerhill Police Station this
morning to discuss the Durham case.

Chief Buckthorn

"Alone? So I can't tag along, huh." Thena looked suspiciously at the note.

Vera agreed that it was a trifle odd. "Maybe he wants to limit the number of nosy journalists. Well, it's hardly a risk to go unaccompanied to the police station."

As she generally had a cordial relationship with the local constabulary in Shady Hollow, she didn't find it odd that the deer would request a chat. Maybe he didn't have any leads and wanted to pick her brain for clues. Buckthorn had been polite enough, although she couldn't say the same for his deputy. Poole was most unpleasant, and never seemed to pass up a chance to say derogatory things about journalists and amateur detectives.

Vera would have to postpone her visit to Chesley at Aster House until after she saw Buckthorn. But with her morning more or less mapped out, she could enjoy a hearty breakfast of blueberry pancakes and fruit salad. Determined to keep everyone's spirits up, she chatted with her friends over coffee about everything *but* the murder. Then Vera gathered up her notebook and hat and said goodbye to the others.

She made her way over to the Summerhill Police Station. Once again, the door was propped open to let in the summer breeze, and Vera entered to find Chief Buckthorn working at his desk. Deputy Poole was nowhere to be seen. Thank the stars for small favors.

The deer looked up at the fox's entrance.

"Good morning, Miss Vixen," he said heartily. "Thanks so much for coming promptly."

Vera nodded and took the seat that he indicated with a large hoof. She was glad he seemed to be in a good mood—he'd gotten rather frosty with her the last time they met.

"I was hoping that we could compare notes on this Durham thing," Chief Buckthorn began. "It seems like I'm not making any progress since we learned that the body had been moved. I got Dr. Reyes's final report from the autopsy," the deer went on, holding up a few typewritten pages. "As expected, the cause of death was two blows to the back of the head, with a heavy object, which you of course helped to locate. Dr. Reyes confirmed that it was indeed the boundary stone that struck him. The blood matches perfectly."

"It's good to know it really was the murder weapon," Vera said, not mentioning that she'd asked Reyes for the same information earlier. At least the good doctor didn't seem to have tattled on Vera for her presumption. How had he put it? Oh, yes. *Buckthorn would be* livid *if he knew* . . .

Buckthorn read from the report. "He bled out from a wound in his skull, though he might have died from the trauma of the blow, even without the blood loss. Durham would have lost consciousness almost instantly. As you surmised from your photos, he was killed near the edge of the site, near those trees where the boundary stone had been removed. Then he was dragged all the way inside the barrow, where the killer set up the rest of the scene with the carved stones and those little figurines."

"Ugh," Vera said with a shiver. "Sounds like the killer really hated him."

"Murder is often the result of passion," the chief agreed. "So it's extremely important that we find all possible motives among our suspects, even a motive that might seem petty to an out-side observer. I've noticed that these academic types can hold a grudge."

"Who are your suspects?" she asked.

"Right now, almost everyone. Very few of the individuals involved have solid alibis. The most common response I got was *I was alone in my room all night*, which isn't very helpful. Even though I'm sure it's true for the innocent."

Vera nodded. "I'm not sure how much help I can be. I've also been trying to rule suspects out. I still don't believe Professor Lee was involved in Durham's murder, despite circumstantial evidence. Lee would never have set up the crime scene that way; she knows too much about death rituals. And I don't think her sister would defend her so staunchly if she thought Ligeia was capable of murder."

"Her sister," Buckthorn echoed, with a significant look.

"*Estranged* sister," Vera pointed out.

"And do you have any theories for the others?" he asked, not looking particularly persuaded.

Vera paused. She wasn't sure how much to tell Buckthorn about her suspicions of Ford, van Hoote, or Chesley . . . mostly because she felt she couldn't prove anything, and she knew that cops tended to leap first and ask questions later. Out loud, she said, "Ford doesn't seem to have any interest in aca-demic power, and thus he didn't tussle with Durham the way that Ligeia Lee did. And van Hoote already has tenure at the college, and everyone agrees that he got along with Durham just fine."

The police chief listened carefully but did not reply.

"Hmm," Buckthorn said at last. "Find anything else?"

"Not anything I'd feel comfortable passing on," said Vera. "I like to confirm my hunches. But for now, hunches are all I've got. What about you? Any leads?"

"I can't discuss any more evidence in the case," Buckthorn said, in a more formal tone.

Vera shook her head. So all the sharing of information was going to be one-sided! It was obvious that the deer only considered Vera to be a source of information, not an investigative partner. Orville had acted that way at first, too, until he'd gotten to know Vera's methods. Well, that was fine. Vera was used to being underestimated. She would pursue her own theory about the relic smuggling without passing it along to Buckthorn. At least, not until it was necessary.

"Well, I suppose that's all," she said, keeping her tone neutral. She rose to leave, and the deer thanked her for coming.

"Oh, just one thing, Chief," Vera said. "Did you ever come to any conclusions about the missing figurines?"

"The what?"

"Both van Hoote and Ford told me that figurines like the ones found around Durham's body had been stolen earlier this season from the workroom on the site," she reminded him. "I was just wondering if you'd made any headway on that case?"

"Do you think the thefts are related to the murder?" he asked, looking interested.

"I'm not sure, but I do know that someone willing to commit one crime is often willing to commit a more severe one later on."

"You may be right, Miss Vixen," he said, nodding. "As for the thefts, I'm afraid that I have very little to go on, and I haven't been able to do much to identify who could be involved. But I have to say, I don't see a connection. Durham's murder appears to be motivated by personal feelings. And surely anyone trying to steal figurines from the dig wouldn't leave several lying around the body."

Vera sighed. "That's a good point. Okay, thanks, Chief."

As Vera walked down Summer Street, she was somewhat annoyed with herself for actually believing that the police chief would tell her anything of importance. Then she heard the town clock chiming ten.

"Oh, I'm going to be late!" She remembered that Lefty had told her he would be arriving today, and the first ferry was due to dock shortly. If he was on it, she wanted to meet him immediately (since it was generally not advisable to allow Lefty free rein in any town).

She hurried to the river and watched as a ferryboat named *Boreal Bess* pulled up and was roped safely to the dock.

Vera's timing was perfect. One of the first passengers on the gangplank was a raccoon wearing a dark linen shirt and pants with a black brimmed hat on his head. (In the winter, he'd trade those out for a dark sweater and a trench coat.) He liked to think it helped him blend into the background.

"Hey, Vera," Lefty called, waving a paw in her direction. "How's it going?"

Vera greeted the raccoon and thanked him for coming. "I hope I didn't interrupt anything," she said.

"Nah, don't worry about it. As a matter of fact, Rhonda was trying to get me to go downriver for a family picnic. *Her* family, you know. No, thanks." Rhonda was Lefty's longtime companion. She turned a blind eye to his extracurricular activities, though she was quite aware of them. However, as Lefty quickly explained, her family was under the impression that Lefty worked as a hospital orderly. Vera had to stifle a laugh at the thought.

As they walked away from the dock and into town along the busy thoroughfare, she discreetly passed him an envelope with his usual fee enclosed within. Lefty nodded his thanks and shoved the envelope into his pocket without looking at it. He and Vera had worked together before, and she always paid him well.

"How are you *really*, Vera?" Lefty asked. "I'm always happy for some honest work, but I'm guessing that you wouldn't have asked me to come if there wasn't something pretty nasty going on."

"Well, it started with a murder."

Lefty covered his eyes with his paws. "It always does!"

"But it doesn't end with the murder. Listen up." Vera gave Lefty an explanation of the events of the past few days, focusing on the missing artifacts and the various suspicions she had about the creatures involved. Despite Buckthorn's skepticism, she was playing with the notion that the killer had been pilfering artifacts and selling them to unscrupulous buyers down in the city. Such an operation would require using several contacts, perhaps starting with a courier to transport the goods in some way, and then a dealer in the city. The more creatures involved the more likely it was that someone would talk . . . if given the right incentive.

"So, do you know anything about the smuggling and selling of historical artifacts?" Vera asked the raccoon. "Anything you can tell me would help a lot."

Probably out of habit, Lefty looked over his shoulder before he replied. When he was certain no one could overhear them, he said, "What you're talking about—lifting and fencing things that are valuable because they're old—is what's called a dusty job. The sort of folk who are into these jobs are specialists. You got to be, because everything depends on you knowing that you're not getting tricked, and everyone you deal with also has to trust that you don't get tricked."

"So you have to have a reputation," Vera guessed.

"Exactly. Whoever is involved has probably been at this a long time. I can't tell you right off who's involved in the dusty racket in Summerhill. But let me rustle around and see what I can sniff out."

"I've got a good lead for you," she told him. "There's a shop called the Bronze Feather, and I wouldn't be surprised if the owner is involved somehow. She's got a few of the figurines for sale, and she's coy about whether they're real or replicas."

Lefty's eyes brightened. "Easy peasy, then. Tell you what. I'll find you tonight and tell you what I've uncovered."

"Thanks, Lefty. And be careful. Someone killed Durham, and that means they'll kill again if they have to."

"Don't worry about me," the raccoon said with a grin. "I'll take this over a family picnic any day!"

Vera bade Lefty goodbye, not wanting to be identified too closely with the admittedly shady character. Lefty always had his ear to the ground, and he'd be able to get to the bottom of what was happening in Summerhill's thriving antiquities business. Of course, it didn't necessarily mean that the murderer would be revealed. But Vera liked to pull on threads—it often unraveled all kinds of interesting secrets.

Secure in the knowledge that Lefty would do his best to find out what was going on at the Bronze Feather, Vera walked over to Aster House, and at the front desk asked for Professor Chesley. She fully intended to quiz the porcupine on a few matters, not least why she hadn't been in her usual stargazing spot last night.

The proprietor was a goat who introduced herself as Eloise.

"You seem young to own a hotel," Vera couldn't help remarking.

"Oh, goodness, I don't own Aster House." The goat laughed. "I just manage it for the couple who do. I grew up in the city, and I've worked in big hotels before, but I wanted a change of pace. I learned about this position a couple of years ago and came up on the next ferry! Luckily, I got the job. Been here ever since."

Vera remarked on how lovely the inn looked (not mentioning that she'd happened to sneak into the top floor suite previously).

The goat was perfectly happy to bound upstairs and knock on Chesley's door but returned soon after with the news that no one answered. "Not a surprise, honestly. She's often in and out at odd hours, since she always goes over to the monument for her work . . . other than cloudy nights, of course."

"Goodness, is the front desk staffed all night?"

"Not officially," Eloise explained. "But my room is just off the foyer there, and I tend to notice when guests come in or leave. Though in fact, Chesley has a key to the front door. Normally, I wouldn't give one to a guest, but she's here all summer and she's a professor at the dig, so it's all right."

A key to get in and out unobserved! That was possibly a very important tidbit of knowledge. Vera said, "I wonder if you happened to see Chesley come back on the night before the murder. She said that the rain curtailed her stargazing."

"What rain? There were a few clouds maybe an hour before dawn, but no rain. I remember that I'd hoped there would be so I wouldn't have to water the hanging pots on the balconies. We've got forty-seven, which adds up to a *lot* of time watering during dry spells."

"You're sure?" Vera asked intently.

Eloise nodded. "Oh, yeah. I count them every time."

"No, I mean are you sure it didn't rain that night?"

"Not a drop, Miss Vixen. I'd swear to that."

"Thank you!" Vera had to leave to digest this new information. Chesley had been quite firm about the fact that she had to leave her customary spot on top of the barrow due to rain. And she knew that Buckthorn had also asked the professor to verify her whereabouts because he'd originally hoped she might have been a witness to what had gone on near the entrance to the tunnel.

But apparently, she had lied about the rain. Why? The most obvious answer was sitting right in front of Vera's face. What if Adelaide Chesley had lied about her whereabouts, pretending she was far from the scene of the crime, because in fact that's exactly where she was? What if she had been the one to kill Ridley Durham at the doorway of the tunnel, and then drag his body inside and set up the sham ritual to cast guilt on her colleague Ligeia, who had been known to fight with Durham constantly? But since Chesley was primarily an astronomer, she had only the faintest idea of what such a ritual might look like, and she didn't have time to get more information because dawn was coming fast, and others would soon arrive at the site.

There was no time to waste at this point. Vera rushed the short distance from Aster House to the police station on Hill Street. Chief Buckthorn was still there, and (less happily) Deputy Poole had joined him.

"Ah, Miss Vixen. I just got an additional note from Dr. Reyes's office. Interesting development: Durham was drunk when he was killed. Reyes noticed some signs that suggested it, and a blood test confirmed it earlier today. Could be a clue, yes?"

"Maybe," Vera said, her mind on other things. "Listen, Chief. Have you seen Professor Chesley at all today?"

"No. Why? Did something happen at the site?" He reached for his hat.

"Not that I'm aware of. I was just at Aster House, and I discovered that she lied about her alibi!" Vera told him, and then provided the details about the weather report and the fact that Chesley hadn't answered Eloise's knock on the door.

Buckthorn's expression went grim. "If she lied about her whereabouts, that's a serious problem."

"I'll stay here, Chief, so you can investigate," Poole offered.

"No, I think you should come as well. Just in case a show of force is needed."

The deer got up and they all left the station (Buckthorn didn't bother to close the door).

"I thought you were patrolling Summers End," Vera said to the wolverine.

"Chief changed the assignment. We got all the evidence we were gonna get, and the professors were all getting salty about not being able to do their work. Dig season's almost over," he added. "Can't wait."

They walked back to the inn, and as soon as Eloise saw the chief, she straightened her posture and lost the genial grin she'd worn before.

Buckthorn glanced around, nodded when it appeared that no guests were present, and said, "Sorry to bother you, Eloise. But I'm afraid I'll need to see the inside of one of your rooms."

"Of course, Chief. Any room in particular, or . . ."

"Chesley's."

"But I just knocked a little bit ago. She didn't answer, and the inn has a firm policy of not violating the privacy of guests without reason."

"I've got a reason," he said, and his tone was enough to make Eloise jump and grab a ring of keys.

"Follow me," she said. The goat led them all up the stairs to the third floor. She knocked again at a door, and then said. "Professor, if you're in there, please say something. The chief is here and wants to talk!"

After a moment, Buckthorn said in a low voice, "Unlock the door, please. And then stand aside."

Eloise did so, looking very nervous. Buckthorn pushed the door open fast, but there was no one on the other side. The bed was made, the curtains open, and the window sash pushed up to let in air. But there was no trace of the recent guest.

Vera noted that Chesley's room was on the other wing of the inn, but with a little balcony that actually gave her a direct line of sight to Durham's suite. The interior of the room was tidy but seemed empty of all personal belongings.

Buckthorn ordered the room to be searched, and he and Poole went at the task with a will. Meanwhile, Eloise and Vera looked on from the doorway.

The police found a battered novel that had fallen between the bed and the wall, though it had evidently been there for some time, considering the dust on it.

"Aw," Eloise said, taking the book from Poole and wiping the cover clean. "*The Oakhill Treasure!* Classic. I loved that story as a kid."

Vera had read it as well and had equally fond memories. "But I doubt it belonged to Chesley," she concluded, flipping through the pages just in case something had been put there.

"I got nothin'," Poole said in disgust after finishing his half of the room. "She must have cleared out fast; it's like she was ready to flee."

"Maybe she was," Buckthorn said. "Okay, I'm going to alert the public to keep a lookout for her. And I'll send word up- and downriver since she may well have already left my jurisdiction."

"Should we tell the Stonehurst scouts to start searching?" Poole asked, a certain dreadful excitement in his tone.

Vera shuddered. She knew exactly what he was talking about. It was rare to resort to such measures, but there was one prison in the woodlands, and it employed a small detachment of raptors. Their main job was to search and retrieve escapees from Stonehurst, but they also could be called upon by local law when needed.

"Oh, no," Eloise cried. "That's rather extreme, don't you think?"

Buckthorn thought about it, then said, "We'll hold off for now, but it's something to keep in mind. I'd much rather deal with this without involving a whole crowd of folks."

Poole looked disappointed but didn't argue.

The chief looked at her again. "We may not have much time. Miss Vixen, if you'll go to Summers End and let everyone there know to be on the lookout for her, I'll spread the word here in town. Depending on when she fled, there might still be a chance of catching her."

Vera nodded. "I'll tell everyone I see. Anything else?"

"Be careful," he said. "If Chesley is our murderer, there's no telling what she might do. But I promise you this. I'm going to do everything in my power to find her."

Vera glanced at the clock on the wall of the room. "Oh,

no. I've got to get to the lodge to help get the students ready for the ferry!"

"Oh, that's right, Ms. Boatwright told me you'd all be leaving today," Buckthorn said.

"Great news," Poole added, glaring at her.

Vera just smiled back. "Most of the group is heading back to Shady Hollow, true. But there's a story here, and I'm going to stay to report on it, along with my intern, Athena Standish. And Lenore is staying, too, obviously, to be with her sister."

"What?" Poole growled. "Chief, tell them they gotta go!"

Buckthorn gave his deputy a sharp glance. "Don't be daft, Titus. Summerhill is open to all. And Miss Vixen has been very helpful so far. Or do I have to remind you of who found the murder weapon?"

Poole turned away in disgust, while Buckthorn just said, "Go help your students, Miss Vixen. There are only a few hours before the ferry is due to leave. And please remember to be careful for the rest of your time here. I can't guarantee your safety, or that of your friends."

"Understood, Chief," Vera replied. She bade goodbye to the goat and made her way out of Aster House and back through town. Every step of the way, she wondered where Adelaide Chesley had gone.

———

Arabella Boatwright should have been a general. Vera watched in awe as the rat efficiently rounded up all the students and persuaded them to pack and clean their rooms, then present themselves for the walk to the ferry, all without losing her temper once. It was truly remarkable.

The chaperones helped, of course, but Vera was still sort of amazed that the whole Shady Hollow school group got to the docks a half hour before the ferry began to load.

"I always tell folks things will happen earlier than they really do," Arabella confided to Vera while they waited. "It just makes things simpler."

Vera vowed to incorporate that wisdom in her daily life.

The ferry captain, an otter, came out on deck and announced that there would be a delay in boarding. "Just be patient!" she added, though she also glanced worriedly at a watch attached to her jacket.

So the students milled around the docks. Fortunately, the young are easily amused, and soon small groups were either peeking under the piers at the mussels clinging to the fat wooden posts or chucking stones across the water, or simply chatting and giggling. But as the minutes ticked by, there was a growing sense of restiveness.

"What's the delay?" Vick muttered, standing with CJ and Georgette. Joshua Chitters sat on his small suitcase.

But even as he asked, Deputy Poole suddenly appeared and stamped his way down the gangplank, nodding curtly to the captain. "All clear. You can let the passengers on now."

"Oh," Vera said, realizing what Poole had been up to. "The police were searching the boat."

"Do they think that the murderer is a stowaway?" Vick asked. "If I killed someone and had to leave town, stowing away on a boat seems smart!"

"Yeah, but it would be smarter to do it right away," CJ retorted. "Not three days later. Anyway, they're not so smart, because they're not on the boat after all. Or we'd have seen Poole escorting them off in cuffs, huh?"

"That would have been so cool," Vick said, his gaze dreamy.

Vera just shook her head, grateful that they would be gone from Summerhill soon. The whole situation was unhealthy for young creatures! She said, "Okay, all of you. Grab your luggage and get on board. Watch out for each other on the trip back downriver."

"Aren't you coming with us, Miss Vixen?" Georgette asked, eyes wide.

"Nah, she's going to stay and solve the crime," Vick said. "Some folks get all the luck."

"If I were lucky, I'd have solved the crime already," Vera told them. "But I am staying here as a reporter, and I'm writing articles for the *Herald*. So you'll eventually be able to read all about it."

Vera and Lenore waved goodbye as the ferry workers cast off and the boat moved slowly into the mainstream. The students lined the side and waved back. Vera heard CJ yell, "Have fun catching the killer!"

Lenore snorted. "He seems to have a different attitude toward detective work."

"That's why I'm glad the students will be out of danger. We really don't know what we're in for, and that's assuming we're successful in finding out what happened."

"We'll do it," Lenore said. "We've got to. Chesley will surface eventually, and we'll go from there."

"We can't be sure she's the killer," Vera said. "Though I admit it looks bad to up and vanish during a murder investigation."

That evening at Rosewood Lodge, the intense quiet was novel. Gerry insisted that Vera, Thena, and Lenore should each get their own rooms for the duration of their stay.

"It's not like we don't have space!" he added with a chuckle.

Vera said, "But aren't you expecting another school group?"

"Not for two weeks. Until then, consider yourselves at home."

"Oh, thank you! We can also help tidy up and get the other rooms ready," Thena said. "It's the least we can do."

In practice, the shift meant that Thena moved next door to Vera, while Lenore kept her room on the upper floor. "Hey, I could sleep in a different bed every night, and that's not even counting naps!" Thena said.

Vera laughed, but the truth was that she was rather distracted, thinking about where Professor Chesley had gone, and if she *was* a danger . . . or was *in* danger.

The whole town had been alerted to Professor Chesley's disappearance, and many folks offered to help look for her, especially because Buckthorn called her a "creature of interest" and was careful to imply that the police were concerned for her well-being. Vera could tell that he was too smart to create a panic among the residents and tourists by saying that a murderer could be roaming the streets.

Late that night, Vera was reading in bed, trying to calm down after the incredibly eventful day. Her choice that evening was one of van Hoote's dry treatises on Summers End. The title of this one was *An Examination of Ancient Woodland Culture Stone Artifacts from a Paleography Perspective*. She'd hoped that by going over the various professors' works, she would learn something useful about the site (or the writer). However, this particular book was only teaching her how to fall asleep. Her eyelids grew heavy as she struggled to stay alert.

"Dolomite . . . quarried and transported . . ." She read aloud in an effort to reach the end of the chapter.

A soft knock on her door startled her into full wakefulness.

"Yes? Lenore, is that you?" she asked.

"It's Lefty!" a familiar voice spoke from the other side. "I got news!"

Vera snapped the book shut and slid out of bed. She pushed her paws into her cozy slippers, then walked to the door.

Opening it, she stepped back to allow Lefty in.

He snuck in quickly and pushed the door shut. "Never do that, Vera!" he scolded.

"Do what?"

"Let random folks in late at night!"

"You're not random. I know you."

"But I coulda just used the name to trick you, and boom! You got a stranger inside with no help to call for."

"Thena's next door," Vera told him. "And anyway, Lefty, you sounded like you when you said, 'It's Lefty.'"

"Sure, but what if someone else made me say it? Say, a crime boss determined to get the jump on a nosy reporter!"

Vera wanted to object, but then she realized that Orville probably would have given her exactly the same advice. "How about I promise I won't do it again, and you tell me what's got you so worked up?"

"Sure thing. Say, do you got any snacks? Snooping is hungry work and I skipped dinner."

Vera retrieved a tin of oatmeal cookies and offered it to Lefty. He took one and nibbled appreciatively.

She waited until he finished the last crumbs, then said, "Well?"

"Okay. Here's what I found out. I cased the Bronze Feather and noticed that when the rabbit closed up shop for the day, she kept the lights on inside."

"She could have just been doing the daily accounts."

"Sure, but when a stoat came and knocked on the back door,

she went and let him in, no questions asked. So she knew him and wasn't worried."

"Were you close enough to hear anything?" Vera asked, without much hope.

"As a matter of fact," Lefty said smugly, "it was a very warm day, and Miss Whatshername left a window open. Just happened that I took a bit of a rest under that window while they chatted."

She leaned forward. "And?"

"Didn't get much, because it must have been a pretty routine exchange. Heard her say that a few expected items weren't available because of Durham's death. The stoat didn't seem too worried, but asked if that was going to happen again, and then the rabbit said the next few months might be tight, and not to make any promises."

"Promises to whom?" Vera mused. "His boss? A buyer?"

Lefty shrugged. "Maybe both. No one wants to disappoint someone who's already given over money, I'll tell you that. They wrapped up the conversation, and I'm pretty sure the stoat passed her an envelope, but they didn't talk about particular amounts, so I can't be sure. Anyway, the stoat left a few minutes later, and she turned off the lights just after."

"Did you follow the stoat? Was he carrying anything?"

"Wasn't carrying anything," Lefty said. "Too obvious. He was wearing a coat, though, and who wants a coat in this weather? I'm sure it was a little bulkier when he left than when he came, though."

"Oh, she must wrap each item up separately, and he can tuck them in his pockets." Vera was taking notes as the raccoon talked.

The thief nodded. "He went back to a boat moored at the docks. Any captain can get fussy about extra cargo, even if it's little, or even if it's personal. But the stoat walked right on and didn't look like he had anything with him, so no questions asked, and the purser won't bother to adjust a manifest later."

"I'll go to the docks tomorrow and talk to the captain," Vera said.

"Good luck with that—the boat left not long after the stoat got aboard."

"Oh, no! That was my best lead. Now I won't know if he was a passenger or crew or anything."

Lefty grinned. "Don't fret. Got the name of the boat: the *Wanderlust*. You'll be able to send a message to any dock or marina downstream all the way to the city and find out where they hauled in for the night. Whenever a boat uses a town's docks, someone's got to register it. Usually the captain."

"And that means I can get the captain's name and their home port. Excellent work, Lefty," Vera said, pleased with the information. Linking the boat used for the transport to the buyers of the stolen goods would be an important step. Even if the captain was completely innocent, she'd be able to trace the movements of the boat and find out exactly who this stoat creature was, whether a regular passenger, or a sailor with a profitable side business!

Lefty was not done passing on what he knew. "There's one more thing, Vera," he said, looking serious. "You should be very careful who you talk to about this. If it goes all the way up and down the river to the city, that means it's a big operation, and that means there's enough money involved to make it danger- ous. And it sounds like it's been going on for a while, which means somebody was being paid to look the other way. Or sev- eral somebodies."

"I'll be careful," she promised.

"Huh, you always say that. Want me to stick around town for a few days? I might be able to dig up more info."

"That would be pretty helpful," Vera said. "I wish I could offer a room here in the lodge, but it might look suspicious."

"No worries," Lefty said, waving a paw to dismiss the idea. "Too fancy for me anyway. There are plenty of places where I can hole up and no one will notice a thing."

"Okay, Lefty. But keep your eyes open. Summerhill isn't as innocent as it seems!"

The reporter closed her notebook and thanked Lefty for his help. He gave her a grin, and then said his goodbyes. Despite the lateness of the hour, she guessed that he would stop in the local pub before he hit the sack. Oddly, the thought of Lefty being near was reassuring. What strange allies she was collecting!

The sudden disappearance of Adelaide Chesley had thrown off her previous ideas. Vera had a lot to think about, and she wanted to share this new information with Lenore. She also wanted to return to the Bronze Feather the next day and ask the owner a few more questions.

As the fox went back to her bed and her interrupted book, she was deep in thought. If someone had been stealing artifacts from the Summers End site, and then funneling them through the Bronze Feather to sell to tourists, as well as into the city through other dealers, had someone killed Durham because he had found out what was going on? Perhaps Vera was wrong to rule out any of the other professors. They could be guilty of something a lot worse than angling for tenure. Ford had lied about where he was working. Van Hoote had apparently absconded with student fees. And Chesley had just plain absconded. What was Vera going to find out next?

Chapter 19

In the morning, the fox first stopped by the next door down and woke Thena, then went upstairs to Lenore's room and rapped on the door. The raven was up and getting ready for the day.

"Wow, do I have a lot to tell you," Vera said when Lenore greeted her.

"Let's rustle up some breakfast and you can tell me then."

Because the large group was now gone, Vera and the others told the Rosewoods that they'd find their own meals for the next few days. Vera figured the couple needed a break.

The friends opted to walk to Front Street Bakery. Vera and Thena took seats at one of the small tables outside, while Lenore went in to purchase the food.

The raven emerged a few moments later with a tray. It held three big ceramic mugs and a plate of various baked goods—because few things are more disappointing than an inadequate breakfast.

Vera accepted her mug of coffee, and then surveyed the options, settling on a zucchini and sweet pepper muffin.

After scarfing down a pecan donut, Lenore picked up her teacup and took a long sip as she listened to her friend relay what she had learned since they last spoke, starting with her most recent meeting at the Summerhill Police Station and ending with her late-night conversation with Lefty. The raven said nothing until her friend was finished, and then she let out a breath.

"Wow, this is way more complicated than I thought!" Lenore said. "Is there any creature in this town who isn't involved in something nefarious? We should definitely talk to Ms. Greenleaf again. She is in this up to her long floppy ears."

"I agree," Vera said, "but we don't want to tip her off that we know what's going on. And all this has got me thinking. Up till now, we've been assuming that Durham was killed for personal reasons. That one of the other researchers was angry about the way he treated them, or because he withheld funding or credit. But what if the motive was more practical?"

Thena nodded, following along as she nibbled at her hot honey cornbread. "You mean that Durham caught one of them stealing objects from the site, and to prevent him from doing anything about it, they killed him to keep him quiet."

"Exactly. But then they tried to make the murder scene look more dramatic, hoping that the police would assume Durham was the victim of an unstable creature who was conducting a weird ritual."

"But they didn't have much time, so they were forced to use whatever objects they had available, which is why Ligeia recognized how inappropriate they were. Which means that Ligeia should be at the bottom of the list of suspects now, because she'd have done the ritual right!"

"Well, I don't know that I'd want to go to court with that defense," Vera said. "Our job is to identify the actual killer, so Ligeia never even has to face a judge."

"I've got a candidate," Lenore said. "When a creature vanishes during a murder investigation, it often means they're the one behind it all."

"Let's not jump to conclusions. Okay, consider all our suspects." Vera got her notebook out again.

"It's a short list," Lenore said. "Other than Ligeia, the only researchers working under Durham this season were van Hoote, Ford, our now-missing Chesley, plus Loring lurking around. And a few graduate interns like Myron. I know Lefty is asking some questions in town to find out how someone would get items to the city to sell. Maybe Buckthorn can help with that."

"I'll talk to him again," Vera said. Then she turned to Lenore. "Meanwhile, you continue to shadow Isaiah Ford. If you notice any suspicious behavior, remember it but don't confront him. Thena, you follow van Hoote. Same assignment. Got it?"

"Yes, ma'am!" Thena said.

For a moment, Vera considered giving Athena a short lecture about how chasing after possible murder suspects was not typical journalism, and that just because a mentor suggests something doesn't mean an intern is required to do it. But then Thena looked incredibly excited by the task of following van Hoote, so it was probably too late. And after all, Thena did specifically request to shadow *Vera*, who'd made something of a habit of exposing murderers in the past. The vole knew what she was getting into.

Thena said she was going to Aster House to try to intercept van Hoote before he got to his room, assuming that the owl was working nights. Vera and Lenore finished their food and then walked through town. They stopped by the Bronze Feather only to see a sign on the door saying the shop wouldn't open till noon.

So they whiled away the time. Though neither of them said it out loud, they were both sort of looking for Chesley. Vera kept glancing down alleys and peeking into back gardens on the off chance the porcupine would suddenly appear.

As they walked up one side street, Vera nudged her friend. "Hey, see that sign? *Roxanna's.* That's the astrologer that Chesley was yelling at the first day we got here. I wonder what she's got to say about the murder."

"You're serious?" Lenore asked. "You want to ask some fortune teller for clues?"

"I was thinking more about asking a local for some insight that we've been missing. We've been talking to the professors and the workers at the site. I bet the townsfolk have seen a side of all of them that we haven't heard about yet."

Lenore cawed in delight. "Excellent! Let's get mystic."

The inside of the fortune teller's shop was dark, with heavy velvet curtains pulled over the windows that obscured even a hint of sunlight. Incense burned in one corner, sending up a plume of smoke heavy with the aroma of rose and oud. Vera sneezed.

"Good day, friends. I'm glad you've come." The fortune teller stepped out from behind a beaded curtain. She was a pika, and her round ears stuck up through the slits in her rather extravagant blue satin turban. (Apparently, she'd left her pointy hat at home.)

"Er, have we met?" Lenore asked.

"Not in this life! But you are seekers of knowledge, and that brings us all together. I can see in your auras that you both deal in words, in wisdom, in truth!"

"Well, I'm a reporter and she's a bookseller," Vera admitted. "So I guess you're right on that count." She was impressed for half a second, and then decided that any fortune teller worth their enchanted salt would study up on newcomers to town, just in case.

"Roxanna Cobb, at your service. Welcome to my humble shop."

"Speaking of services, what do you offer?"

"A full range of divination options, depending on your needs! Paws read, cards spread, star charts drawn, all of it. Do you have a preferred method?"

"Er, I have to admit that neither of us are exactly fortune-telling regulars."

"Skeptics, huh?" Roxanna winked. "Well, we all start some-where. What sort of knowledge do you seek today?"

"We want to know who offed Ridley Durham," Lenore said bluntly. "Don't suppose you've got a deck of cards with that answer."

The pika ignored the sarcasm. "Cards? No. For such a query, I think we need something else. The murder occurred at Sum-mers End, on Summers End. That is cosmic in both place and time, and that suggests we look to the cosmos for clues. Come and sit. As it happens, I've been curious about the murder as well, and I've drawn up a star chart for the day in question."

Vera and Lenore sat at a round table covered in purple velvet cloth. The pika unrolled a big sheet of paper on which the stars visible on that night had been carefully mapped out. Along the edge, representing the horizon, a line of trees had been hastily sketched.

"Ah, here we are," said Roxanna. "The constellations speak to us if we know how to listen. The night of the murder was full of portent. In the east, the stag ascendant rose late—er, that's these five stars here, here, and here," she added, tapping a paw on the star chart and drawing a rough shape that a very drunk or nearsighted creature might call a stag's head. The pika went on. "And high in the sky, we see the scales, which of course relates to justice."

"Or reptiles?" Vera asked.

"Not those kinds of scales. The serpent is located here, in the southern sky." Roxanna made a squiggly gesture over some other dots.

"Okay, scales for weight. That constellation would be helpful if you're at the grocery," Lenore murmured. Vera jabbed a paw into her side to hush her up.

Roxanna continued. "Here in the west, the ram sets, flanked on the left by the ship."

"What's that mean?" Vera asked. "It's not like Durham drowned. He was conked on the head."

The pika frowned, irritated. "Look, the constellations are what they are. The ram is *always* next to the ship. I can't really change that. They're called the fixed stars for a reason, okay?"

"Okay. But what do you think it means?"

"Perhaps we should move to a different method to refine the question. Let me brew some tea and we'll read the leaves." She bustled off, obviously somewhat miffed at her clients' mundane outlook.

"What a bunch of nonsense," Lenore muttered to Vera. " 'Refine the question'? The question is who killed Durham! That doesn't need any refinement."

"I think we just have to go with it," Vera whispered back.

They waited a rather long time for the pika to return. When she did, she bore a tray with a small teapot and two plain white cups on plain white saucers. She poured the tea, and then instructed them to drink up. "Leave a little bit in the bottom. You'll then swirl it around clockwise and invert the teacup onto the saucer. The pattern the tea leaves fall into will reveal the universe's answer to your query."

Vera and Lenore dutifully sipped. Thankfully the tea seemed quite ordinary, and except for the loose leaves it was pleasant to drink.

"Very well, swirl it around . . . yes. Now quickly invert!"

Vera placed the cup upside down on her saucer, and Lenore did the same.

"We're asking the same question, aren't we?" Lenore asked, sounding skeptical of the whole enterprise. "Shouldn't our leaves look the same?"

"You are different creatures, with different experiences and outlooks. You will come to the truth in different ways." With a flourish, Roxanna lifted the cups.

Vera looked at the two sodden images revealed there. The tea leaves on her own saucer conglomerated in a large lump, with a scattering of tiny bits around it. Meanwhile, Lenore's leaves had made a rather pretty crescent shape.

"Aw, yours looks nicer," Vera said. "Kind of like the moon."

"Indeed!" the pika said. "A clear sign! The moon is a symbol of night, when the murder occurred. And it is a symbol of wisdom, indicating the answer *will* be found, in time. A crescent moon, hmmm, the night of the murder, there was a crescent moon, setting after midnight, I believe. The moon saw the murder occur, but will the moon help us unmask the killer?"

Roxanna turned to Vera's saucer.

"Sorry," Vera said. "It's just a lump. Like a little hill of leaves."

The pika looked up at Vera, her eyes gleaming. "What an instinct for tasseomancy, Miss Vixen! You call it a hill, and of course the murder occurred at the mound known as Summerhill. But you see, all the leaves surrounding the hill . . . to me they say *Look beyond, there is more.* The monument is there and will be there. But your answers are beyond it. I think you would do well to look for more clues in the town of Summerhill. Examine the many entities and creatures whose lives depend on the ancient Summerhill, the old monument that gives our new town its reason for existence. That is where you'll find what you seek."

The pika suddenly slumped back in her chair, putting a paw to her forehead. "Oh, dear. Connecting with the mystic is always so enervating. I must rest."

"Maybe have a cup of tea," Lenore suggested, deadpan.

"I shall do just that, in a moment. That'll be twenty, please. And tips are welcome."

Vera pulled out the money from her bag and thanked the pika for her time. The two friends left the shop and emerged, blinking, into the bright afternoon.

"What was *that?*" Lenore muttered when they were far enough away that the astrologer couldn't overhear them. "Talk about a scam!"

"I thought it was sort of interesting," Vera said. "She's right about one thing. We shouldn't focus exclusively on the site and those who work there. The whole town of Summerhill depends on the fame of the monument to prosper, and Ridley Durham was entangled in a lot of folks' lives here in town. I bet we *will* benefit from looking at this murder from another angle."

"Well, I'm up for whatever you think we should do . . . unless it means breathing in more of that incense! I refuse to get my star chart done or look into a crystal or tell anyone about my dreams."

Vera chuckled. "I don't think you'll need to do any of that. But how about we stop by the pub and talk to some locals before we approach Greenleaf again? There's no better place to pick up information about what folks really think. And we might pick up a clue we didn't even know we needed."

"And we can get something to eat," Lenore declared. "I'm starving. You know the real problem with tasseomancy? It doesn't come with cookies."

The news about Professor Chesley's disappearance the previous morning was still the biggest news in town, and creatures of all types kept showing up at the police station to report sightings of her, although none of them panned out. Vera tried to follow up with the witnesses, talking to them after they gave their tips to Buckthorn. Chesley had been spotted at the docks. Chesley had been spotted at the local diner, stocking up on sandwiches. Chesley had broken into a house. Chesley had been seen running away from town, into the green woods, where no houses were.

In every case, whether it was Vera or Buckthorn or Lenore or someone else who checked out the clue, no trace of the porcupine was discovered.

"It's most likely that she left town and traveled through the woods until she reached someplace with a dock, where she got onto a boat," Buckthorn told Vera after a long and unsuccessful day of searching. "I've sent wingmails to the next couple of towns both up- and downriver, telling them to be on the lookout for any unknown porcupine. But so far I've gotten no response. If I don't get a break in the case soon, I'll have no choice but to call in the Stonehurst team. Their approach is . . . uncompromising, but they get the job done."

Vera shuddered. She'd hoped that the fearsome team of raptors wouldn't be necessary. But she knew that it would be a difficult task to track down the professor if she had that much of a lead on them. "Okay. We'll keep looking, of course."

"If you find any trace, inform me immediately," Buckthorn ordered. Since hearing of Chesley's broken alibi, his demeanor had grown steadily more concerned, and he didn't look as if he'd slept a wink.

Vera promised the deer that she'd keep alert for news of Chesley and report anything she learned. Buckthorn gave her a grateful nod, and then immediately had to turn his attention to a stoat who'd come in with the news that a porcupine had been seen lurking up in the Hilltop neighborhood.

Vera quietly left the station, thinking hard. Why had the astronomer chosen to leave when she did? If she was the killer, why didn't she leave immediately after the murder . . . or stay even longer? What had happened to change her plans? "And did she take her telescope?" Vera wondered out loud.

Of course, perhaps Chesley hadn't chosen to leave on her own. She could have been targeted by the murderer as well. Vera hated the idea that there might be another victim to be found, but she couldn't discount the possibility.

While thinking these gloomy thoughts, Vera strolled up Summer Street, looking at the neat and tidy homes and businesses on either side, and greeting whoever she met with a polite nod, too distracted to offer more.

And then she saw Professor Ford, sitting at one of the outdoor tables at the pub, soaking up the sunshine. Now there was an avenue for investigation! Professor Ford was hiding something. It was time to discover just what that lizard was up to.

"Oh, hello, Professor Ford," Vera said, walking up to him as casually as she could. "I was hoping I'd run into you today."

He looked inquiringly at her. "Really? In that case, have a seat and tell me why."

Vera sat down, but before she could start in on some small talk, a squirrel hurried over and asked Vera if she wanted a drink.

"Oh, yes. Iced tea, please." The sun had gotten very warm indeed.

After the squirrel left, Vera smiled at Ford. "Summerhill is a charming town, isn't it? I'm glad I came . . . even though the circumstances haven't been exactly happy."

"Yes, I noticed that you stayed even after your group went home," he noted, his eyes unblinking and alert.

"Well, I'm staying in my capacity as a reporter. And a friend."

"I see. And just what about this town do you find charming?"

"Oh, um, lots of things. Everyone is so friendly."

"It's a tourist town. Of course everyone you meet is friendly," Ford said with a snort. His mood seemed subtly different from usual. Less avuncular. Sharper.

Before Vera could reply, the squirrel returned with her iced tea, with a sprig of mint jutting out of the top of the glass. "Enjoy!" the server said.

"See?" Ford noted with a chuckle. "So friendly."

Vera tried another tack. "There are a lot of interesting places for such a small town. That occult shop is quite an experience, plus all the souvenir stands, not to mention the crafts and antiques shops."

"Yes, you were at the Bronze Feather," Ford said. "You and your friend Lenore."

So much for subtlety, Vera thought. But there was no sense in denying it. "Yes, it's true. Lenore's just mad for antiquing, you know. And Ms. Greenleaf's shop is full of fascinating items!"

"And did you buy anything she's selling?" Ford asked.

"Er, no. The items we were interested in were a bit on the pricey side."

"Pricey? Or priceless?"

Vera leaned forward. "That's the real question, isn't it? What's your interest in the figurines she's selling? Or should I contact Chaparral College and just ask them what's going on with Professor Isaiah Ford?"

The lizard flashed a grin. "They couldn't tell you."

"Who could?" Vera challenged. "No more games, sir. The more I've been investigating this murder, the more I think it's not as simple as professional jealousy gone too far."

Ford looked at her for a very long time, his gaze flat and impossible to read. Then he said, "Do you know why I got into studying archaeology?"

"Why?"

"Because I love learning about the past, and, more than that, I love knowing that a thing I've learned is *true.* Archaeology is about real things. Objects that creatures actually used and kept or threw away, or hid from others, or gave as gifts . . . things that were part of their lives. And years later, we can pick them up again and study them and know that our ancestors really did something. Say I found pieces of a cup, carved out of stone. I put them together again and I know that someone, a long time ago, was thirsty and wanted a drink and they used that very cup. Not one like it, but that specific item. It's a special connection to the past, to hold an object like that."

Vera nodded, thinking back to the pitcher that van Hoote had shown her.

Then Ford went on. "Over the course of my career, I ran into frauds and fakes, which was annoying enough. But worse than that was when a real artifact disappeared. Or perhaps showed up someplace it shouldn't be . . . like someone's private collection. That's not just taking an object. That's stealing from our whole past, sneaking little bits of the truth away, leaving us—*all* of us, all of society I mean—less able to understand ourselves. It enraged me."

"I get that, a little," Vera said. "I don't study the past, but I do try to find out the truth of a situation, so that everyone who reads my articles will know what really happened. Sometimes it's not an important thing, or it might not seem like it. I've written articles about spelling bees and quilting frolics. But sometimes I write about murder. And no matter what, I want every word I write to be the truth."

"You understand, then," he said. "I got so angry about missing artifacts that I decided I had to do something about it. So I left my teaching post and started working for an organization dedicated to finding lost objects like that. One such item was that obsidian hatchet I showed the students the other night. The organization lets me bring it along because they know I'll protect it, just as they know it's an important tool for teaching."

"I see," Vera said cautiously.

"I don't expect you to take my statement at face value, but I can supply proof if you like—it would take a few wingmails, and I'd prefer not to do it until I can conclude my work here. The risk of being exposed is real, and then I'll lose all my progress."

"Let's say I believe you, for now," Vera warned. "What happened next?"

"Last year, we heard that some artifacts had been taken from Summers End. My job was to join this season's dig and find out everything I could, with the goal of stopping the thefts once and for all. I'll show you something important, Miss Vixen. But you have to come to the site with me."

Something in Vera told her she could trust Ford. So, after quaffing her tea, she followed him out of town and back to Summers End, where she was not completely surprised when Ford led her to the building where the professors all had workspaces, and where the closet of artifacts had been rifled.

Ford opened the door, then moved directly to his own worktable. He unlocked a drawer and removed a small bone object from within.

"Look at this," Ford said, flicking the small figurine toward Vera with his front claw.

She picked it up in one paw, lifting it to the light. It was a figure of a weasel holding its paws up in greeting, carved from a single piece of bone, grown creamy yellow with age. She tilted it to see the bottom, and there was the hollow where the marrow had once been. The carver had skillfully used a slight curve of the material to suggest that the weasel was bending over slightly, as if beginning a bow. The engraved lines were shallow but stained with some dye that had faded over time, leaving the figure's face a mere suggestion, the idea of a weasel more than anything else. It was, she suddenly felt, a very beautiful piece.

The carver chose to etch the lines on it because they knew this chunk of bone was meant to be weasel shaped.

"This is real," she said softly. "I mean, it's really *old*. Authentic. You or someone else dug this up from the site."

"Indeed," Ford said. "I recovered it from a dig pit earlier this summer. I had kept it stored separately because I was performing some tests to see what kind of animal bone it was. I have hopes of linking the carvings of Summers End with Red Rock Canyon by establishing that both sites made use of bison bone, which they traded over the plains and up rivers. That was my stated purpose, anyway. There was another reason. If it had been stored with the other figurines, it might have been among those that were stolen this season."

"How many have gone missing?"

"Just this season, nearly a dozen. May not seem like much, but the excavators won't keep unearthing such artifacts forever, and each one is unique. Thank goodness Buckthorn locked up the ones found with Durham's body at the police station until the investigation is over. They're safe there. The previous ones, not so much. About a dozen a year, maybe a few more . . . Add that up over the years the site has been studied . . ."

Vera did some very quick math and arrived at a number that appalled her (granted, any number over zero would be troubling, but this was beyond the pale). "There are that many collectors who want these artifacts?"

Ford sighed. "Hard to say. Some collectors undoubtedly buy more than one. Perhaps a small number actually have the bulk of the stolen items. Some collectors are insatiable and strive to own as much as they possibly can. It is my hope that we can track down the seller and recover some of the artifacts. But the authorities would have to move quickly, catching the collectors by surprise."

"Otherwise, they'll have time to hide all their stolen items," Vera guessed. "Also, such collectors are likely to be wealthy and influential, making it more difficult to accuse them of a crime like buying stolen property."

"Exactly. So you understand the need to keep a low profile. Because discretion is key to success, I kept up the ruse of being an active professor. Most folks never questioned it. But then again, my own investigations have never overlapped with a murder."

"Wait a second," she said, remembering something. "Durham found out you weren't at your college anymore; I uncovered a letter about it. Did he confront you?"

Ford snorted. "He wanted to, but he didn't dare. The fact was that Durham was facilitating the removal of the artifacts from the site."

Vera gasped.

"I know it," said Ford. "But unfortunately, I have no hard proof. And that's what I need, Miss Vixen. I need to know every link in this black-market chain. I need to know exactly how they're alerting buyers and how they're moving the goods. While I could have accused Durham in public and made his life awkward, that wasn't the goal. I want to shut the whole thing down. And it's maddening because whoever is involved is very careful. It's nearly impossible to pin any aspect of the operation down."

"I've got a friend in town who might be able to help you with that," Vera said, thinking of Lefty's unusual skill set. "But this brings us right back to Emmeline Greenleaf at the Bronze Feather. Am I right that you suspect her?"

"Almost from the start of the summer, when I arrived here," he confirmed. "I'd heard of her shop before, and I went in to check it out, again maintaining my pose as a professor. She tried to bribe me into giving phony certificates of authenticity for those fakes she's got in that case."

"Those are fakes?" Vera asked. "They're so expensive!"

"They're decoys. If Chief Buckthorn or any other member of law enforcement came to her shop to arrest her for selling historical artifacts, she'd just admit that they were replicas. A much smaller crime! But I think she sells real ones under the table. I once found Greenleaf's name in some papers Durham tried to hide from me. But when I tried to draw her out, she refused to tell me anything about the stolen items."

"Why not tell Chief Buckthorn about it, then?"

"He already knows," Ford said. "Van Hoote reported more disappearances earlier this summer. Selling artifacts is a crime, but not a very important one for an officer of the law who's dealing with a whole town's worth of problems. And let's not forget, Summerhill gets a lot of business from tourists who like to buy such things."

Vera said in disgust, "It looks bad for all the businesses if one gets called out for selling something they shouldn't. So the other owners tell Buckthorn to turn a blind eye. The only folks who really get hurt from buying her fakes are strangers who'll be gone in a day or two, and all they've lost is money."

"Exactly," Ford said. "But if we could *prove* that Greenleaf is actually passing along real artifacts, it would be a different matter."

"Okay, Ford," Vera said. "I think that the thefts and the murder are linked. So let's work together on exposing this black-market scheme."

"What do you need from me?"

"A complete list of all the missing artifacts, for previous years, too, if you've got it."

"I do," he said. "What else?"

"Anything you've got on Ms. Greenleaf will help. We need to figure out the process they used to move each artifact, and maybe then we'll see where simple theft turned to murder."

"I'll get you the information right away," he promised, a light in his eyes. "Let's go to Aster House. I've got a locked case in my room."

"Hold on there, Professor. You talked about discretion, and you're right. It's probably better if we're not seen working together."

"But this could be exactly how I find out what's happening!" he protested.

"Patience is a virtue. My friends and I will start on this, and we'll check in later tonight, okay?"

"While I'm just waiting around!"

"Not just waiting around," she told him. "You mentioned decoys. Well, now *you're* the decoy. And by the time the folks behind the thefts—and maybe the murder—figure out you're not working alone, we'll be able to shut them down."

Chapter 20

After her conversation with Ford, Vera quickly found Lenore and Thena so she could relate all she'd learned.

Lenore in particular was deflated, perhaps because she'd been so sure that by tracking Ford to the Bronze Feather she'd uncovered a nefarious plan.

"Well, so much for Professor Isaiah Ford being our secret antiquities thief," she said with a sigh.

Vera nodded. "It was a good theory, until the facts ripped it to shreds. Still, I think we learned some important information. Plus, now I'm pretty sure we can trust Ford's statements in general. So his alibi for the murder and his testimony about what he saw on the site can be considered reliable."

"I'm glad," Lenore said, looking anything but glad. "I do like him. But I was just sort of hoping that by showing someone else—anyone else—was a better suspect, Ligeia wouldn't have to worry about Buckthorn arresting her after all. The disappearance of Chesley is suspicious, but I bet both Buckthorn and Poole still consider Ligeia the top contender, especially now that Ford is out."

Thena was more sanguine about the revelation of Ford's real work. "It makes sense," she said. "And I have to say that all the replies I got when I asked about him were highly complimentary. His old college would take him back in a heartbeat."

"Oh, by the way," Vera said, "did you happen to get any other information from our hedgehog?"

"Only the lack of it," Thena admitted. "When you mentioned the missing figurines maybe being relevant before, I asked about the professors having any possible connection to missing artifacts, but Ms. Jeffries didn't have anything to say about it. At least, not that she was willing to tell little old me."

"More likely she really doesn't have anything to tell," Vera said. The reporter believed, and Ford's information confirmed, that the illegal moving of artifacts had been kept very quiet. After all, the more creatures that knew about the operation, the more likely it was that someone would blab. Also, the fact that Lefty had heard about this smuggling ring but didn't want to get involved told Vera that whoever was in charge of things was dead serious about dealing with any creature who let sensitive information find its way to the authorities or any other animal who was not directly involved in the scheme.

She nibbled thoughtfully on a raspberry pastry and wondered how to proceed. The group was once again at the Front Street Bakery, having found the quiet little business to be an excellent, if temporary, headquarters for their sleuthing.

Then, from the corner of her eye, she noticed a small wooden stand. A smile lit her face. Of course! A newspaper! That was always a great way to learn about something you might be missing. Vera dashed over and picked up a copy of the *Summerhill Star*. It was a weekly paper, and this was the first edition since Durham's death. The front page was naturally all about the crime, and Vera would read it later. First, she wanted to check out the rest of the paper, to get a sense of what made the news in Summerhill.

Vera flipped to the next page, scanning the densely written columns (not an inch of paper was wasted). In the bottom corner was a rare bit of open space, and printed there was a poem.

Huh. The famous poet Mr. Loring deigned to have his work published in a minor local paper? That seemed out of character.

"What are you frowning at, Vera?" Lenore asked.

"Loring's got a poem in here. Quite a coup for the *Summerhill Star*."

"Yeah, it's not exactly a literary journal, is it? But maybe he has some deal with the editor. Read the poem out loud," Lenore instructed.

"You asked for it." Vera cleared her throat and began to recite:

> To glide o'er the endless snow
> Glistening with diamonds under paw and ski
> For a thousand years will the raccoon race
> But he races alone—who will come to see?

"Wow," said Lenore. "That's . . . terrible. I've read some bad poems in my life, but that's just embarrassing. Are you sure it's really *the* Keats Loring who wrote it?"

"Says here 'An original verse by acclaimed poet Keats Loring, winner of the Granite Prize.'"

"Yup, that's him. They only give the Granite Prize out every five years, you know. It's a huge deal for a writer to win one."

"You're up on your prizes," Vera said.

"I have to be," Lenore explained. "I always stock the books by the prizewinners in every category. I read his winning collection, and it was excellent. I can't believe he put his name to that piece of drivel. A paean to a skiing raccoon? Come on."

While Lenore was talking, Thena narrowed her eyes and looked down the street. "Hey, there's van Hoote. I'm going to shadow him, just in case. Meet you at the lodge later!" The tiny vole was off like lightning.

Vera was still looking at the paper, thoughts zipping around her brain, tracks crisscrossing each other . . . not unlike that of a slaloming raccoon. "A winter poem in high summer. And the image. We've seen this before."

"We have?" Lenore looked confused. "I feel like I'd remember such a bad verse."

"Not the verse, the idea. One of the carved figurines around Durham's body was a skiing raccoon."

Lenore tipped her head, her gaze suddenly sharp. "So we did. But did Loring ever see it? He was never inside the monument with the rest of the group!"

"No, and he once told me he didn't have any interest in the dig—he was staying here to absorb the landscape. But now I'm not sure that's all he's here for."

Her friend leaned forward. "What's on your mind? What do we need to do?"

"We need to find back copies of the paper for the entire summer. Last year's, too, if we can."

"I noticed that there are always several newspapers and magazines at Rosewood Lodge. Maybe Gerry and Cora keep back issues, too. And if they don't, we can see who keeps copies in town."

The two of them retired to the lodge, where the last few weeks' issues of the *Star* were easily procured. Vera then walked over to the small cottage where the proprietors lived. The first door was open to let in the summer breeze, so Vera knocked and called out a hello.

"Who is it? Come on in!" came Cora's cheerful voice. "I'm here in the front room."

Vera stepped into the sunny cottage. She immediately spied Cora, who was seated at a table with a ledger book open in front of her and a pen in her paw.

"Oh, Miss Vixen. Please take a seat, I just need to finish adding up this column or I'll forget my place."

Vera sat down in the chair opposite, waiting for her hostess to complete her task. Meanwhile, she looked around the room, which seemed to function as an office during the day, but a dining room after hours, to judge by the dish-filled hutch on one wall. There were also a few photos on the next wall, and Vera got up again to get a closer look. One depicted Rosewood Lodge as it looked just after it was built. Several squirrels posed in front of the building, dressed in the fashions of the day, with top hats and walking sticks or long gowns and wide-brimmed bonnets.

Behind her, Cora put down the pen and sighed. "Well, that's all done! You'd faint if you knew what our grocery bill comes to every month when we've got a full house! Talk about hungry mouths to feed. You're looking at Gerry's grandfather there. He bought the land for the lodge and employed half the town to build it. He was a real entrepreneur. He knew folks from all over would want to see Summers End, but he also knew they would prefer comfortable accommodations. Before he built Rosewood Lodge, visitors mostly had to sleep in tents, or rent a room in someone's house in town."

"We've got it much better nowadays, especially with our meals catered, too," Vera said with a laugh.

"My goodness, I do hope it doesn't sound like I was fishing for a compliment."

Vera shook her head. "Of course not. And this photo over here is newer—is that you and Gerry at the site?" The more recent image showed the squirrel couple standing in front of one of the tall stones that surrounded the central hill, which rose in the distance behind them. Next to the couple, a familiar figure stood tall and confident. "Wait a moment. Is that Professor Durham?"

Cora nodded. "That was taken shortly after our wedding. It was Durham's first year at the site and he stayed at Rosewood Lodge all summer. He took us on a special tour for a wedding present, into the monument itself on the day of Summers End, plus all the little side chambers and nooks and crannies."

"So you must have known Durham very well."

"Oh, he was always friendly to us both, and always recommended the lodge when folks asked him about where to stay, so I'm grateful." Cora was chattering quickly. "But I wouldn't say either of us knew him well. It's funny. I loved the tour, and thought I'd visit so many times, but as it turned out, we both work so much that we haven't got a lot of time for visiting, even though the site's so close. But you haven't come to ask me about the origins of the lodge."

"The reason I ask," Vera said bluntly, "is that I heard that Durham had a falling out with Gerry, and that's why the professors don't stay at Rosewood Lodge anymore."

Cora swallowed nervously. "Um. I . . . er, I don't know why you'd listen to mindless gossip like that, Miss Vixen."

"It's not mindless if there's evidence to support it. The fact is that Durham used to stay here. But for the past three dig seasons, he and all the other professors have roomed at Aster House, even though it's much more expensive to do so. What happened, Mrs. Rosewood?"

Cora glanced out the window, as if searching for her husband.

"He's in the kitchen, cleaning up after cooking for all our students the past few days," Vera said. "Should I go and get him so he can tell me the truth?"

"No," Cora said quickly. "It would only upset him. I'll tell you."

Vera was patient, knowing that the squirrel would need a moment to gather her thoughts.

"We have a daughter. Her name is Aisling, and she went to university largely because she grew up close to Summers End and was inspired to study archaeology. When Durham met her and found out that she was from Summerhill, he got very friendly with her and even made sure she got a position as an assistant up at the school. It paid for her tuition, and she was very excited about it. Aisling looked up to Durham as a mentor, and she believed he saw potential in her."

"But he viewed her in a different way," Vera guessed.

"She was a resource to be exploited," Cora said with a pinched expression. "He made her do extra work and all manner of menial tasks. But fetching him coffee was one thing. She discovered that he'd swapped her name with his own on a paper she submitted! Not just adding his—he plain stole her work! But when she confronted him about it, he told her that if she told anyone, he'd ruin her career. He'd tell folks that she was a bad scholar who'd formed an inappropriate attachment to him. Can you imagine?"

Unfortunately, Vera did not have to imagine, having heard all too similar stories before. Aloud, she said, "But Aisling must have told someone anyway, because you know about it."

"Oh, it happened here. *Here*, at our home, right at the end of the dig season. Aisling confronted him just outside this cottage, but she didn't know Gerry and I were home at the time. Well, Gerry turned so red I thought he might boil over. He stormed out and told Durham that he overheard it all and that if Durham didn't leave the grounds at once, he'd smash his smug face right in."

"How did Durham react to that?"

"He blustered at first, said Gerry misunderstood. Aisling was mortified, poor darling, but she stood up for herself, said that she'd ignored a lot of things Durham did over the school year but stealing a paper was a step beyond. Said she wouldn't keep silent. That's when Durham started to threaten all of us, said he'd get the lodge shut down and all sorts of other nasty things. Gerry told him to get his things and leave immediately, or he'd ask the chief of police to escort him off the property. Durham never could stand any affront to his image, and having Buckthorn show up would certainly do that. He left, but he said he'd make us pay. And he did—the next season, he arranged for all the professors to stay elsewhere, and he's done so every season since. Won't say that it hasn't had an impact. But we've still got the student groups, and other visitors who couldn't care less what some university professor says about our place."

"But Durham did return to the lodge," Vera noted. "I saw him give his welcome speech to the students the first night we were here."

Cora nodded. "Summers End is the reason we're in business, and Durham is—well, was—a big part of that. We never exactly spoke the rules out loud, but Durham and Gerry and I had a little understanding after the incident with Aisling. He can show up and play his part for the school groups, but the moment the show's over, he leaves. He knew that if he tried to push things further, we'd spill the beans about the way he stole Aisling's work. And we knew that if we pushed further, he'd make it even harder to get guests to stay at the lodge. Not a happy solution, but it worked."

"You could have gone to the university anyway," Vera said.

"Actually, Aisling did. But whenever she asked about the progress of her complaint, they always had a reason why nothing was happening. Eventually, she stopped asking. She told us she learned a lesson . . . just not the one she expected to."

"I'm sorry to hear that Aisling had to go through all that. Is she still at the university?"

Cora shook her head. "She was so disappointed with the administration's lack of response, she transferred to a school in the city. I think it was too difficult for her to face everyone and still keep what happened under her hat. But she's doing well where she is, and she comes back to visit us often."

"Just not during dig season," Vera guessed.

The squirrel gave a snort. "Exactly. I suppose you think all that's a motive for murder."

Vera paused, but then shook her head. "Motive, maybe. But if either of you hated Durham enough to kill him, you'd have done it right away. And honestly, I don't see you or Gerry waiting around to whack Durham on the back of the head, particularly on the morning when you know a crowd of folks will show up to see it."

Cora actually laughed at that. "Nah, we're too busy getting breakfast ready. Well, are you satisfied? Is that what's brought you here, Miss Vixen?"

"In part. Actually, I was also wondering if you had any older issues of the *Summerhill Star*. I wanted to look something up from earlier this year."

"Oh, indeed I do!" Cora looked so relieved to be discussing a quotidian subject like newspapers. "I never like to waste a thing, and newspaper has so many uses after it's been read. Come along."

A short while later, Vera brought the old copies of the newspaper to her room, where Lenore was waiting. (She had not been shiftless during that time—she was looking over the photographs Vera had taken inside the monument and was making a list of all the objects around Durham's corpse.)

"Well, I think we can cross a couple of suspects off our list." She explained what Cora told her about Aisling and the stolen paper. "It supports what we've heard from others, about Durham taking credit and exploiting graduate students, or whoever he found useful. But I really never thought the Rosewoods killed Durham. Sure, they despised him for what he did, but they're practical, and they figured out a sort of détente."

Lenore nodded. "Besides, could a squirrel, or even a pair of squirrels, actually hit Durham hard enough to knock him out, and then drag him down the tunnel? And have the time to set up the scene with the candles and figurines?"

"I can't picture it, especially because I saw both Cora and Gerry before dawn that morning. Cora was filling mugs with coffee, and Gerry had trays of fresh baked muffins. If they'd been at Summers End, they couldn't have been minding the oven!"

"Muffins make the best alibi," Lenore agreed. "Well, I'm glad we can cross them off, not least because they're our hosts. Now, what are we doing with the newspapers?"

"Take half of these," Vera said, offering some issues to her friend. "That will make the work go faster."

"What am I looking for?" the raven asked.

"Primarily poems by our peacock pal," said Vera. "I have a little theory and I'm curious to know if there's anything to it."

"Anything else?"

"If you happen to see any mention of Durham or another professor from the dig, circle the article. You never know what tidbit might prove helpful."

The pair paged methodically through issue after issue. Lenore held up one page from May. "Here's an article covering the arrival of this year's research team. Says: 'With the university's spring semester done, it is now time for the professors, students, and helpers to resume their study of our favorite prehistoric site. Led by Professor Ridley Durham, the team anticipates another fruitful season. As usual, many school groups will visit the site over the next few months.' And there's a picture of everyone." Lenore held the page higher, showing the black-and-white photograph of the professors lined up in front of one of the tall stones circling the site. Durham was in the center, beaming out at the viewer. Chesley was next to him, smiling awkwardly. Van Hoote looked downright pompous, while Ligeia stood at one end, unsmiling. And Ford was next to her, his expression difficult to read thanks to a smudge of ink. There were a few other figures as well, identified as graduate students and assistants.

"Loring's not in the image," Vera noted. "I wonder if he was asked, since he's a professor, too."

"You think he was jealous?" Lenore asked.

"Not sure. But if he . . . ah, here's a poem!" Vera jabbed a paw at a spot in the paper she held. She read aloud, " 'An original composition by famous poet Keats Loring. The *Star* is honored to be the first to publish a series of poems by the writer, all composed this summer and inspired by the site of Summers End and the surrounding landscape.' "

"Huh, so he must have some arrangement with the editor of the paper. Or they're friends. What's the poem?"

Vera took a deep breath, then read:

> *A swallow carves her swoop in the blue,*
> *An artful curve, wingbeats made gold*
> *By a benevolent summer sun*
> *Seven centuries spun out could not create another.*

Lenore tipped her head side to side, considering. "Better than the most recent one, I grant you."

"It's okay," Vera agreed. "Not stellar, but kind of interesting." She reached for her notebook and jotted down: *Swallow.* Then she reached for the next paper.

"So what's your theory?"

"I think these poems are how the sellers of the stolen artifacts are advertising their wares to distant buyers. They don't dare move the figurines before they've got a sale lined up, but they need to communicate what they've got to buyers they might not know already. So they come up with this idea: a newspaper can show up anywhere and no one thinks anything of it. Copies of the *Summerhill Star* get loaded on boats going downriver, all the way to the city. And there, folks in the know are sure to find a copy in one way or another."

Lenore held up the paper she'd been scanning and gestured to the masthead. "Guess who the paper thanks for its generous support?"

"The Bronze Feather."

"Yep. There are several other businesses named as well, but I bet Greenleaf forks over money to ensure that enough copies get printed so they can send them downriver."

Vera nodded. "And once the downriver readers get their copy, they know to look for the information in a poem. It will tell them a few details about the specific figurine. A swallow, or raccoon, or whatever. And another line in the poem tells them the price. Seven centuries means it will cost seven hundred for the swallow. Our skiing raccoon will fetch a thousand, or at least that's where the bidding starts. Interested buyers must have some predetermined way to contact the sellers, and one by one the artifacts are sold and shipped downstream, never to be seen again in public."

"And no one will get to study them, and no one will ever see them in a museum." Lenore snapped her beak in frustration. "Ugh, what a dirty racket! You really think Loring is working with them?"

"Yes, but maybe not by choice. When I ran across him in the woods one day, he was working on a verse that could have been about one of the figurines. He clearly hated what he was writ-

ing, and he didn't even pretend otherwise. That's what makes
me think that he's being forced to participate in some way."

"Huh. It would be awkward to ask. What if you're wrong?"

"Worse, what if I'm right?" Vera shuddered, thinking of what
a desperate creature might do to protect such a secret.

Chapter 21

Vera felt that the discovery of Loring's involvement was their best lead in a while ... assuming it panned out. She said, "We should talk to Ford right away. I'm sure he'll want to be there when we confront Loring."

"Yes," said Lenore. "And the next question is, where do we find Loring? He's not staying at Aster House with the others."

"No, van Hoote told me that Loring is renting a room from someone in town. Ford's been here all summer, so he probably knows where that is."

It was tiny Thena who went to Aster House to slip a note under Ford's door and then leave before anyone got too curious about whom she was there to visit. A few hours later, the group met up outside the now-quiet Rosewood Lodge. Ford was excited to hear about their theory of the poems-as-advertisements, but confessed that he actually didn't know where Loring was staying.

"He's been awfully secretive about it," Ford said. "He'll come to the pub for drinks, but he's never invited anybody over. I assumed it was snobbery, but I guess it had more to do with protecting his involvement in the black-market operation."

Lenore said, "Sounds like a job for Lefty. He's good at finding things out quickly, especially when others want to keep them secret."

It wasn't difficult to get word to Lefty (he and Vera had a running system of leaving notes in public places like a pub or a messenger office), but they did have to wait for the raccoon to get the message and then show up. It was after dark when he finally arrived at the lodge, skulking in while munching the remains of a sandwich.

"What's up?" he asked the group after being introduced to Ford as a "freelance finder" of misplaced items. Lenore, to her credit, did not laugh at this description, and Thena wasn't well acquainted enough with Lefty to know his true vocation.

Vera quickly explained how they deduced that Loring's poems were the method by which the sellers of the stolen figurines alerted potential buyers of the goods available.

"Pretty smart," Lefty admitted. "I never would have thought of that."

"So we need to find out where he's staying, and quick."

"Easy peasy," Lefty replied. "I know where he is. Saw him go into his place with groceries while I was poking around."

"Good work, sir!" Ford looked quite impressed. "And where was that?"

"He's in a little backyard guest cottage. On Mulberry Court. The one right behind the Bronze Feather."

"*What?*" Vera couldn't believe she'd overlooked such an obvious connection. "You mean Emmeline Greenleaf has him right on her own property, next to her store?"

"Makes sense when you think about it," Thena said. "If he's working with the ring, why not?"

Ford grunted. "It's enough for me. Time to go find out what this peacock knows."

The whole group journeyed to town, moving separately so as not to attract attention, though few creatures were on the streets at the late hour.

Vera chose to trot the long way around, and she approached the property on Mulberry Court from the backyard of the next street over. She glanced at the main house and saw that while the lights on the first floor, where the shop was located, were all out, one light burned in an upper window. That was probably Emmeline Greenleaf's bedroom. She worried that the passage of so many bodies would alert the rabbit that something was up, but Lenore lit down on silent black wings, Thena barely disturbed the grass, and Ford seemed to have a gift for quiet. Lefty, of course, didn't have to be told how to remain hidden.

Vera turned her attention to the guest cottage. It was small but quite homey, with an overhanging roof in the front and a single rocking chair underneath, and several pots of flowers surrounding the area. It seemed a fine place to relax and think about poetry, so perhaps it wasn't a surprise that no one questioned Loring's presence, if the neighbors had even noticed.

She motioned to the others that she would knock on the door, and that they should remain out of sight until she could step inside. Lefty was already moving around the back of the cottage, just in case Loring tried to escape that way (much as Lefty would intend to do if the roles were reversed).

Vera knocked softly, saying in her most entreating tone, "Professor? Are you there? I need your help!"

After a moment, the door cracked open, and a beady eye peered out. "Who's there?" Loring demanded.

"It's me, Vera Vixen. I've got a question about some of your poetry."

"At this hour?"

"It's a very important question. I don't think I could sleep if don't know the answer."

He pulled the door open wider. "Well, come in, I suppose."

"Oh, thank you!" Vera gushed, stepping in and herding him backward in the process. "I hope you don't mind if a few of my friends join us. We're all obsessed with poetry lately."

Loring goggled at the sudden appearance of Lenore, Athena, and Ford. But it was the way Lefty stepped up from behind him that really got the peacock distressed. "I say, what exactly is going on here?"

"Simple, Keats," said Ford. "We just need to know why you've been using your award-winning poetry skills to move stolen goods."

Lenore just held up one of the newspapers and gestured to his poem in the corner of the page.

Loring froze for a second, then just staggered back and collapsed into a chair by the window. "Oh, I knew this would happen someday. How'd you find out?"

Vera was pleased the peacock didn't try to deny it. She said, "We happened to read the poems you published this summer in the *Star*. Let's just say they weren't worthy of your reputation."

"They weren't worthy of kindling a campfire," Lenore said with a sniff. "And why would a famous poet publish in a small-town weekly? Didn't make sense."

"Unless you had a different reason for doing it," Ford added. "Each poem was a coded message, telling buyers what figurines stolen from Summers End were available to buy, and what the asking price was."

"I had to do it!" Loring said, looking at each of them in a pleading way. "It was the only way I could stay out of trouble!"

"Trouble with *who*?"

The peacock quailed. "I can't say."

"You'd better," Ford said, stepping forward. "If you don't tell us now, you'll be telling the authorities later, probably from the wrong side of a jail cell door. Now talk!"

Loring sighed. "Look, I've made some mistakes in life, and one of them was getting into more debt than I could get out of easily. I made it big with my work, and I was living big . . . but a bit beyond my means, you know. And I had to get some money quickly, and I heard about this lender . . ."

"Oh, I know what comes next," Lefty said. "The lender was happy to give you the money, but with some pretty harsh terms."

"I was sure I could pay it back, but then I didn't get a grant I was counting on. And my expenses kept going up . . . I had to borrow a little more . . ."

"So you owed your lender back, and you couldn't pay. Who is it?"

"He's down in the city. He's called . . ." Loring's voice dropped. "He's a badger called Bernard Giles."

Lefty whistled. "Bernie the Claw? Wow, I'm surprised he didn't toss you in the bay."

"He was going to," Loring said miserably. "But he didn't want to lose his whole investment. So he said he was going to let me 'work off the debt.' But as far as I can tell, that means I've got to do whatever he says for the rest of my life. I'll never work it off."

"That's usually how it is," Lefty said, not unkindly.

"You've heard of this criminal?" Ford asked Lefty. "I'm not from here, so I don't know all the names."

"Bernie's a heavy hitter in the city's underworld. Got a lot of irons in the fire, so it makes sense that he's somehow involved in this racket, too. I would not go within a hundred miles of Bernie if I could avoid it."

"I wish I'd known that," Loring said. "But I didn't really know who I was involved with till it was too late. He ordered me to come to Summerhill for this dig season. Greenleaf was my contact here. She told me to stay in this cottage and gave me a bunch of little assignments, like taking a package from the store to a boat, or reporting on what items had been dug up by talking to the workers at the dig. But what she really used me for was writing up these horrible little ditties for the newspaper."

"Did the editor of the paper know their purpose?" Vera asked.

Loring shook his head. "Not at all. She's this sweet old bird who prints the paper as a sideline. She also runs the candy shop, you see, and she likes all the businesses to put their ads in the back. She didn't know my work, but she knew I'd won a big prize, so she was happy to print anything I gave her. I could have offered her my grocery list and she'd have put it on the front page. All she knew was that my poems were part of a deal with the 'local business community,'" he concluded with a sad laugh.

"Did Greenleaf ever tell you who else was involved?" Vera asked. "One of the workers on the dig site had to be complicit, or it would be too difficult to keep stealing artifacts. That's why Durham was killed, right? Because he interrupted a crime?" She withheld the fact that she already had been told he was linked to the thefts—it could be helpful to pretend you knew less than you did.

"I can't say what happened the night of the murder. I wasn't there. But Durham wasn't interrupting anything," Loring said simply, "because he was the one letting those objects go."

"You knew that?"

"Earlier this summer, I overheard Greenleaf talk to him. They didn't know I was close by. I didn't hear much but I could tell he was involved. I think he got into a fight with Greenleaf, maybe because he thought too many items were getting shuttled into the black market. They were getting greedy, and folks were starting to notice."

"True enough," Ford grunted.

"I don't know if it was Greenleaf who killed him," Loring went on, "but I know she wasn't in her house that night, because I saw her coming back along the side path at maybe four in the morning. I didn't say anything to the police because I was too worried about what would come out about my own, er, issues."

"Okay, what about Chesley? Why did she vanish?"

"I've got no idea," Loring said. "You've got to believe me! I wouldn't put it past her to be involved, too. The whole summer, she was very aloof and almost rude. Plus, she's always around the site at night."

"She's an astronomer," Thena pointed out, a little exasperated with the peacock.

"Sure, but that doesn't mean she's not also a criminal! I'm just saying I wouldn't be surprised, especially with her sudden disappearance after Durham's death. Maybe it wasn't Greenleaf who offed him. Maybe it was Chesley."

Looking at her notes, Vera said, "Let's talk about the thefts a little more. So you wrote a poem for each missing figurine. What, one a week?"

"More or less. I hated every minute. I've had writer's block ever since I got into debt, and having to write that drivel is only making it worse. It's one thing to owe money to a nefarious criminal, but now I've had to compromise my artistic standards, too." He looked disgusted with himself. "I'll never be able to show my face among real poets again."

"Your latest poem is about a figurine of a skiing raccoon. But that figurine wasn't stolen. It was placed by Durham's body and it is now in police custody."

Loring only ruffled his feathers. "I never see the figurines. I just write up something based on the details Greenleaf gives me. Maybe she thought it would be available, but the murder messed things up." Then his eyes widened, and he said, "Oh, no, it got published, which means Bernie's going to be expecting to make money off it. Oh no, oh no."

"You're in a pretty deep hole," she agreed.

"I know!" Loring sagged back in his chair, his feathers drooping. "But I don't know how to get out."

"Well, I've got an idea," Ford said.

Loring looked up hopefully. "You do?"

"I work for an organization trying to stop the thefts. If you come with me right now, we'll confront Greenleaf, and with your evidence, I can send her to jail and break the black market's connection with the town. If you cooperate fully, I can ensure that your debt will be paid off, and the public won't know who the informant is. Then Bernie won't have any more reason to come after you."

"Oh, really?" Loring stood up, his manner revived. "I'll do it! I'll do anything, just get me out of this mess!"

Ford nodded. "Let's get Greenleaf and stop this racket once and for all."

"And we're all going," Vera said, "because we don't know exactly what Greenleaf did, but I think we can all agree that she's dangerous."

Chapter 22

The group left Loring's cottage and crossed the backyard, climbing onto Greenleaf's back porch. Vera noted that the same light was still on, but that the house was quiet. Hopefully they'd be able to catch the rabbit without a fuss.

Lefty didn't bother to knock—he just jimmied the back screen door open and walked in, the others following. The house had an eerily empty feel. Vera directed Ford, Thena, and Loring upstairs, while she, Lenore, and Lefty headed for the front of the ground floor, where the shop was located.

Getting into the shop was easy, because the connecting door was wide open. Vera lit a lamp and hurried in, only to find what she feared. The case holding the high-priced figurines had been ransacked, and they were all missing.

Lenore looked at the jewelry. "Most of the good stuff is gone," she said. "Greenleaf must have noticed us in Loring's cottage, guessed what it meant, and cleared out."

Just then the others rushed in, and Vera knew they had found no one upstairs.

"What do we do now?" the peacock asked, frightened.

"We get help." Ford pointed to Loring. "You're coming with me. There's a private boat kept at the docks that I can use in an emergency, and this is an emergency."

"Where will you go?" Vera asked Ford.

"There's a prearranged meeting place in the next town upriver. I'll be able to get Loring to a safe place away from Summerhill—he's our most important witness now—and send for help via wingmail. With luck, they'll get here by morning. I'll let them know to look for Greenleaf, too. She must have left just a short time ago."

"We'll go find Buckthorn," Vera said. "He should be at the station, since he's still working on Chesley's disappearance. He'll be able to start the search for Greenleaf, too, and hopefully we can catch a thief and a murderer at the same time."

"Good luck," Ford said. "See you tomorrow. And be careful! The folks we're dealing with are ruthless. Come on, Loring. The sooner you're out of Summerhill, the safer you'll be."

"Yes, sir!" Loring looked like he'd follow Ford anywhere.

After the bearded dragon and the peacock left, Vera turned to Lefty. "Thanks for your help. We'd never have gotten this far without you. But I'm guessing you don't want to come to the police station with us."

"Not my scene," he agreed, looking oddly introspective. "In fact, I gotta tell ya, Vera, I'm sort of looking forward to getting back to Shady Hollow. This place seems nice on the surface, but there's so much going on underneath, I have to wonder how it got that way. All these black-market shenanigans and the nastiness among the professors . . . it's not right."

Vera nodded, and had no urge to crack a smile. Lefty had hit on an important point. The fact that he himself was on the wrong side of the law more often than not just meant that he understood how dangerous things could get.

"Okay, we're off to tell Buckthorn everything. Consider your job done. Stay out of trouble, Lefty."

He retorted, still with a worried frown on his face, "Advice you might want to take someday, Vixen!"

Vera started walking away. When she turned back to say goodbye, Lefty was no longer there.

Vera, Lenore, and Thena left the Bronze Feather and hurried from Mulberry Court onto Summer Street. It was very late now, and the town was wrapped in a deep, sleepy silence. The air was mild, and the leaves of the trees rustled in a light breeze. The moon had not yet risen, so the only light came from the stars above and a few scattered lanterns or candles in random windows.

Thankfully, the police station was one of those buildings with lit windows, and when Vera and Lenore rushed in, Buckthorn was awake, pacing around the office.

"Chief Buckthorn, we've got a lead!" Vera said without preamble.

Lenore added, "Technically, we've lost a lead."

"Tell me everything," the deer ordered, indicating they should both take a seat on the absurdly cushioned chairs. He himself continued to pace, his hooves clomping on the floorboards. Behind him, a few of the leftover art pieces from the building's salon days had gone askew, perhaps tipped out of place during the chief's ruminations. In fact, the whole place was in minor disarray. One of the cell doors was partly open, and it was clear that it had been converted into a closet. At the moment, it was a very messy closet, with several items on the floor or about to fall off a shelf. Buckthorn must have been looking for something inside.

"We think Emmeline Greenleaf is involved in the murder," Vera explained. "We know she's involved in the theft of the artifacts from the site."

He paused. "Did she say that?"

"She didn't say anything," Lenore told him. "When we went to confront her just now, she'd scarpered. Took the figurines that had been in the case in her shop, and some jewelry, too. I'd say that means she doesn't intend to come back."

"That scheming rabbit," Buckthorn said, shaking his head. He was standing right by the front door, and he kicked it closed in frustration. "I should have known."

"How?" Thena asked.

He blinked, then sighed. "She's always been out for herself. She always looks so calm and pulled together, but whenever I spoke to her, I got the sense that she couldn't be fully trusted. What put you onto her?"

"Actually, Keats Loring did," said Vera, and gave him the details of the newspaper poems. She didn't say anything about Ford's role, partly to respect the discretion the lizard needed to work, and perhaps partly to simplify things.

"Loring confessed his part just like that?" Buckthorn asked, frowning. "What else did he say?"

"Not much. He said Greenleaf kept him ignorant of other

details, though he realized Durham was involved, too. He thinks Greenleaf might have been the one who killed Durham," she added. "You sure you don't want to take notes on all this?"

"Later," he said. "At the moment I'm just trying to figure out what to do next."

"You'll need to start a search for her," Lenore said.

"You bet I will. I already alerted the team from Stonehurst to come up as part of the hunt for Chesley. I'll add Greenleaf to the list. I'll get them all and tie this off. I hate loose ends!"

Meanwhile, Vera was thinking hard. "Greenleaf has the sang-froid to kill, but I still can't picture her dragging Durham all the way across the site and into the tunnel. Maybe if Chesley was in on it and they both did it, but then why would Chesley vanish first . . . and it still doesn't explain how they got a feather to plant under the body to frame Ligeia . . ."

Buckthorn shook his head. "Worry about details like that later. Let's agree that Chesley and Greenleaf are in on this together. It's quite likely that the two of them will make a final attempt to round up every valuable artifact they can before they flee."

"No sense being sneaky about the thefts anymore, you mean," Vera said. "They'll grab all the ones they can find, whether they're in storage or inside the barrow."

Lenore squawked, "Oh, no! Ligeia's there right now!"

"You three head to Summers End," Buckthorn ordered. "I'll follow as soon as I send this wingmail and get Poole as backup. If you do encounter Chesley or Greenleaf, just stall them as long as you can. I'll take care of the whole situation when I get there."

"Come on," Lenore urged. "There's no time to lose!"

Chapter 23

Vera, Thena, and Lenore burst through the door of the police station and bolted down the street, Vera running as fast as her paws could carry her, while Thena scampered alongside. Lenore flew low overhead, dodging tree branches and lampposts.

At that hour, the town was eerily quiet, the residents and visitors snug in their beds, dreaming, blissfully ignorant of the turmoil stirring just outside.

They left the last few homes behind and plunged into the forest along the path past Rosewood Lodge, so recently bustling with students and now nearly empty. Not a single light shone in the Rosewoods' cottage.

They finally reached the site and rushed directly to the low building the professors used for work. The windows were lit, and the door was open. Inside, Ligeia was startled by the sudden arrival of Vera and Lenore. Thena arrived a moment later, panting with exertion.

"Oh, great, you're here. Nothing seems disturbed—" Ligeia started to say, but her sister cut her off.

"We know who's behind it all!" Lenore told her. "Greenleaf is selling the artifacts from the site, and she was using Loring to advertise. We think she and Chesley were working together, and they'll try to steal whatever they can from here before they disappear forever!"

Ligeia gave a low whistle. "They can't steal artifacts if they can't find them!" She whipped out a key from her worktable drawer. "All of you, take boxes or bags, whatever you can. We'll fill them with every artifact in this place and then hide them until Buckthorn can arrest them."

Thena nodded and jumped toward a stack of boxes. "Let's get moving!"

Vera and Lenore followed the vole's lead, and a few moments after Ligeia unlocked the closet, the creatures had gathered nearly all the cataloged figurines.

"There are more in the tomb itself," Ligeia said when they finished. "We left a lot of them in place in their niches so researchers and visitors can understand how they're used in practice."

"Greenleaf isn't going to respect that," Lenore said with a snort. "She'll clear out every nook and cranny. Let's get over there! With luck we can stop her and Chesley in time."

"Or at least catch them in the act," Vera added.

They blew out the lamps and left the workroom, moving toward the barrow at the very center of Summers End. Vera cautioned the others to move quietly to avoid alarming the criminals if they were indeed inside.

Just as they reached the long, low altar stone in front of the entrance, Buckthorn emerged from the gloomy forest edge. He was absolutely silent—an impressive feat for someone his size.

Vera and the others waited for him, and when he reached them, he said in the softest possible tone, "Poole will be here in a few moments. Any sign of our quarry?"

"Not yet," Vera responded, just as quietly. "We retrieved all the figurines in storage, so Greenleaf can't sell those, at least." She pointed to the boxes and sacks they'd put at the base of the altar stone.

"Excellent." He looked elated. "I'll get them to the station as soon as possible."

Meanwhile, Ligeia had been listening at the entrance to the tunnel. She whispered, "I don't think anyone is in there. No sound, and not a flicker of light."

"We must have got the jump on them," Buckthorn said. "If you four are willing, could you gather the rest of the artifacts from in there so I can get them all together under lock and key? I'll watch right out here to keep anyone else from approaching the tomb. And Poole should be here soon to assist."

Ligeia was clearly eager to safeguard the remaining figurines and dove into the tunnel almost before Vera could offer her one of the empty sacks. At the same time, Lenore stretched her wings once, saying, "Ugh, underground again. I really don't like being so cramped in there."

Vera nodded, feeling sympathy for her friend, who was so used to the open sky. Her feathers showed only as a slightly reflective gloss against the night. Hopefully, they'd soon be done with retrieving the figurines and both ravens wouldn't have to contend with tight spaces again for a while!

"It's a shame," Thena said as she went in. "Even though it's to protect the artifacts, I wish we didn't have to move them from their spots. Think of all the ancestors who will be wondering where their stuff's gone!"

Vera had already followed her inside several steps, and she paused as the vole spoke. "You know, Thena, that's a good point. We were so focused on protecting the items, we forgot they already are protected. We can just close up the tunnel. Right, Chief?"

She turned around as she was speaking and saw Buckthorn standing directly in front of the entrance.

"I'd prefer it if all of them were in police custody," he said, loud enough to echo down the tunnel. "It won't take you long."

"But Thena's correct," Ligeia said, having come back to the others. "If we can keep the artifacts in place, it's much more respectful to the dead."

"Not to mention how much work it will be to replace them all," Vera agreed. "I think—" She broke off, because something just caught her eye . . . a slightly reflective gloss against the night.

"Chief, why do you have that?" she asked, pointing to the feather sticking out of Buckthorn's pack.

He reached back and stuffed it farther inside. "Oh, no reason."

A bad feeling slithered down Vera's spine.

Lenore had picked up on Vera's change in focus. "A raven feather," she said. "You reported that one feather was found under the body. Why do you have more now?"

"Because *he's* the one who planted the first one," Vera said, looking at the massive deer, and suddenly the scene was crystal clear. "Just picture it! A large, strong creature had just dragged a body into a tunnel and wanted to frame someone else for the crime. When he showed up later, in an official capacity, to remove the body, he could easily slip the feather he brought along under the edge of the corpse, and then point it out to the doctor in town who's there as well."

Buckthorn's countenance went cold. "It's very dangerous to spout such lies."

"You claimed to be investigating the murder," she went on, "but what did you ever do besides put Poole on guard duty and ask basic questions of witnesses? You always wanted Ligeia to be the obvious suspect, so there was no point in trying to pin it on anyone else, especially because you already knew what happened!"

"Watch yourself, Vixen," he warned.

But Vera was too riled up. "If we wanted to see the figurines from the crime scene, the ones you took into evidence, would you be able to produce them? Say, the one of the skiing raccoon? Or is that one already on its way downriver, with Loring's latest poem advertising its arrival?"

Buckthorn snorted and moved a step toward her.

Lenore spread her wings wide enough to brush the sides of the tunnel, blocking Vera from his view. "Come on, Vera," she said urgently. "We've got to get out of here and find someone who will listen!"

Buckthorn's eyes narrowed. "Even if you do manage to yap to someone, who will believe a murder suspect, her sister, and some reporter who's obviously just out to smear my good name?"

"Excuse me?" Vera asked coldly. (It is a pity that glaring does not incapacitate an individual, for our story would end much faster if it did.)

He smirked. "I've served Summerhill for years. You are inter-lopers. I run this town. No one will take your word over mine."

"They will when we present the evidence alongside our word!"

"What evidence? The figurines will be gone. Greenleaf will be gone. Loring will crumple the moment he realizes that his lender will never, ever allow him to get to a courtroom alive. Durham can't exactly speak up for you. And Chesley is who knows where? She might be dead in a ditch . . . I hope."

"That attitude must be why you're such a popular cop," Lenore muttered.

He grinned at her. "Oh, I know how to impress the voters. And I know what they really want. Peace and quiet. They'll do pretty much anything to achieve that. So they'll accept my account of the murder; they'll believe Ligeia is the killer if I tell them she is. And they'll do that because they just want life to go back to normal."

"I believe folks want the truth," Vera said. "Yes, peace and quiet are nice. But not when they come at the expense of justice."

He snorted. "Ugh, a reporter with ideals."

Lenore angled herself between him and Vera. "She's got more than ideals. She's got the story. And we'll expose you for the lying, opportunistic murderer you are."

He gave a low, chilling laugh. "Not until you get out of this grave. And you can't do that if you're dead." With those words, he stepped outside the entrance and pulled the heavy wooden barrier across it.

Chapter 24

The four creatures hurled themselves against the barrier, but they couldn't shift it against the weight of the buck outside. They tried several times, but then heard Buckthorn call out to someone, "Bring a bunch of rocks over here. Got the criminals inside, and I don't want them wiggling out."

"Yes, sir!" came the eager voice of Poole.

"Oh, no. The wolverine's out there, too. Now we really can't make a break for it." In her frustration, Vera smacked her paw against the wood, which stung badly.

"We're trapped!" Thena squeaked. "We're going to run out of air."

"Calm down," Ligeia told her. "This is a big tomb and there's plenty of air. Plus that barrier isn't airtight. Even if we're stuck in here for hours, we'll be fine."

"Plus other creatures will come to the site sooner or later," Vera added, cradling her paw. "We just have to wait Buckthorn out."

Her confidence was misplaced, however. She heard Buckthorn's low laugh just as the odor of smoke started to drift in through the gaps in the wooden planks.

"Hard to breathe smoke, huh?" he called through the barrier. "Goodnight, ladies. Sorry you'll miss the sunrise!"

"We have to get out now!" Thena said, pushing ineffectually against the wood. Then she coughed, and Lenore pulled her back.

"Uh," Lenore croaked. "I don't care if the ghost of Ridley Durham is in here. I'd rather deal with that than a killer determined to silence all of us. Now come on. Let's see if we can find a place to hide farther back, a place that's lower than the smoke!"

"The farthest side chamber," Ligeia ordered. "Follow me."

While they were talking, Vera found and lit a lantern, the small flame guttering and throwing grotesque and twisted shadows against the stone walls. The tiny group stuck close together as they moved farther into the tunnel.

Just before they reached the far end where the calendar stone stood in the darkness, Ligeia disappeared into the left side chamber, the one decorated with images of bears. They all piled in behind her.

"So now what?" Lenore whispered. "We just wait?"

"I can sneak out," Thena volunteered. "If I can get to Rosewood Lodge, I can find someone who will listen."

"Shhh!" Vera waved her paw at them to hush them. "Did you hear something?"

They all held silent for a long moment. Vera thought she heard the scrape of the barricade being moved. The long stone tunnel muffled and distorted sound, though, and she couldn't be sure. After a moment, she turned to her friends. "Maybe I made a mistake."

"Or maybe you didn't. We might only have a few minutes," Lenore said. "Let's try to think of a way out of here! Preferably one that doesn't lead us directly to a fire or a waiting deer."

"Yeah," Thena said nervously. "This is an amazing place, but I don't want to die here."

Despite the urgency of their situation, Vera couldn't help but be entranced again by the painted image of the bear on the far wall. The paint seemed fresh even after millennia. Vera shivered, as if her fur was being ruffled by some long-ago breeze.

Then Vera glanced down at her forepaw and saw that her fur really *was* being stirred by some shift in the air. "There's some kind of wind coming from a crack or crevice over here," she told them. "I think . . . I think this wall might not be a wall. Maybe it's a door!"

Lenore spread her wings in front of the wall and closed her eyes. Then she said, "There's open space behind this stone. You're right! I can feel the air moving, so it must go farther into the ground."

"Let me see," Ligeia said, moving up to the wall. "There was an old account of a researcher who claimed that they found secret passages in old barrows. No one put much stock into the stories because they seemed so much like pulpy adventure tales. But I've always wondered why this wall didn't have any niches in it. It set it apart from all the others in the barrow. Now let's see . . ."

Together, they poked and prodded along the edges of the wall, trying to find some hinge or a mechanism that would cause it to open. Thena focused on the floor but had no better luck.

"There's got to be something," Ligeia fretted.

Vera lifted the lantern and noticed something she'd missed before. "Ligeia, look up! There are stars painted above the bear's head. When you told the story of Princess Bear back in the tea-room, you said she mapped the constellations."

The raven nodded. "Yes, there're all there, just a bit faded from time. There's the ram and the ship, the serpent, the polestar . . ."

"The polestar! Try pressing it!"

"You're not supposed to fiddle with cave art!" Ligeia objected.

"Sister mine, we are being *hunted by a murderer*," Lenore squawked. "Press the stupid star!"

Ligeia did so, fluttering up to get a better angle, then pushing hard.

Nothing happened.

She tried again, pushing around the edge.

Nothing happened.

She sighed and gave it a final jab with her beak, more out of annoyance than hope.

Still nothing . . . until they all heard a grinding sound.

Vera and Thena leaped back as the entire wall angled inward, allowing a rush of cold dry air past them. Both ravens instinctively raised their wings against the draft, and Ligeia kept looking up and down at the retreating door.

"The whole thing still works?" she said, gasping. "There must be a hidden lever or pulley that gets activated when the button is pushed. Basic mechanics known at the time, but brilliant engineering, better than some construction today!"

"Old ways are the best ways," Lenore said with a shrug.

With the door all the way open, a rectangle of darkness was revealed. Vera held the lantern in front of her and leaned in, illuminating a narrow passage extending down into the earth. "Is this a natural cavern?" she asked in wonder.

Ligeia stepped forward, brushing her wingtips over the damp surface. "Partly natural," she said. "But look here, and here! These are marks, both from stone tools and animals' claws. Whoever did this worked very hard to make this passageway navigable. And there must be a reason. Come on."

"It might be collapsed farther on," Lenore said worriedly.

"We'll find a way through! I'll be able to sneak under any collapse," Thena assured her. Vera admired her tenacity. Of course a vole wouldn't have the same concerns as the birds, and it might be very useful to have the small creature along.

So the little group ventured onward, down, down, down. The air was not exactly damp, but it had a clamminess to it, and Vera wondered who the last creatures to breathe this air before them had been. Those creatures might be centuries gone.

"I think there's something up ahead," Ligeia said. "I can feel a tiny bit of a breeze."

"I feel it, too," Lenore agreed.

The group proceeded, more carefully than before, not knowing what lay in store for them. Thena volunteered to go first, crawling slowly along the cold surface to test the stability of the floor and check if any dangers lurked.

"It seems safe," she said after a long moment of silence. "It's big and mostly empty."

Vera held the lantern closer to the ground to ensure no one would trip. The ravens moved in close behind her until they all reached the larger chamber.

They stopped short when the lantern light reflected on something, a gleam hovering in front of them.

"What's that?" Lenore asked. "Vera, hold up the lantern!"

Vera did so and took a few cautious steps forward.

"Oh, my stars," Ligeia whispered. "It's *her*."

"Princess Bear," Thena breathed.

It was indeed. Vera regarded the scene in front of her in awe. At the far wall of the cavern, there was a niche cut out of the rock, and inside it, the remains of a bear, still wearing the remnants of some ceremonial garb. Metal twinkled at them as it caught the glow of the lantern. Bronze bracelets gleamed softly, and a silver headdress still covered the skull. Stones of many colors had been placed all around the body. Amethyst, moonstone, citrine, and peridot formed a rainbow, and each stone had been etched with some symbol of a thing the giver had wished for Princess Bear to take on her journey. Offerings of food, or tools, or clothing, or toys all surrounded the sleeper. And besides the stones, there were piles of gold and silver. Some coins, but mostly objects and jewelry crafted with care.

"The sun's and the moon's gifts," Thena said, pointing to each pile. "Gold for the sun and silver for the moon. The legend is true!"

Ligeia was weeping, her head tucked under her wing as she cried.

"What's wrong?" Lenore asked in alarm.

"Nothing!" Ligeia sobbed. "Everything is just as it should be! Look, this is the evidence we've needed! Even this far back, creatures were civilized and cared about each other. All this was left

with our nameless princess . . . it means the living had enough
to offer something to the dead. It wasn't all struggle and hunger
and scarcity and cold. It was . . ." She trailed off, unable to finish.

"Belief," supplied Vera.

"Hope," Thena added.

Lenore nodded. "Memory."

She stepped up to her sister and laid her head on Ligeia's
neck. "You did well."

Ligeia wept harder. "Thank you! Don't tell Berenice and
Annabel I cried."

"Never," Lenore swore.

As they continued to gaze in wonder at the scene, Lenore
sidled up to Vera and whispered, "We can never, ever let Lefty
know about this place."

"Agreed," Vera breathed.

"Also, I really hope we get to see Lefty again, because that
would mean we get back to Shady Hollow and we don't end up
dead."

"Also agreed."

Finally, Thena sighed and said, "Um, we still have the little
problem of how we're getting out of here. Buckthorn isn't just
going to give up, and I'm sure he doesn't believe we just vanished into thin air."

"You're right. We either have to go back the way we came
and hope that he's not camping out for us there, or we can try
to find a different way out. I've been feeling that breeze again.
It makes me think there are more passageways. Maybe one of
them will lead out in an unexpected place."

"It's going to be dawn soon," Ligeia said. "If we get out and
can avoid Buckthorn and Poole, then we could find help. He
can't just kill us in broad daylight when other folks are around."

"Okay," Vera said. "Let's focus on that breeze. Everyone, close your eyes and try to feel where it's coming from."

They all did so. Vera's paws only led her to the entrance to the tunnel that they had used before, but the ravens (perhaps more attuned to such things) had both met at the far wall, which was mostly lost in shadow.

"There's something here," Ligeia said, her wings out and feathers splayed wide. "A natural vent, maybe."

"Could just be a crack in the bedrock," Lenore said. "Just . . . over . . . here!"

The sudden crash of falling rocks made them all shriek in alarm. But the rocks tumbling down from a gap in the wall were only pebbles, and Lenore was unhurt.

"It's not just a gap! It's bigger than that, worn down by water running past. I think we can all get through . . ."

They all crowded around, peering in where Lenore was pointing.

"Wait, there's a bigger rock wedged in here," her sister said, disappointed. "Thena could get through, but I don't think we can."

But Vera got an idea. "If we take some of those smaller flattish stones in the corner and stack them up just next to it, we can sort of lever the big rock out of the way."

"Basic mechanics to the rescue again!" Ligeia cawed. "Let's do it."

The four of them worked feverishly to move and stack the stones, and by wedging a few under the big rock, they were able to shift it just enough to let it roll to the bottom of the tunnel, resting on the floor of the burial chamber.

Without waiting, Thena scurried into the passage. "That was the only blockage," she reported. "There's one more biggish rock, but you can easily move it to get through."

"Can you see the end of the tunnel?" Lenore asked.

"No, but I can smell fresh air, so it can't be far. I'll go and take a look," Thena said. "I'll give a holler if it's all clear, and then you can move those last few bigger rocks and follow me." The tiny vole crawled through the rubble, and they lost sight of her. Only a few scratchings and the odd clatter of falling pebbles indicated that she was still working her way out.

"Wonder what she'll find," Lenore said, "or where she'll pop up."

"I'm all turned around," Ligeia admitted, then pointed to the side of the passageway. "I think north is that way, but it's so . . . underground . . . that I can't be sure. We might be just below the—"

She broke off as they all heard a sound that made their hearts quiver. A thin, small scream echoed down the passage.

"That was Thena!" Lenore gasped. "Something's happened to her!"

She started to tug at the one rock blocking the way for larger creatures, but stopped when a new voice called down the tunnel.

"There's no use in hiding anymore!" came Buckthorn's deep tones. "Come on out and join your little friend. I don't want to have to tell you what happens to her if you don't."

Vera groaned and leaped to help Lenore move the rock. "Ugh, this is all my fault. I should have sent her back on the ferry with the rest of them! Come on, let's move this thing! Buckthorn didn't sound very patient."

The rock suddenly tumbled out of its place, leaving the passage clear. Vera said, "I'll go first. But if either of you get a chance to fly free, do it, and get to whatever help you can find. We don't have any other choice."

The fox wriggled and squeezed through the narrow, twisting

tunnel. It was longer than she'd expected, but at the end she inhaled a whiff of cool night air. Just as she pushed her head and forepaws through, she was abruptly grabbed by two strong paws.

Poole tugged her out the rest of the way and practically threw her onto the grass in front of the towering deer.

Vera winced as she saw Thena under his front hoof, held fast by her tail. The vole looked so scared that Vera thought she might pass out.

"Ah, Miss Vixen," he said calmly. "So nice of you to join us. Now we can finish our discussion. It's fitting, really, that this happens at Summers End. Because unless you cooperate with the law, this is going to be the end for you and your friends."

Chapter 25

It took Vera a second to realize where they were, and she was surprised to see that the escape tunnel let them out almost exactly where they'd come into the barrow—by the long, low stone near the entrance, the one called the altar stone. The massive rock had been concealing the tunnel for centuries, until she and her friends scrabbled their way under it from the inside.

Unfortunately, their escape had only led them to a trap.

Vera stood very still, not wanting to provoke the deer. "Let Thena go, Chief," she told him. "She's not the one you want."

"She's insurance."

"She's innocent!"

"Send Chesley out to me and maybe I'll let the vole go!"

"Chesley? She's not with us!" Vera was genuinely confused. In a flash, she realized that Chesley must have some hold over Buckthorn, and he must want to find her in order to silence her. "I haven't seen her in days."

"Don't lie to us," Poole snarled. "You're in cahoots with the porcupine."

"The only cahoots happening are the ones your boss is in charge of. The thefts and black-market sales of artifacts. Probably made as much or more through that than he did from his official salary."

"What's that now?" Poole demanded. "Who's making extra money?"

"Oh, you haven't cut Poole in on your little side gig," Vera said to Buckthorn, enlightened.

"What's she talking about?" the wolverine asked his boss.

"Ignore her," Buckthorn replied calmly. "She's just trying to confuse you and thus divide us so she and her confederates can escape. Which they won't because I won't permit it."

"We're gonna send them to Stonehurst Prison, ain't we, Chief?"

"Oh, I think we'll send them to the bottom of the river."

"Ha!" the wolverine barked. Then he blinked in confusion. "Wait. What?"

"Do as I say, Poole. That's how things work, remember?"

Just then, there was a commotion at the edge of the clearing, and a crowd of creatures approached the site from the path leading to Rosewood Lodge. Vera saw the Rosewoods and most of the guests from Aster House, plus Eloise bounding alongside. Several other townsfolk were there as well. Dr. Reyes, who was already dressed for the day. She even noticed Roxanna Cobb in a purple turban.

Buckthorn saw them and snarled. *"Civilians,"* he muttered.

"Who's that at the lead?" Ligeia whispered.

"Oh, my stars, it's Lefty!" her sister cawed in astonishment. "He didn't leave town right away after all! He must have got suspicious about Buckthorn and then called up a posse. I never thought I'd be so happy to see that rascal."

"Vera!" Lefty called. "I overheard the convo in the station! Never trust a cop, you know. Anyway, I started knocking on doors and roused all the folks I could get! Everyone's an early riser today, huh?"

"Lefty, you're a gem," she called back.

"What exactly is going on here?" Dr. Reyes asked, moving to the front of the crowd.

"I'm arresting these four miscreants for the murder of Professor Durham," Buckthorn announced in his most authoritative tone. "Everyone disperse. And ignore anything they might say."

Vera stepped forward. "Buckthorn is the killer! And I can prove it!"

No one ignored *that*. The whole crowd surged closer, and creatures all murmured and whispered among themselves.

"Your chief of police is a criminal himself," Vera went on. "Not only did he kill Durham, he was involved in the sale of artifacts stolen from Summers End as well. In fact, that's probably why Durham was murdered—an argument over who was getting how much money. Greed was the motive."

"Utter nonsense," Buckthorn said, with no trace of discomfort. "The fox is just trying to confuse everyone so she can help her raven pal escape justice. Ligeia Lee is the killer."

"I'm just telling the truth," Vera insisted. "And now there are so many folks here to witness it that you can't pretend you're really solving crime. You're at the heart of the crimes."

"That's true!" a voice called out.

Vera whirled to see Professor Ford. "Ford's here! He must have come back early!" Vera whispered to Lenore.

The bearded dragon hurried up to the front of the crowd. "I can vouch for her account of the thefts of the figurines. I've been investigating the black market myself."

Buckthorn was momentarily shaken, but then he just said, "Theft is very different from murder. And Ligeia Lee killed innocent creatures to keep her secrets."

"Ligeia didn't go near Durham!" a voice called out from the crowd. Everyone turned to look as various creatures shuffled and made way for the hidden speaker to emerge. Then Vera heard a chorus of gasps when Professor Chesley stepped into the open.

She pointed to Buckthorn, saying, "I know because I was up on Summerhill when Buckthorn dragged the body from the woods outside the ring of stones all the way into the barrow."

"Did you see him break into the laboratory and bring the figurines?" Vera asked.

"No." Chesley shuddered. "I lay down the moment I realized something weird was going on. And the moment Buckthorn and the body disappeared into the barrow, I ran away. I was terrified he'd see me if I stuck around."

"And you left your telescope behind!" Vera said. "I remember when you told me that you always have it with you. But Ligeia said that she saw it unattended on the top of the hill that morning. It took me a long time to notice the discrepancy." That lost detail had been bothering her subconscious for so long.

"It's true," Chesley said. "I was so scared. I think it was the first time in my life that I abandoned my telescope. I wanted to go back to check on it and make sure it was safe, but I didn't dare."

"If you knew Buckthorn was the killer, why didn't you come forward right away?" Lenore asked.

Chesley rolled her eyes. "Oh, sure, and who was I supposed to tell? The chief of police, maybe? Or his snarling deputy? I'd have been thrown in a cell on a trumped-up charge before I got a whole sentence out. Or more likely, I'd be whacked in the back of the head just like Ridley . . . another death to blame on an innocent creature."

"But you did let everyone assume the accusations against Ligeia were true," Vera pointed out.

"I wouldn't have let it get all the way to a conviction!" Chesley said with a certain amount of offended pride. "That wouldn't have been right. I did intend to speak up and tell some proper authorities as soon as I could get away safely. But that was the problem. I couldn't get away, first because it would look weird to leave, and then because everyone was searching for me. It wasn't safe to step outside."

"Outside of where?" van Hoote asked. "Where were you hiding? The whole town got torn apart in the search for you!"

"Well, the fact is that I stayed with Roxanna. Her home is above the occult shop, so I hid out there while I waited for some opportunity to leave or be able to confront Buckthorn safely. Honestly, the worst part was the patchouli. And the fact that I couldn't go outside and use my telescope."

Vera nodded. "So you went into hiding, because your original plan wasn't working anymore."

"Exactly. When the murder happened, I figured my safest bet was to say nothing and pretend that I wasn't anywhere near the site. Luckily, Buckthorn didn't see me when he was bringing Durham's body in, because he had to concentrate. He couldn't look up. And then I snuck away as quickly and quietly as I could. I was sure he'd be right behind me, but as it turned out, he spent more time taking those artifacts and staging that weird little death ritual."

"Ha!" said Ligeia. "I told you that the scene made no sense! And it was because Buckthorn isn't any kind of scholar. He just grabbed some things and arranged them randomly."

"Okay. So shortly after you and then Buckthorn left the site, Ligeia must have arrived. She hoped to catch Durham alone and talk about why he wanted to deny her tenure, but of course, she never saw him because he was already dead and inside the tunnel. The larger group got to the site just before dawn, and the body was discovered at sunrise."

Lenore piped up. "And Buckthorn showed up again, ostensibly because van Hoote alerted him, but in fact he already knew what happened. But he interviewed everyone just like he normally would. He's a good actor, I've got to admit."

"But Buckthorn had to wait to interview you, Professor Chesley. It gave you time to settle on your story," Vera said.

"Yes. I didn't know if someone else would mention that I'm usually on-site during the nighttime hours. If they did, Buckthorn would be extra suspicious. So when he found me at Aster House later that morning, I claimed that some rain swept in at three thirty, well before he arrived, so he wouldn't have any inkling that our paths had crossed. I said I just went back to the inn and slept the rest of the night and into the morning till he knocked on my door. And he bought it."

Vera sighed. "Yes. Until I stupidly mentioned that someone

else could prove that it hadn't rained at all. That information was all he needed. He realized that you were very likely a witness who could confirm that he was the killer."

"I'd been jumpy ever since the murder," Chesley explained. "And I was pretty sure Buckthorn would start to connect the dots. He's been in charge of Summerhill for a long time because he's clever. I'm surprised he let you snoop around as much as you did, Miss Vixen. Though he didn't know how *much* you snooped. I happened to see you and a pal break into Durham's room that night while I was stargazing from my room. I was worried for a bit that you and Buckthorn were allies. So after I heard you were looking for me, Miss Vixen, I decided to move house, as it were."

"The astronomer hiding out with the astrologer!" Ligeia said. "It was the perfect cover. No one would suspect you two were friends. You constantly bickered."

"Well, as it happens, we're more than friends," Roxanna said, stepping up to hold the porcupine's paw. "And bickering is one of the things that brought us together."

"It does add appeal to dig season," Chesley admitted, smiling. "But you can all see why I didn't dare show my face—I didn't want to put Roxy in danger, too."

"The danger was real. Buckthorn had a stranglehold on this town," Dr. Reyes declared. "And if he realized that Roxanna—or anyone—was working against him, he'd have done something permanent to them. He was subtle about most of his dealings, but the fact is that he treated everyone else like he owned them. It's high time he's dealt with. I'm just sorry it took a death to do it."

Buckthorn stamped his hoof. "This is nonsense. You can't

accuse *me* of a crime. I'm the one in this town who takes care of the crime!"

"Yeah," said Gerry, the proprietor of the lodge. "You take care of it by doing most of it yourself."

"I don't have to listen to this blather from a bunch of strangers," the chief said. "Listen, friends. This nosy reporter and her retinue aren't even from Summerhill. How could they know anything about how we do business here?"

"Starting to get a little tired of the way business is getting done round here," said a coyote. Vera recognized him as the one who ran the bakery on Front Street. "Maybe it took a stranger to show us what was wrong."

"Poole," Buckthorn called out angrily. "Do something about this crowd. It's getting to be a problem."

The wolverine stepped up, his eyes fierce as he pulled out his nightstick. "You got it, Chief."

"Oh, no," Lenore whispered.

The deputy continued, "Lawrence C. Buckthorn, you are under arrest." He glared at his boss.

"What?!" Buckthorn said, looking at Poole as if he'd never seen him before. "That's not what you're supposed to do!"

"I think it is. Way I see it, you need to come with me to the station and get comfy in one of our nice cells until we can sort this whole thing out. Got a problem with that . . . Chief?" Poole growled.

Buckthorn looked around the assembled crowd, and then to the edge of the forest.

"You won't make it," Lenore assured him. "And even if you did, you'll have a flock of birds on your trail, and *you* can't run faster than *we* can fly."

The deer snorted and dug in his hooves, as if he meant to

leap away. But Poole simply jumped in front of him and put his bulky, squat self firmly in the way.

There was an agonizing moment when the two beasts stared each other down. Vera had to give Poole points for bravery. Not only was he blocking the escape route of a twelve-point buck, but he was also facing down his superior officer.

"Don't do it, Chief. Only cowards run," Poole growled.

The phrase seemed to cut through Buckthorn's rage. Maybe it was something he had said himself, in his role of upholding the law. The deer shook his head, and didn't look at anyone as he said, "Fine. Let's get this over with."

Poole led his former boss down the path to town, flanked by an escort of newly civic-minded townsfolk eager to see that Buckthorn made it safely into a locked cell.

The small group who remained all looked at one another, blinking as if coming out of a dream.

"Wow," said Thena, her voice shaky. "That was scary for a little bit."

"But it's over now," Ford said. "And everyone at Summers End will sleep easier knowing that the mystery is solved."

"More than one mystery!" Lenore added, looking proudly at her sister. "We solved a mystery much older than the murder of Durham, and I think it's way more amazing. Seriously, Ligeia. After you reveal your latest find, you won't have any trouble getting funding for Summers End. You've made the find of a lifetime!"

"Several lifetimes," Vera added.

Ligeia said, "I just hope that this means we can use Buckthorn to take down the rest of the black market he was dealing with."

"Oh, I bet he'll talk," Ford said. "There's not that much honor among these thieves. Once the operation is shut down, not only

Summers End, but a host of other sites will be much safer from plundering. And I don't know that it would have happened without the efforts of our new friends from Shady Hollow."

Vera felt warm to the tips of her ears when everyone's attention settled on her. "Well, we just wanted to find out the truth."

Lenore added, "And protect the innocent."

"And write the story!" Thena pointed out, in true journalistic fashion.

"There's a lot of thanks to go around," van Hoote declared. "And I for one would like to begin by getting the first round of coffee! Come along, friends old and new. We may not be together much longer, so let's celebrate the time we have."

"Hear, hear!" Ford agreed. "Last one to the café buys the second round!"

The procession to the café was, to say the least, a speedy one.

And as the dust settled behind the departing group, the stones of Summers End once again stood silent, keeping time in the slow and steady way it always had and always would, no matter what small dramas played out upon it.

Epilogue

Three days later, after speaking with the various authorities who arrived in Summerhill to settle matters (well after the danger was past, she couldn't help but notice), Vera and her companions finally returned to Shady Hollow. They'd bidden a fond farewell to the Rosewoods and the remaining professors. Van Hoote had been horrified to learn of the potential motive they'd found for him and was able to produce receipts showing that the student fees he collected had been given to Durham . . . who had really been the one to pocket them. Vera was glad, because she would have hated to tell her friend Heidegger bad news about his cousin.

Vera stopped in Roxanna's shop to buy some tea for Athena, who was heading back to the university for the fall semester. Lenore tagged along, and even purchased a book about tasseomancy.

"It's good to support local businesses," she said, ever the practical raven.

"I'm so glad you came by before, too," Roxanna said. "I really wanted Adelaide to talk to someone, but she was too nervous. So I tried to pass on a few clues via the divinations."

"*The stag ascendant,*" Vera recalled. "You were talking about Buckthorn running the operation. And you told us to focus on the town, not the dig. You were trying to steer us away from the theory that the murder was driven by academic infighting."

"Yes," the pika said. "But I was afraid to be too blunt about it. Though as it happened, everything worked out! Destiny at work!"

Vera, Lenore, and Thena were provided seats on a fast boat downriver. (Lefty, unsurprisingly, had vanished from Summerhill the moment proper legal representatives showed up, which was probably for the best.)

The journey home was swift and uneventful, a situation all three agreed was ideal.

After a long sleep and a leisurely morning, Vera once again stood in her living room and regarded her comfy little home with joy. Travel was all well and good, but there was nothing quite like sleeping in one's own bed and sipping tea from one's own cup. She puttered around a bit, dusting a shelf at one point, moving a chair closer to the window at another. She was fully committed to the idea of not writing one word of her article for BW until after noon, mostly because she was amused to think of the skunk pacing a trench in his office as he waited for the piece.

There came a knock at the door. Though not loud, the knock had the distinctive heaviness of a large creature. And she knew exactly which creature it was.

Vera opened the door to see her beau standing there, cap tucked under one limb, and in the other paw a bouquet of late-summer flowers: daisies, bee balm, coneflowers.

"Why, good morning, Officer," Vera said sweetly. "I'm not in any trouble, am I?"

"We can decide that later," he said in his usual gruff tone. He offered the flowers. "Wasn't sure if I'd actually get to give these to you, or just put them on your tombstone."

"Wow, that's a Lenore-worthy comment." Accepting the bouquet, Vera asked, "Have you talked to her?"

"I did get a brief report," he said, "when I stopped by the bookstore just now. The dispatches sent downriver weren't exactly reassuring. But now that you're back, I want the full story."

"Funny, that's just what BW said." Vera moved to the kitchen and filled an old jar with water to place the blooms into. She then looked at her rather empty larder. "You know, I think we should continue this discussion on the way to Joe's. I haven't got any decent food here."

The bear nodded, and held the door open for Vera, who quickly gathered her bag and hat. As they walked down Shady Hollow's main street, the sunlight poured down on them . . . but was there also just a hint of crisp dryness in the air? And was the light slanting a bit more than yesterday? If Vera had any doubts about the seasons' turn, they were put to rest the moment they walked into Joe's Mug, where a chalkboard sign proclaimed that the dessert of the day was an apple, pear, and apricot cobbler.

"I'll be getting that," Orville said, pointing to the sign.

"Sure, but what are you getting for dessert?" she teased.

Joe himself directed them to a booth by the windows so they could see the passing scene as they ate. Once tucked into their seats, with coffee mugs in front of them and their orders placed, Orville leaned back.

"Okay, Miss Vixen, star reporter, let's hear it. I only know what happened from your letters and the various messages sent to and fro. I must be missing a lot."

So Vera filled him in on the whole adventure, starting the moment she stepped on the ferryboat going upriver. She explained the journey's descent from a boring chaperone role for rambunctious students, to the finding of the body, through the investigation . . .

". . . which no one told you to do!" Orville mentioned at one point.

"But it's a good thing I took it upon myself," Vera countered, "considering that the creature technically in charge of the case was none other than the killer."

The bear snorted in disgust. "Giving the whole profession a bad name. I'm glad you exposed him. Okay, go on."

While diligently consuming her fruit cobbler, Vera related the final details, including the harrowing chase and the surprise discovery of the secret tomb far below, an unexpected twist amid an already twisty experience.

"That's amazing," he said at last, after she told him about the find. "And the whole thing was dangerous! You knew that Buckthorn was a threat, and you still goaded him into action. You ought to have been safer about it."

"Do you really think that would have happened?" she asked, with a skeptical look.

After a moment, Orville just shook his head. "Don't know

why I even bring it up anymore. Vera Vixen *will* get into trouble. It's guaranteed."

She gave him a little smile. "Glad you understand the situation."

He seemed about to protest—or start a lecture—when he frowned, looking out the window.

"What's this now?" Orville muttered, gesturing to the street outside. Vera looked and noticed Lenore flapping her way over. "You'd think we'd get one day without some sort of alarm."

Moments later, Lenore entered the diner, peering around at all the tables until Vera waved a paw at her. The raven hurried over.

"What's up?" Vera asked, noticing her friend's ruffled state. "Something wrong?"

"No, but still a bit of a surprise. I just got a wingmail from Ligeia. She says she's just heard from the university, and they've appointed her the new head of research at Summers End."

"Oh, that's great news! And fast."

"Ligeia thinks that they were worried she'd leave for another institution if they didn't offer her some kind of promotion. She's already been contacted by a few rival schools, especially because Ford put in a word for her. Turns out that our bearded dragon pal has got rather a lot of clout, despite having technically retired. Her discovery, plus the whole scandalous murder thing, has made her a bit of a celebrity in certain circles."

"She worked hard, and she deserves to be head of the site. I'm sure she'll do wonderfully."

"She said she's helping get the whole place ready for winter, and then she's taking a short sabbatical, partly to rest, but also to start writing a book about finding the tomb."

"Ooooh, you can host the launch at Nevermore," Vera said.

"Then the town will finally get to meet a member of your family."

"Funny thing about that," Lenore said. "Ligeia is going to take her sabbatical here. She intends to rent a room at Bramblebriar."

"She's not staying with you?" Orville asked, puzzled.

"We're taking things bit by bit," said Lenore. "When you've avoided your family for years, you don't want to jump right back into the nest together."

"That sounds very sensible," said Vera, who lived alone and loved it.

Lenore added, "And Vera, she wants to talk to you about your whole investigation so she can include the right details in her book. So everyone will meet her, and much sooner than I ever expected."

The raven then said goodbye, since she needed to return to the bookstore.

After they paid the check, Orville stood up, saying, "Well, suppose I should get back to the station, too. Not that we've had any crime to worry about. You were gone . . . Lefty was gone . . ."

She laughed. "Are you saying you want me to leave again, just to give you a quieter life?"

"No, I like it better when you're here."

As a rule, Vera wasn't the swooning type, but she did feel just a touch swoony right then. "Well, all right. I guess I will stick around."

"In that case, do you want to join me for a picnic dinner sometime this week? I'm not sure you've ever been to Sunset Point. It's not just a clever name."

"I've been, but not actually at sunset."

"Then we should go . . . er, unless you think things like that are silly." He looked suddenly concerned.

Vera shook her head. "If I've learned anything this summer, it's that few things are more important than taking the time to notice things like sunrises and sunsets. You never know how many you'll get."

"Great. I'll get a dinner basket from Brocket's and pick you up about an hour before sunset. Days are definitely growing shorter," he added. "We've had a run of fantastic weather, but summer is just about over."

"Summer always ends," she agreed. "But it'll return on schedule. Like clockwork. And meanwhile, we have the rest of the year to enjoy."

Orville took her paw in his. "Let's start today."

The End

Acknowledgments

Getting our books from idea to bookshelf is a job too big for any one person. So we must first give a final shout-out to our first editor at Vintage Books, Caitlin Landuyt, for taking us on and helping us bring Shady Hollow to life. Caitlin, the next round at Joe's is on us. We also cheer the whole team of copy editors, publicists, and designers who help make the books the best they can be. On the bookselling end, we would also like to thank Jason Gobble, Penguin Random House rep, for picking up the early indie versions and seeing a glimmer of gold inside. And thanks to Daniel Goldin, owner of Boswell Book Company, for first stocking those indie versions and talking them up to everyone looking for a quirky little mystery. And, of course, we want to thank the many librarians, booksellers, and reviewers across the world who have shared and championed our books. It is so gratifying to see people enjoying our stories and the world we've built.

Read more from
Juneau Black

The Shady Hollow
Mystery Series

"My new favorite comfort reads."
–Sarah Weinman, *The New York Times*